CHAPEL COVE ROMANCES

WHEN LIFE BEGINS AT FORTY...

A Chapel Cove Romance
~ Book 3 ~

By

USA *Today* BESTSELLING AUTHOR

AUTUMN MACARTHUR

Contact Information: autumn@autumnmacarthur.com

Scripture taken from Holy Bible, New International Version®, NIV® Copyright ©1973, 1978, 1984, 2011 by Biblica, Inc.® Used by permission. All rights reserved worldwide.

Cover Art by Marion Ueckermann: www.marionueckermann.net

Edited by Deidre Lockhart.

Cover Image ID 204139390 purchased from Depositphotos © 4pmphoto
Logo Image Chapel ID 164957864 Depositphotos © verity.cz

ISBN: 9781097641796

To Alexa ~

For her wonderful help with the first draft, and for being a dear friend.

Dear Reader

Nai and Mateo both carry heavy burdens of guilt, doubt, and insecurity, and struggle to learn a lesson that's not always a simple one to learn.

Life doesn't feel easy and light all the time, and for some of us, none of the time. We encounter trials and tests and hurts that can sometimes make us feel God is a long way away from us.

But Jesus tells us we can hand those burdens over to Him. He promises us rest for our weary souls when we surrender control to Him, walk with Him, and let Him lead us.

My prayer for all of us is that we may know His peace and His rest and His love, today and everyday.

Blessings,

Autumn♡

*"Come to me, all you who are weary and burdened,
and I will give you rest.
Take my yoke upon you and learn from me,
for I am gentle and humble in heart,
and you will find rest for your souls.
For my yoke is easy and my burden is light."*

~ Matthew 11:28-30 (NIV)

PROLOGUE

Saturday, April 13

"WE SHOULD never limit our dreams to only five things. God has many, many more wonderful things for us."

As Naomi Macnamara turned her key in the trailer's front door lock and shoved a shoulder against the door at the right place to stop it from sticking in the warped frame, her friend's words at last night's slumber party echoed in her ears. Just as if Kristina was beside her repeating them, instead of pedaling back down the long driveway with Clarise.

God had better have wonderful things planned. Because, apart from her friends and Aunt Ivy, there wasn't too much wonderful in her life right now.

Thankfully, the other girls agreed to ride their bikes to

Kristina's house and wait for her there, rather than stand giggling and chatting outside the dilapidated single wide. To make sure they didn't wake Mom up, not to hide the mess the ancient trailer home was in. Embarrassment, and the risk of Mom being mean to her in front of her friends, stopped her from ever asking them here.

Not to hide the truth. No point even trying.

Everyone in Chapel Cove knew about Mom. Even though they didn't know yet she *wasn't* like her mom. The measuring stares she'd intercepted Clarise's parents giving her told her that. They'd done it last night, yet again. Assessing her, deciding if she was good enough to be allowed in their nice house, to be a friend of their daughter, whether she'd lead Reese astray.

No danger of that. The last thing she wanted was to be like Mom.

As quietly as she could, she tiptoed past Mom's bedroom, avoiding the creakiest spots on the floor. The worn and cracked vinyl showed where they were. Soft snores and the unmistakable odor of liquor oozed out the half-opened door.

At least, only one set of snores. Phew! Mom hadn't brought anyone home last night.

Never drink alcohol. Something she'd vowed as part of her determination not to make the choices Mom had. But she couldn't write that on her Before-I'm-Forty list. Their ambitions were supposed to be positive and upbeat. Dreams to aspire to.

What could she write that would compare to Reese's grandiose plans and Kristina's wonderful ones? Though Kris was the shortest and the youngest of them all, she often sounded so much older and wiser than not quite thirteen.

Made her feel like a little kid in comparison.

So here she was, standing in her bedroom like some stupid statue, staring at the too-short faded floral curtains. Waiting for inspiration. For some idea of what to put in the tin to be dug up when they were forty.

She didn't have a clue. No more idea than she had about what to write on her list.

Last night, when her friends wrote their lists, she'd pretended to keep hers secret. Told them to be patient, they'd only need to wait twenty-seven years to find out.

Truth was, she'd written nothing yet. Wasn't sure she dared write what she really wanted. God surely would have good things in store for Kristina and Reese. Their optimism and confidence deserved rewards.

Harder to imagine He planned wonderful things for her. She couldn't remember her own father. He'd died when she was a baby. And the string of "uncles" Mom provided weren't good examples to help her imagine her heavenly Father.

Still, one never knew. Maybe it was time to start believing good things could happen for her, too. Time to believe she could make some decisions about her own life since she was a teenager. Go live with Dad's older sister, Aunt Ivy, instead of here with Mom. Maybe even change her name, the way Clarise decided from now on she'd be called Reese.

Taking a deep breath and straightening her usual slouch, she grabbed the pen and paper and scrawled a list.

Stand straight and tall. Right, an easy one for starters. So what if she was already taller than all the boys in their grade except Mateo Rodriguez? So what if Mom kept reminding her how ugly she was since she'd gotten so tall and lost all trace of her baby cuteness?

Pay to get braces and fix my teeth so I can smile more. Yes! Good one. She'd already started saving the little bits she earned babysitting and math tutoring. Someday, she'd save enough to fix her teeth. Hopefully, long before she turned forty.

Get a scholarship for college, leave Chapel Cove, and never come back. Definitely. With an education, she could make something of herself. Leave behind what the mean girls like Olivia called her — trailer trash.

Believe Jesus really does love me, even if my mom doesn't. Huh? Where did that come from? Of course, she knew Jesus loved her. Didn't she? Her heavy scribbles to cross it out before anyone else saw it tore right through the paper.

Go on a mission trip and make a difference. There. Nice and safe. That one she could let her friends see.

Four items on her list would have to be enough to satisfy the girls. Unlike Kristina, believing a zillion good things could happen to plain ordinary her just felt too big a stretch.

Next, something to put in the tin. Something special. Super-special. So special not even her friends could see. Too special to dare write on her list.

She scrabbled in her nightstand drawer till she found what she wanted. Tearing another page from Reese's notepad, she sketched a million-dollar bill. If she was rich, maybe then Mom would start treating her differently.

She laid her silly little treasure on the bill and then folded the page over and over till the little package hid what lay inside. The girls wouldn't guess what it was that way. If it came true, she'd let them see it when they turned forty. Once done, she tossed it into her backpack along with Reese's notepad and pen.

Now to stealth an escape from the trailer before Mom woke up. Someday, she'd leave all this behind. And she never would come back.

CHAPTER ONE

Twenty-seven years later…

NAI MACNAMARA couldn't refuse Aunt Ivy's request, much as she wanted to. Her aunt had been so much more of a mom to her than her birth mother, after all. Still, she *could* try to get Ivy to change her mind.

As Ivy matched her in stubbornness, she didn't hold out much hope.

"Are you sure? I'd far rather stay here with you, help you to recover, and then drive you back to Chapel Cove when your cardiologist lets you leave the hospital."

Smiling, Ivy patted her hand. "Nonsense, child. I'm fine. This whole thing has been a lot of panic about nothing."

Nai's gaze darted to the cardiac monitor above Ivy's bed as the faint beeping noise accelerated. The "panic about nothing" included Ivy almost dying yesterday.

At least her aunt's no-nonsense manner remained intact. Even if her heart muscle wasn't.

One eyebrow raised, Nai threw Ivy a no-nonsense glance of her own. "Right. Of course you're fine. That's why Dr. Moreno said he'd need to keep you here another five days or so, when most patients get to go home the next day."

No matter how much Ivy tried to minimize it, her heart attack had not been a little thing. The cardiologist who'd just left the Coronary Care Unit made sure Nai knew the truth. Ivy had ignored chest pain for days, pain signaling her heart muscle was starved of oxygen. Though surgery had fixed the main blockage, today's tests showed she'd be left with some permanent damage.

Ivy waved a dismissive hand. "These medical men. They do fuss so. Dr. Jeff, back home, is just as bad. I don't need you here babysitting me. The bookstore and my pets, on the other hand, will be in serious need of someone sensible to babysit them."

"Lucille...?" Surely, the friend who minded Ivy's on Spruce and the menagerie during Ivy's annual week of vacation with her in Austin could take care of things.

"Sorry, child. Lucille's in Denver, spending time with her daughter. Her sixth grandbaby is due to arrive any minute." Shaking her helmet of salt-and-pepper hair, Ivy grimaced. "I know you vowed never to go back to the Cove, but if we leave Violet and Fern in charge, anything could happen."

If even a fraction of the stories Ivy told about her bookstore staff were true, disaster did seem possible.

Not just possible. Likely.

Nai sucked a breath through her teeth. She *couldn't* say no. Back to the hometown she'd been only too glad to leave behind.

A hint of a flush colored Ivy's cheeks. "Besides, um, normally I make sure to rearrange things before anyone goes upstairs. With this happening, I haven't."

"No, I guess you couldn't." Tidy to the point of being called a neatnik by her college roommate, Nai shuddered to think what condition the living quarters over the bookstore would be in.

Ivy was a sweetheart. And a well-loved sweetheart, as the number of concerned messages the nurses passed on and the number of visitor requests the nurses turned down indicated. It got so bad they'd begged Nai to let the townsfolk know Ivy couldn't see anyone but close family yet.

But as well loved as she was, Ivy's untidiness and book hoarding were notorious.

Housework came a very poor last on her To Do list.

Clearly guessing what Nai's expression meant, Ivy chuckled. "Yes, it's about as bad as you're thinking. You know what I'm like. Once I open a book, that's it. The building could collapse, and I wouldn't notice. Plus, I'd love to have you fix up the downstairs apartment for me. It's full of books at the moment."

"So, you're following doctor's orders after all?" Surprise she made no attempt to hide arched Nai's brow, though she kept her voice low to avoid disturbing other patients. The nurse had already touched a finger to her lips to tell them to shush when Ivy argued with the cardiologist a little too energetically, making her heart monitor beep louder and faster than it should.

"I suppose I'm going to have to." Ivy released a sound somewhere between a huff and a sigh. "You heard Dr. Moreno. He won't discharge me unless I do. Even if he would, Jeff will nag me to death if I don't avoid the stairs for the first few weeks. But you're the only person I'd want going through my things to bring what I need downstairs." No doubt about her note of triumph. Ivy knew she had the clincher Nai couldn't refuse.

Nai eyed her, lips pulled to one side. This wasn't the first time Ivy had tried to persuade her to visit Chapel Cove, though a cardiac arrest made this her most spectacular attempt. Far more persuasive than mere invitations spiced with not-so-subtle hints Mateo Rodriguez had returned to help his grandpa, joined the local police force, and remained single.

7

Her life in Austin was fine, just fine, without Mateo or any other man. Hadn't her aunt supported her determination to be different from Mom, to choose a career over marriage, to believe she amounted to more than her reflected value in a man's eyes?

She didn't want to return to her hometown.

She didn't want to see Mateo again.

She didn't want to not have a choice. But right now, none of that mattered. For Ivy's sake, she'd have to.

Frowning as her rental car's back wheels slipped on the rain-slicked surface, Nai slowed around the curve. The road from Portland to Chapel Cove turned out way more dangerous than she remembered. Wipers worked furiously on her windshield against the downpour, and the headlights barely penetrated the shrouding gloom.

Welcome home. It's spring in Oregon.

And the rain wasn't about to stop any time soon. Because of the slower trip and lingering longer than she should with Ivy, getting her set up with a stack of books and a few sets of pretty pajamas, she'd be way later getting to the bookstore than she wanted.

Nerves knotting her stomach, she clenched her fingers around the steering wheel's smooth surface. A truck passed her at high speed, spraying her vehicle, the driver oblivious to the road conditions. After easing to the roadside, she flicked her hazard lights on and rested her head against the steering wheel.

Fatigue and frustration burned behind her eyes. Normally, she was Ms. Organized, no matter what. But after a sleepless night racked with concern for her aunt and a predawn rush to catch the next available flight after Reese called from the hospital, the six a.m. via Phoenix, she couldn't recall when she'd last felt so ready to fall apart.

At times like this, faith would come in handy. But she'd left that behind in Chapel Cove. If she'd ever had it.

She lifted her head and peered out into the curtain of rain. Unlike her mother, who used to go from yelling to laughing in a few seconds, Nai never allowed herself to succumb to emotional extremes. Emotional *anything*. She pushed her hair back behind her ears and resolved not to fall apart now.

Sitting here stewing wouldn't get her where she needed to go or help her do all she needed to do.

She needed to keep moving. And make a list. Juggling the bookstore, Ivy's pets, and all the work she'd promised her boss she could do remotely would be a challenge, but she could do it. All it needed was enough organization.

Leaning forward as far as her seat belt allowed, pulling her shoulders back, and keeping her head high, she eased onto the road again. And almost immediately needed to tap on the brake to negotiate a sheet of water spread across both lanes. Once out of the water, she pressed on the accelerator. A straight stretch of road allowed her to pick up some speed.

Her eyelids drooped, and her head bobbed forward. Jerking upright as she realized how close she'd come to falling asleep, she stiffened at the curve ahead. Did she miss the sign? As her vehicle entered the bend faster than she wanted, she hit the brakes.

Too hard.

The car skidded to the shoulder, tires squealing as they grasped for purchase and failed. With a white-knuckle grip, she tried to recall what Mateo taught her. Not to wrench at the wheel, but to steer gently out of the skid. A single-word prayer consumed her.

Please!

Holding her breath, she wrestled the sedan into the middle of her lane. Air whooshed out of her lungs as she released her grip a fraction.

I'm okay.

I'm okay.

I'm okay.

Thank You.

She'd prayed more in the past twenty seconds than she had in the past twenty years.

The only blessing from the near-accident, besides surviving and not meeting Mateo again as a mangled roadside wreck, was an adrenaline-fueled jolt of energy. Her mind was clearer, and since the rain eased off to something less of a deluge, the road was, too. The tightness in her chest loosened.

Still, her body begged for rest. Number one thing on her To Do list once she arrived at the bookstore. Get some sleep. Everything else could wait.

When the brightly lit Welcome to Chapel Cove sign appeared alongside the town limits, relief mingled with her frustration.

She didn't want to be here. But at least, soon, she could rest.

Driving through the well-remembered streets felt like driving back into the past. Back to the shy and insecure teen she'd been, desperate to escape the Cove. As if moving away would erase her history. It hadn't, it seemed. Merely let her ignore it. Already, the shame she thought she'd outrun began to bite, shrinking her smaller and smaller with each house and storefront she passed.

The Cove hadn't changed much, but she had. She *had*.

She parked at the curb outside Ivy's on Spruce and peered through the rain at the bookstore. Ivy's business and home, and her home, too, for her last few years in Chapel Cove. Some of her happiest memories of the Cove centered on her time at the bookstore with Ivy.

From what she could make out in the streetlights, little had changed here, either. The same wraparound porch graced the clapboarded Victorian. The same pointed tower she'd imagined as a castle fit for a fairy-tale princess when she was a little girl rose from one corner. The same moss-green paint with darker green and white trim.

Though peering closer, she groaned at peeling paint and missing pieces in the white gingerbread cutouts decorating the porch.

Knowing Ivy, the paint wasn't only the same color, but the same old paint job. The one she, Kristina, and Mateo had helped his contractor granddad with in junior high. Could be, that was the last time anyone with maintenance skills came near here.

Ivy might not have been joking when she said the place could collapse around her and she wouldn't notice.

Better add "get a contractor to check the building" to her To Do list.

That list was growing, but that shouldn't worry someone like her, used to juggling projects with hundreds of items, not just three or four. Fix up her aunt's apartment? Care for a few pets? Face the town she never wanted to see again? A cinch compared to managing Jesse Buckley, the impractical-but-genius billionaire she treated more like a younger brother than a boss.

A cinch. Right. Add "ignore the nagging that this optimism is ungrounded" to the list. Too bad the list was easier to ignore. All she could think was — *I'm back. Right back where I started.*

Not a happy thought.

As soon as she had the bookstore organized and Ivy on her feet, she'd do as she'd done all those years ago. Leave and shake the dust — or should that be, *mud*? — of this place off her feet.

Even with the unexpected gift of Reese and Kristina being home as well, she didn't belong in Chapel Cove. And neither her aunt, her friends, nor Mateo Rodriguez could make her change her mind. She had no intention even *thinking* of Mateo, especially not of wondering what sort of man the boy she'd known grew into.

Time to do something constructive. At least, send Reese and Kristina another text letting them know she'd arrived safely. Maybe by the time she hit send, the downpour would have stopped.

It hadn't.

And it hadn't after she texted Violet and Fern, Ivy's bookstore employees, to tell them she was here, either.

No point waiting any longer for the rain to ease. Best thing to do was get into the bookstore, up the stairs, and find a bed. Good thing she'd packed light, only a carry-on bag for the few days she'd planned in Portland. Lugging a heavy suitcase and holding an umbrella at the same time would be difficult.

Especially considering she'd forgotten to pack an umbrella. Not like her to be disorganized, but she could blame her worry over Ivy. Again, tears blurred her eyes as she stared at the bookstore through the sedan's rain-washed side window. Just fatigue and concern for Ivy. That's all.

Nothing to do with any thoughts of Mateo and what-might-have-beens. Being here, knowing he lived farther down Spruce Street and could drive past any minute, that hadn't reminded her of him.

Not one bit.

She shoved the car door open with more force than needed, grabbed her small suitcase from the back seat, and sprinted for shelter. Once on the porch, the suitcase deposited on the worn timber boards and her hands fumbling to scrub the raindrops from her face, she began to give thanks for not getting completely soaked.

Her hands flopped to her sides. She'd left her handbag and Ivy's door keys in the sedan. Her gratitude vanished faster than Ivy once a new cozy mystery from her favorite author arrived.

With a sigh, Nai looked out at the rain, now sheeting down. Nothing here to hold over her head. No choice but to make a run for it. Bracing herself, she dashed out into the downpour and along the crazy-paved path toward her car. As the cold droplets pelted her, a pickup truck slowed beside her rental, then stopped in front of it. A tall, dark-haired man got out and opened a colorful golf umbrella before sprinting toward her.

Fear shivered through her, pounding her heartbeat. Then relief sagged her. She knew this man. Or at least, knew the boy he'd been.

Mateo.

Droplets blurred her vision as they landed on her glasses, which, unlike the windshield, didn't have wipers. At least, she'd blame her hazed vision on the rain and not the feelings seeing him brought cascading back.

"Let me help you, Naomi." He lifted the umbrella, holding it over them both. "I didn't expect to see you here. Is Ivy doing okay?"

As she gazed into his concerned face, handsome one side, marked by scars on the other, she forgot about the storm and even her exhaustion. All rational thoughts vaporized as her heart fluttered in a way it hadn't done since she was a teenager.

Of all the men in the world, of all the streets in Chapel Cove, of all possible times, Mateo Rodriguez had to drive his vehicle down Spruce Street exactly when she returned. How could that be a coincidence?

If she still had her faith, she'd almost believe God set this up.

Almost.

CHAPTER TWO

WHILE THE deluge pelted down outside the umbrella's dry circle, Nai simply stared at Mateo, unable to erase a memory from her mind.

They'd been caught in the rain together and shared an umbrella just like this, but with heads close together, laughing. Until their eyes met and the laughter fled. And then... and then... Mateo brushed his lips against hers, plunging her into a whirlpool of sensations and emotions she'd never experienced. Her first kiss, at sixteen.

So startling and unexpected she'd run away from him, heedless of the soaking rain.

Her heart raced for days afterward, and she couldn't easily face the boy she'd been friends with for years. Keeping him at arm's length while pretending nothing had changed kinda helped.

Kinda.

Leaving Chapel Cove helped a *lot*.

She'd thought.

Apparently, twenty-five years later, grown-up and confident, she still had difficulty facing him. She *was* grown-up now. Wasn't she?

Since driving down the main street, she wasn't so sure. Seemed she'd been zapped into the past.

Managing to find her voice, she squeaked two words. "Thank you."

Huh? Was this the same woman who got on the plane this morning? It didn't sound like her.

Her voice emerged small and weak, not her usual brisk and competent tones. How could such a simple meeting slam her straight back to fifteen, a riot of shyness and hormones?

His navy blue jacket couldn't hide his broad shoulders, muscular torso, and biceps. A beard circled his strong chin. Hard-earned wisdom settled in the creases radiating from his brown eyes. He was all grown-up, too. For reasons she refused to admit to herself, her heart beat faster. Just as it had after that kiss.

As Mateo returned her gaze, something unreadable flashed in his dark eyes.

Realizing she hadn't answered his question, she glanced down to her soggy suede loafers. "Aunt Ivy's doctor wants to keep her in Portland a few more days. But she insisted I come home today so she didn't have to worry about the bookstore."

Home.

The word slipped past her lips without her intending it. Chapel Cove hadn't been home for years.

She ignored the whisper asking her: Is Austin?

"Makes sense." Mateo nodded. He probably knew all about Ivy's unreliable assistants. "You take the umbrella. I'll bring your luggage inside. It's in the trunk?"

She grasped the umbrella handle he held out to her. Still warm from his palm, it eased some of the chill in her fingers. Almost as if they held hands. The thought fluttered her heart even more.

Obviously, their meeting affected her much more than him. Though according to Aunt Ivy's hints Mateo remained single, he wouldn't be holding a torch for a girl he hadn't seen since their teens.

She wasn't holding a torch for him. Really, she wasn't.

"Thank you." She sounded like her aunt's parrot. No, wrong, from what she heard on her phone calls with Ivy, the bird usually sounded more intelligent than she did now. *Pull yourself together, girl.* "I… I have no more luggage. Just my handbag. Under the passenger seat."

As she stood, still staring at him, he held out a hand to her.

For her to take? Surely not. Confusion furrowed her brow.

"The car key." His tone held a deliberate calm. "So I can get your purse for you."

Oops. She clicked on the key fob she'd forgotten she clutched, opening the doors, then stepped nearer the car as he reached in for her handbag.

To keep him covered by the umbrella, not to stay near him.

When he straightened, bag in hand, she clicked again to lock the sedan. The huge umbrella wobbled in a sudden gust of wind. Mateo's hand shot out to steady it, engulfing hers.

She gulped, her mouth and throat dry. This was getting ridiculous.

But she didn't pull her hand away.

"I'll see you to the door and safely inside." The rumble of his baritone voice shook something deep inside her.

Together, they hurried to the porch. Protected from the rain and wind under its wide sheltering cover, he took the umbrella from her, closed it, and braced it against the wall. While she scrabbled in her bag for the house keys, he waved a hand in front of the light fixture secured to the wall.

"This should be set to come on automatically when someone steps onto the porch. It needs repairing." He pulled a small flashlight from his jacket pocket and shone it on the door lock so she could see to insert the key. "I could —"

She jumped in with a reply before he uttered his inevitable offer to do the job. "I'll get someone to have a look at it. It and a lot of other things around here will need fixing." That sounded far better. More like her usual cool, calm, and collected self.

The door swung open, and as she stepped into the big room, the familiar scent of books greeted her. Slightly musty from all the older books, but still comforting. During the day, the aromas of coffee and pastries from the attached coffee shop would add to the coziness.

Oh, how much she'd loved this place! Her oasis, her safe haven.

But it didn't feel the same without Aunt Ivy.

She flicked on the light and turned to thank Mateo and get her suitcase. Despite his umbrella, the rain had soaked his jeans from the knees down, and his face and hair were almost as wet as hers.

"Come in, dry off, and have a cup of coffee." Where had those words come from? She wanted less time with him, not more. "Um, if you want to. You were on your way somewhere when you stopped."

Please, let him say he couldn't come in.

Her small suitcase in one hand, he stood just outside the door.

"I'm due on duty soon, but not for twenty minutes or so." He gazed at her, forehead creased. "You don't have to invite me in if you don't want to."

Just like years ago, he seemed to read her mind. And she could hardly tell him the reason she hoped he'd refuse. Her ridiculous hormones working overtime again.

But for a man who could easily drive home and change his clothes, he showed little sign of wanting to do so.

Her gaze took in his wet clothing and the droplets in his hair, eyebrows, and beard. Sending him out into the rain was hardly neighborly. "You got wet helping me. Offering you a towel to dry off and a warm cup of coffee is the least I can do."

She forced her lips into a smile. Plenty of practice looking cheerful no matter what. Those skills wouldn't fail her now — now when she had no idea *what* she felt.

Mateo shifted from one foot to the other and ducked his head as if he was still the shy teenager she'd once known. "I missed you when we stopped being such close friends. I'm sorry things went wrong."

Not just that kiss. The junior prom. She didn't need reminding. She didn't want to talk about it. Her heart still ached over her mother's taunts when he stood her up.

But she wasn't that girl anymore. She didn't achieve all she had by being a wimp.

"Enough, already. The past is in the past, and we'll leave it there." Her best I'm-in-charge-here tone. Nice if she could believe that when it came to her feelings for Mateo. "Let's get us both dry and warm."

A slow grin spread on his face. "You've changed, Naomi. You didn't use to be so assertive. Good for you." He sounded as if he meant it.

"It's Nai, now. I stopped being Naomi a long time ago." She reached for the thermostat and turned up the heat. "Follow me." Her tone emerged more clipped than she'd intended. His smile stirred something inside her. Something she didn't want to reappear.

As she dodged stacks of books to reach the staircase leading to the apartment upstairs, she cringed more than a few times. Books piled up everywhere, almost blocking the stairs and creating a fire hazard. Two paintings hung crooked. Fuzzy dust skulked like a living thing on the stairs and along the walls. The floorboards squeaked with every step, and the faded pink walls could do with a fresh coat of paint.

Lips pursed and head shaking, she scooted around yet another teetering stack. In her condo, she kept her books organized by subject, size, and then color. No sign of *any* organization here. Detective stories were in the romance section and vice versa. A book lover's nightmare.

Had it been this bad when she'd lived here? She couldn't recall.

Compared to the trailer she'd shared with Mom, Ivy's had seemed an oasis of calm and order. But now, compared to her super-organized life in Austin? Chaos.

And she didn't even have Aunt Ivy's pets here yet!

The stair railing wobbled as they climbed upstairs. One more thing to add to her list. If she could find a screwdriver, she'd fix that herself.

After unlocking the green door labeled Private and throwing it wide, she stepped through into Ivy's big open-plan living and dining room. She removed more stacks of books from chairs and waved for Mateo to take a seat. Nothing had changed in twenty-five years, the same floral sofa cover, the same dining table and chairs. All just grown more faded and dusty. "I'll just grab you a towel."

She switched on the ancient electric heater Ivy used to supplement the even more ancient central heating, then dragged her tired feet to Aunt Ivy's bathroom and snatched up two towels. They smelled almost as musty as the old books, but at least they were dry. Rusted faucets and chipped tiles raised a grimace, as did the litter tray in need of emptying.

Welcome home, here's your litter scoop. Her least favorite job when she'd lived here.

Returning to the living room, she found Mateo standing in front of the heater. He'd removed his jacket, and his damp T-shirt clung to him, revealing muscles he hadn't sported as a weedy teen. Steam rose from the lower legs of his jeans.

If she kept staring at his chest and arms, steam would soon be rising from her, too. Though his white T-shirt was wet from the rain, she couldn't really suggest he take it off as well, could she? She swallowed hard and dragged her gaze away as heat crept up her neck.

No. She couldn't.

And he wouldn't want to, anyway. The boy she'd known was painfully conscious of the scars on one side of his chest, arm, and face, scars the crueler school bullies taunted him about. Lifelong reminders of a childhood accident, one she guessed scarred him on the inside much more than on the outside.

Compassion constricted her rib cage, and she steeled herself against it. She was in town to help her aunt, not rekindle old feelings. Especially toward a man who'd caused her scars of her own, scars on her fragile teenage heart, giving Mom so much more to taunt her with.

Drama queen thinking, more like a sixteen-year-old than a woman of nearly forty.

But true.

She handed him a towel and averted her eyes as he rubbed his face, neck, and hair with it. Lightning flashed, bright through the uncurtained windows. She winced and then winced again as a thunder crash followed.

"The storm must be right overhead." He moved to draw the drapes, then stepped closer, as if trying to protect and reassure her.

Protection she didn't need. She wasn't a child, scared of storms.

It made her jump, that's all. Straightening herself to her full height, she focused on drying her own skin and hair. No doubt her long black locks hung in straggly wet strands, not adorably tousled like his dark hair.

"I'll put coffee on and change into dry clothes. Can you wait a few minutes?"

"Of course. I wouldn't want you to get a cold." Oh, his smile, so soft and sincere, warming her like sunshine. She'd always been a sucker for Mateo's smile.

Turning away, she dashed to the kitchen and cringed. This place could use some cleaning, too. If the café's kitchenette downstairs was in the same state, Ivy's on Spruce might have difficulty passing the next food hygiene inspection.

Well, one more item on her To Do list.

After rinsing out the coffee maker container, she found a can of coffee in the cabinets. Soon the coffee was brewing. Simply inhaling the enticing aroma gave her a much-needed lift. A much-needed distraction from Mateo, too.

Then a shiver reminded her about her wet clothes. With a wave at Mateo as she picked up the suitcase he'd carried upstairs for her, she hurried into a bedroom, the one she'd used when she first moved in with Ivy. Books covered the bed. Even more books piled in the next guest bedroom. Feeling like Goldilocks, she opened the door to Ivy's room.

Hardly "just right", but at least here she had fewer books to shift from the bed.

Surveying her meager luggage almost sank her spirits again. Expecting a couple of days sitting around in hospital waiting rooms, she hadn't brought anything fancy with her, only casual clothing. Not that she should wish to dress up for drinking coffee with Mateo.

She scooped up a pair of jeans and a simple long-sleeved T-shirt, the color of the spruce outside the bookstore, and then changed without risking a glance in the mirror. Her sodden loafers, the only shoes she'd brought with her, looked decidedly unappealing. So did Aunt Ivy's carpets. Going barefoot was *not* an option.

Instead, she slid her feet into the sheepskin slippers she'd sent Ivy at Christmas and hurried into the kitchen.

Mateo had beat her there. She found him pouring coffee into a mug that matched her T-shirt.

"I hope it's okay that I went ahead. Here's your coffee." He gestured to a mug on the counter, already filled with coffee, and judging by the enticing scent, caramel macchiato creamer. He'd even wiped the countertops down.

Tenderness mixed with her gratitude, and she smiled. Despite her taller-than-average height, she needed to tilt her head a little to meet his eyes.

"Thank you. But I take my coffee black, no sugar." No need to add those unwelcome inches on her hips and waist again.

Her mother's insistence she constantly diet when Nai did her reverse ugly duckling had ripped her apart. Not her fault she turned into an unattractive duck of a tween and teen after being a beautiful swan of a toddler. But Mom seemed to think it was.

Set free from Mom, she'd fallen into comfort eating it took some serious willpower to overcome.

"I'm sorry. Here, have mine." He offered the mug he'd just poured. "I'll be fine with this one." The regret in his caring eyes and downturned lips made her change her mind. Somehow, she didn't have him tagged as a caramel macchiato kind of guy.

So he stood her up for the prom? There were worse things. He'd never mocked her. Never blamed her for everything wrong in his life. Never snatched food from her hand and thrown it in the trash, making her crave the forbidden snacks even more.

Picking up the first mug and carrying it to the dining table, she smiled. "It smells so good. I can make an exception."

Instead of sitting, she deposited the mug. Why not make it even more of an exception? She'd hardly eaten all day, after all.

"Be right back." Returning to the kitchen, she opened the yellowed Tupperware box that, when she'd lived here, usually held treats left over from the café. Yes! She gave one of the pastries a tentative poke and a sniff. No way to know how long it had been here, probably since Saturday. But it smelled and felt fresh enough. Almost.

Judging by the lack of any other food in the kitchen, Ivy must subsist on coffee and leftover cakes.

Nai snatched a plate from the cabinet, placed the freshest and least soggy-looking of the pastries on it, and returned to the table. "Here we go. I hope you like two-day-old almond danish."

Not that she intended to please him. Okay, maybe a little bit.

Mateo laughed. "My favorite! I'll give thanks." He bowed his head. "Dear heavenly Father, thank You for this food. Please bless it to our bodies. Please help Ivy recover from her heart attack and please keep my grandpa safe and well. And please help Naomi — I mean, Nai. We ask this in the name of Your Son, Jesus Christ, amen."

After a long pause, she added her own amen.

Mateo's faith had always been stronger than hers. She'd tried to find her path to God, the effortless trust in Him her friends seemed to have, yet somehow her faith got lost along the wayside.

But it touched her how Mateo included her in his prayer.

One sip of her hot, flavorful coffee, and warmth spread through her. She forgot how delicious coffee with creamers could be. The second sip, and then the third and the fourth followed soon. She pushed the plate with pastries toward him.

He bit into one, and she tried to drag her eyes away as he licked a flake of almond and a few sweet crumbs from his lips.

"It's been a long time, Nao — sorry, Nai. Remember how we used to work at math problems together, but then we competed with each other at every test, to see which of us would come first? My best friend and my biggest rival." He chuckled. "You motivated me to try extra hard, with math and with chess."

"Of course, I remember." How could she forget?

But she remembered even more. Sitting close to him over their math books or a chessboard, their heads nearly touching. So close she could easily reach out to him if she wanted. And once she entered her teens and their childhood friendship became charged with emotions she hadn't understood, oh, how she'd wanted!

A wave of awareness rippled through her as it had so many times all those years ago. Then she'd been too shy to show her attraction. Pretended to ignore his tentative attempts to hold hands. Fled the one time he kissed her. Ached over the disaster of their junior prom. Insisted they were only friends.

And now…?

Now she'd tuck those feelings far away. Back in some long-distant recess of her mind. Where they surely belonged.

It worked. She and Mateo talked about old times and classmates and "where are they now" like the friends they'd once been. They carefully avoided any touchy subjects like proms or kisses or her determination to leave the Cove.

But her eyelids felt so heavy. She drained the mug, hoping the caffeine would kick in and keep her awake. The sleepless night and long exhausting day were taking their revenge.

Her eyes closed, and her head nodded forward. She forced her eyes to open, lifted her head. Her eyes closed again, and she forced them open once more. No way would she fall asleep in front of Mateo, face down in the pastry plate. Mateo, of all people.

Absolutely no way.

CHAPTER THREE

WHAT SHOULD I do, Lord?

Mateo wasn't usually this indecisive, but he'd need to leave for work soon. As Naomi's head nodded forward onto her chest and her words trailed off midsentence for the third time, he'd been quick to move the empty coffee cups and plate away from her. A throw pillow grabbed from the sofa would cushion her head if she ended up leaning on the table.

Though the pillow — ugh! Even an undomesticated guy like him could guess the pet-hair encrusted item didn't belong on a dining table. But what choice did he have? God willing, she'd wake before he left. But even for the short time he'd be in the kitchen washing up their mugs, he couldn't leave her to risk smacking her head on the oak tabletop.

He solved the problem by wrapping the pillow in the towel

Naomi had used to dry her hair, before placing it in front of her. Her beautiful hair, jet black and poker straight in her teens, now sparkled with scattered silver strands. Still-damp tendrils curled around her temples and cheeks, framing her face as if it was a precious portrait.

In sleep, her face held a softness and vulnerability he figured she'd rather no one saw.

Naomi looked good at forty. As good as she'd looked at eight when he'd told her he'd marry her when she grew up. As good as she'd looked at sixteen when he'd kissed her for the first and only time.

Dragging his focus from the girl he'd once loved, he carried the dishes into the kitchen and washed up. After a fruitless search for a clean dishcloth to dry them, he left them to drain. When he returned to the big room, Naomi hadn't moved. Chin on her chest, her slow even breaths formed quiet, ladylike snores.

Time he left. He'd need five or ten minutes at the patrol house to change into his police uniform before starting his shift.

And time she went to bed.

"Nai. Nai, wake up, you need to go to bed." No response.

He gently shook her shoulder. That at least got *some* response. She murmured something inarticulate, and her dusky eyelashes flickered on her cheeks. But her eyes stayed shut, and she didn't move.

He couldn't leave her like this. What sort of good cop, let alone decent friend and neighbor, would he be if he did? All too easy for her to slip forward off the chair or fall sideways. She could be hurt.

A hand on her shoulder and a gentle shake, followed by a more vigorous one, failed to elicit more than a mumble he couldn't decipher. She'd most likely had a sleepless night of concern for her aunt, followed by a long day of travel. And hospitals weren't the happiest places to be. He'd spent too much time there himself when his grandma was ill.

As he gazed at Naomi, a warmth he didn't try too hard to define flooded his chest.

Only one option.

In the bedroom she'd used to get changed — Ivy's? — he lowered her suitcase to the floor and turned down the bedclothes. Beside Naomi again, he bent his knees, slipped one arm under her jeans-clad legs and the other around her back, and then scooped her up against his chest.

His arms tightened around her as he staggered a little. Carrying a full-grown woman was nowhere as easy as they made it look in the movies or in those romance novels his grandma had loved. He'd read them to Abuela when she was too tired to read herself.

Stories full of petite heroines and superhuman heroes. But he was far from a Superman, and lovely Naomi was far from petite.

She still didn't wake, snuggling into him. Lurching steps took them to the bed, and he lowered her onto it. Despite his protesting knees and back, his arms took their time sliding from under her, seeming reluctant to release her.

It really *was* time to go. After pulling off her slippers and dropping them to the floor, he spread the comforter over her. As he removed her ebony-framed glasses, an impulse he couldn't explain impelled him to bend and drop a gentle kiss on her forehead.

"Sleep well, Naomi."

He took the stairs two at a time, clicking the latch on the entrance door and checking it before he dashed for his truck through the steadily falling rain. Too late, he realized he'd left the umbrella on the bookstore porch. It could stay there. There'd be a spare at the station. Plus, he wouldn't complain about the excuse to drop by tomorrow.

The next few days would be interesting with Naomi Macnamara back in town. Whether good interesting or bad interesting he couldn't decide. He'd leave that in God's hands.

But one way or another, interesting.

Under the shelter of a shared umbrella, Nai stared at Mateo as he held her hands. His gaze roamed her face, and he leaned closer to her and closer again. Her heartbeat stuttered, then went into overdrive as she moved toward him. Feather-soft, his lips brushed her forehead. Any moment now, their lips would meet and...

Something wet plopped onto her forehead, so different from the sweet touch of his lips. No matter. A little rain couldn't distract her from the delicious anticipation.

And again. Plop, right between her eyes.

This couldn't be right. His umbrella had a leak? She opened her eyes and looked up, seeing only darkness as another drip hit.

No Mateo. No umbrella. Instead, a bed and a damp one at that. The pillow was soaked. Even if she'd cried herself to sleep, which she'd never done, no one could cry that many tears.

Where was she? She'd been having a cup of coffee with Mateo. And then...

Another droplet splashed her face as lightning lit the room. Though she winced at the unexpected flash, it showed familiar surroundings. Aunt Ivy's room. The same cabbage rose wallpaper she remembered. Pink and green, the colors Ivy loved.

Nai sat up, reached for the lamp, and clicked it on. The bedroom came into focus, dusty and heaped with books like the rest of the place. Rain pelted the windows and thrummed on the roof while thunder rumbled.

So the storm hadn't stopped.

Looking up, she groaned. Sure enough, the ceiling was leaking steady drips. But the house had an attic. Did that mean the leak in the roof was bad enough to flood the attic and trickle through to the second floor?

Great. So she was back in Chapel Cove, the one place she'd vowed never to return to. She'd have Ivy's eccentric staff and unruly pets to deal with. Not to mention, Ivy herself, no sooner over her near-death experience than plotting how to flout her doctor's orders. A bookstore and living quarters filled with dust and disorder. A health-hazard café at risk of being shut down. A stack of work beckoning her in Austin.

And a six-foot-two hunky package of memories and emotions she didn't want to revisit. No doubt, while she and Mateo were in town and single, everyone would try pushing them together again.

With all this, God gave her a leaky roof, too? Seriously?

A moan escaping, she leaped to her feet. Or rather, *tried* to leap to her feet. Wet cotton wool stuffed her head, and her limbs, somehow made out of cooked noodles, showed little inclination to obey it.

What time was it? After fumbling on the nightstand for her glasses and jamming them in place, she glanced at her watch. Only three a.m.

No wonder she felt so lousy.

But how did she end up in bed? Had she been so dopey she didn't remember crawling under the comforter?

Uh-oh. Warmth tingled up her neck. Last she recalled, she'd forced herself awake after nodding off while chatting with Mateo. Not awake enough, obviously. Had she fallen asleep right in front of him? Honestly? Sound asleep.

Cringing, she slapped her forehead with both hands. Her stomach clenched.

Mateo, of all people.

If that wasn't embarrassing enough, he must have carried her to the bedroom.

How had he managed? Tall and average build for her height, she wasn't exactly a lightweight. At least, they'd already been upstairs. Strong and muscular as he was, even he couldn't lug her up those stairs.

Of course, a caring person like him couldn't leave her to sleep in the plate of pastries. But, really, tucking her up in bed?

Her face flamed. Things just got better and better.

Come on, Macnamara. Let's get practical here. No need to dwell on a little embarrassment. Or even a lot of embarrassment.

With a deep breath or two to calm herself, she forced her unwilling limbs to move. Searching closets and the mudroom, she located a bucket to hold the drips until morning.

Please God, it would stop raining by then.

Grunting and straining, she managed to move the heavy mahogany bed a few inches. Some more heaves gained extra inches. And again. Finally, she dragged the bed sideways, just enough that the leak missed it.

The bucket could catch those drip-drip drips. The wet pillow could go in the mudroom. She'd wait till morning to dry it. The rest of the bed, thankfully, remained fine.

Done. Now she could sleep again.

She hoped.

Surveying her work, Nai frowned. What if the bucket overflowed, and water leaked into the store below? Worse, what if the attic was flooded? The entire ceiling could collapse.

Some welcome home for Ivy.

Pulling her shoulders back and lifting her chin, she tried hard not to flinch at each flash of lightning and crash of thunder. Only one thing to do. Go up to the attic and see.

After climbing the steep stairs, filled with dread of what she might find, her heart sank. No visible flood. Phew! But several large buckets stood under drips.

Most only held an inch or so of water, but one, the one over Ivy's bedroom where the drips fell fastest, had filled to overflowing. So this wasn't a recent problem. And Ivy's stopgap solution wasn't good enough.

Roof repairs. Another item to add to her list.

She scowled at the big five-gallon bucket. No way could she carry that down the attic stairs without it spilling. There'd better be another bucket somewhere.

There was. Back up the stairs again. She wouldn't miss the gym while here.

Holding her breath in case the full bucket toppled, she edged it out of the way and placed the empty one under the leak. Nothing more she could do. If this one leaked, the bucket below would catch the drips. And she'd just have to hope it didn't damage the ceiling too much.

Kristina's brother, Roman, did home-maintenance work. He should be over that accident Kris said he'd had months ago and able to fix the roof. So, she didn't need to ask Mateo and his granddad to help.

She'd text Kristina first thing in the morning.

In the meantime, she'd get some rest. A spare bedspread from the linen closet would serve as a makeshift pillow. Much as she'd love to sleep in, she set her cellphone alarm for seven a.m. Provided it stopped raining, that gave her enough time to check the attic and the roof and speak to Roman before the bookstore employees and customers started arriving.

And if it didn't stop raining, she'd need to find a lot more buckets — fast.

This return trip to Chapel Cove shaped up to be the worst week of her life. Once she had Ivy settled back in and safe to leave, she'd escape on the next flight.

Surely, nothing more could go wrong. Could it?

CHAPTER FOUR

WHEN HER alarm chimed what felt like mere minutes later, Nai muttered something unfriendly to her phone, half-opened her eyes, and pressed snooze.

A sound stopped her from going back to sleep, though her head hurt and her eyes felt as if somebody trickled sand into them overnight. She was used to getting up early, but not after missing most of two nights' sleep.

What was the sound nudging at her? Birds chirruping. The occasional vehicle passing by on Spruce Street. Nothing else.

And that was it. Nothing. No rain hammering on the windows or the roof.

It stopped. Almost enough to make her want to give thanks. When she managed to force her eyelids all the way open, sunlight filtered through the faded hand-sewn, book-patterned curtains.

After dismissing the alarm, she put on her glasses and peered at the bucket beside the bed. No new drops joined those already there. The bucket in the attic hadn't overflowed.

She slogged into the bathroom, splashed cold water on her face, and stared at her reflection. Beneath stuck-out hair that refused any attempts at styling, dark circles shadowed her hazel eyes. No wonder her mother called her ugly so often. No wonder she'd chosen a career over marriage.

Not that she'd actually been offered the choice.

Her chin raised, and she eyed her reflection. No negative thinking. *Someone* found her attractive, at least once in her life. If Mateo hadn't, why else would he have kissed her?

That was a long time ago. And then he embarrassed you.

Best to ignore that nasty voice. She had more important things to think about. The leaky roof and all those buckets. As fast as she could, she dragged a hairbrush through her hair and gave her teeth a sketchy brush. Forget changing her sleep-crumpled clothing. The sooner she checked the damage up there and sent a message to Kristina and Roman, the better.

Before Mateo arrived to check on her.

Somehow, she knew for sure he would.

She grabbed a gray sweater from her suitcase to ward off the chilly morning air. There used to be a ladder in the storage lean-to behind the house, and almost certainly, there still would be.

As she passed the kitchen, she debated grabbing a cup of coffee. Her stomach perked up at the thought of food, but she shook her head.

First things first.

Halfway up the tall wooden ladder she'd wrestled to its full height, she paused, hands clenching on the rungs. Being so high in the air made her a bit... uncomfortable. It took every ounce of her willpower to ignore her quivering tummy and push herself farther up. Her tummy quivered as she reached the top. The steep-sloped roof could have its disadvantages.

To make things worse, the sun hadn't dried up all of last night's rain yet. Raindrops still sparkled all over the roof. Pretty, sure. But the worn asphalt shingles some long-ago builder replaced the original cedar shakes with were, most likely, slippery.

She really should leave it. Just ask Kristina for her brother's assistance. And if Roman was still out of action after his accident, ask Mateo. But the image of Mom, needy and flaky, always desperate for a man's help and attention — a different guy each month, it seemed — flashed in her mind.

The mom she'd vowed never to become. So what if some people might say Nai's stubborn independence was equally unwise.

She swallowed as she surveyed the slick shingles. This was a bad idea. A very bad idea.

But walking on the roof? Way easier than asking Mateo for help. Less risky, too. She'd taught herself a lot of things, some by attending classes, some by searching on the internet. Did all her own maintenance on her apartment. No need to beg for a man's help. Ever.

Without shingles and the other necessary supplies and tools, she couldn't do much. But she did need to determine the extent of the damage. Maybe she *could* fix it herself. At least once she knew what she'd be dealing with, she could do the research and decide. If she stretched, she could just reach the first rung of the narrow rusted metal ladder attached to the roof.

Feet scrabbling for a grip on the shingled surface, she hauled herself up and then climbed higher. The subdued roar of a motor on the sleepy street made her twist to glance down.

Vertigo engulfed her.

So far down to the ground. And despite only seeing it last night in the rain, the black truck looked familiar.

If she'd wanted to beat Mateo, she was too late.

Forget Mateo. She hadn't come this far to give up. The main leak should be just the other side of the roof ridge.

"Nai, what are you doing up there?" Mateo's concerned voice hit her in the back.

Best not to look down. That vertigo was no fun. What did he think she was doing? Enjoying the view?

Though as her head crested the roof to peer over the ridge, the view across the Cove to the sea really was spectacular. A spectacular distraction she didn't need. Just like Mateo. What she'd come up here for was to identify the leaky spots. She'd simply need to let the ladder go and inch crabwise till she spotted the damaged shingles.

"You shouldn't be doing that. You know I'd be happy to help you. Please, come down." His voice sounded louder, far nearer, and the extension ladder rattled against the guttering.

The moment she glanced over her shoulder, her foot slipped on the shingles, and she lost her grip on the slick roof ridge. She gasped as she slid down the wet, rough surface.

Arms windmilling, she tried to grab onto something. Anything. But her hands only caught air. Finally, they connected. But clawing for a grip on the roof ladder only spun her sideways, before gravity tore her loose. Her heart pounded in her throat.

Please, don't let me fall all the way down!

Thwack!

She slammed side-on into something solid. Or somebody. Mateo's chest. The ladder he stood on shook, and for one terrifying moment, a painful meeting with the ground felt inevitable. For both of them.

Somehow, Mateo held strong. The ladder steadied, but not her heartbeat.

"I've got you."

Sandwiched between the roof and Mateo on the ladder wasn't the best place to be right now. Or ever. Though when she looked into his dark eyes, so close to her...

Shutting her eyes, she turned her head away from him. If only she'd taken the time to brush her teeth more thoroughly. The roof didn't care about her morning breath, but Mateo might.

"I wouldn't have slipped if you hadn't distracted me. I was doing fine till you came along." Her words popped out, sulky and petulant as a spoiled five-year-old. Though it happened to be true. She *had* been doing fine.

Still, hadn't she just nearly sent both herself and Mateo flying off the roof? He'd risked his life to help her.

Thankfully, he didn't mention that tiny detail. "The roof leaked last night, I'm guessing? That's why I stopped by on my way home from my shift. I noticed a few cracked shingles a while back, but Ivy's as stubborn as you are and refused to let me look at it. I'm not a trained roofer, but Grandpa is. So why don't you let us take care of it?"

"I..." No further words emerged.

The position she was in wasn't one she wanted to have this conversation in. Not that she *wanted* to have this conversation. Though, ridiculously and quite inappropriately, a pleasant wave of sensation spread through her at being so close to him, pressed against his firm chest.

Surely just adrenaline over how close she'd come to falling. Nothing more.

"Officer Rodriguez, what are you doing up there?" A young female voice floated up to them. "And is that Ms. Nai with you? I have Ms. Ivy's dogs and the parrot." Yapping accentuated her words.

Nai cringed. It must be Fern. Just the way she'd wanted her first meeting with one of her aunt's flaky employees. Including the animals in the mix so soon only added to the fun.

"I'm checking where the rain is getting in," she called back. "The roof leaked badly last night. Right over the bed."

Mateo's laughter rumbled through his chest. "That explains everything. Should I be grateful you didn't try this stunt last night during the storm?"

No doubt, her chest pressed against his spoiled the effect of her eyeroll. At least, ever so slightly.

"Let's get you to the ground." His voice softened. "But first, you need to be the right way around. Head down is never a good way to do a ladder."

Between him heaving and a lot of awkward groping with her hands and feet, she managed it, toes wedged in the solid old metal gutter and fingertips burning, rubbed raw from scrabbling on the shingles.

"Mateo and Naomi, Mateo and Naomi, Mateo and Naomi," the parrot screeched.

Her face flamed up again. "It's Nai now," she muttered under her breath. Who taught the stupid bird to say that, anyway? She certainly hadn't. The rescue parrot moved in with Ivy not long after she moved out.

Of course, the parrot didn't hear her and continued screeching, as if competing with the yappy dog to make the loudest noise.

"We'll have to take this a step at a time." Mateo stayed focused and showed no sign of reacting to the bird's annoying chant. Yet. "Nai, let me help you, please? This is not the time to be Ms. Independent."

Not much of a choice. If she didn't accept his help, there was still a chance of knocking the ladder and both of them to the ground.

Probably, right on top of the yappy dog and the annoying parrot.

A plus, yes, but…

"Okay. You win."

"Good. I'm pleased to hear it." His note of about-time satisfaction suggested he'd squeeze every inch of mileage from her admission. "I'm going a few steps down. Then I'll guide your feet to the ladder rungs. You'll need to slide a little to do that."

Not exactly what she wanted, after fighting so hard to get where she was, into a position that finally felt secure. "As my only alternatives are waiting to grow wings and fly down or asking Fern to call the fire truck to come rescue me, like I'm a kitten stuck up a tree, I suppose I'll have to."

Mateo chuckled, apparently not in the least offended. "That's my Nai. So, I'm going to take hold of your right foot now."

Good thing he warned her. When his strong hand grasped her ankle, she almost jumped off the roof, even *with* the warning. Without the benefit of wings, her meeting with the ground wouldn't be pretty.

"Lift your foot, so I can shift it to the ladder. It could feel like you're unsupported. But trust me. I've got you. And God's got you."

Trust. A commodity she'd always been short of. Life taught her to do it herself. No need to trust anyone. But her "secure" position wasn't secure at all. She'd *have* to trust Mateo.

Just this once.

God, she still wasn't sure about.

Mouth dry, she swallowed. "Okay."

After the longest minute of her life, both her feet were firmly on the ladder rungs, and her hands grasped the top rung. The breath she'd held escaped with a whoosh.

"Good girl." Mateo's approval raised her hackles. She wasn't a dog or a child. She didn't want to be grateful to the man. "Now all we need to do is climb down the ladder."

When she stepped onto solid ground again, her legs trembled, and she clung to the ladder with one hand. Grinning, a slender girl with spiky blonde hair and a hippy-styled dress held a hand out for her to shake, oblivious to the fact her employer's niece almost fell on top of her. "Nice to meet you, Ms. Nai. I'm Fern. I brought the dogs and Oscar back."

As if to confirm her words, the little beige dust-mop dog, all hair and noise, resumed his yapping and danced around Fern's legs, tangling her in the leash. The larger mutt with short, wiry brown hair gave out a few barks but at least stayed in one place, either better behaved or because Fern held the leash firmly. The parrot, resplendently plumaged in green and red, stared at Nai with his orange eyes and continued to squawk.

Nai strained to hear the girl. How had her organized life become such a mess?

Letting go of the ladder, she stepped near Fern. Oops! Her legs gave way, and she flopped onto the damp grass, resting her head on her bent knees. "Sorry. Two sleepless nights. I guess they've caught up with me."

"Aw." Fern's lips turned down. "I guess you're worried about your aunt. We all are. I'll just take the dogs for a quick walk before they go inside. It's almost time to open the café."

Mateo squatted beside Nai and slipped a supportive arm around her shoulders. Her accelerating heartbeat did little to ease her lightheadedness. "Did you have breakfast?"

"Not yet." She shook her head. "It seemed more important to check the roof."

"I'm sure you could repair a roof if you put your mind to it. But would you want a person who's never done anything in Excel updating the formulas in your spreadsheets? Besides, I think you might find your hands full, with these guys to care for." A twinkle appeared in his eye as he gestured at the departing dogs and preening parrot.

How she hated it when he was right. A long breath escaped her. "And I'll still be working remotely for my boss, too. Okay, no DIY. I'll hire Kristina's brother. I'll take the animals upstairs, grab something to eat, and phone him now."

And brush both her teeth and her hair. And change into clothes she hadn't slept in. And check with the hospital to let Ivy know everything was running smoothly—as in, she hadn't killed anyone or anything.

Yet. She choked down a snort.

Doing her best not to lean on his support, she stood, then waved him away. "I'm fine."

Mateo let her go. "*You* might be fine, but I don't know about Roman. He could be up to doing some work again, though last time I saw him he was still on crutches."

Crutches? Nai grimaced. "Oh. I hoped…"

She *had*? Had she honestly hoped for anything? Or had all hope fled along with her sanity when she crossed that invisible barrier beside the Welcome to Chapel Cove sign?

"I don't want you to let me do the job so I can score points over you. It's just…" Mateo glanced at his feet, brow furrowed, and loosed a heavy breath. "Grandpa could use some distraction. He's missing Gran terribly. He walks around the house, touches her things, and sighs. Or even worse, spends hours doing nothing but stare at the chair she used to sit in. He's not eating enough. I'm worried about him."

Her heart constricted. Too much time with Mateo, and she'd end up in Coronary Care, too. But she *did* feel for his worry and grief. "I'm so sorry, Mateo."

Hearing the name started the parrot screeching again. "Mateo and Naomi, Mateo and Naomi. Mateo and Naomi should get married."

Pretending her face wasn't flaming, Naomi picked up the bird's cage. "Oscar, I'll need to teach you to say something different. How about 'Never in a million years.'"

For once, the perfect line. Usually, she only thought of them way after the event. So why did she spoil the effect by peeking at Mateo to see how he reacted?

He laughed and shook his head. "I like Oscar's line better."

He couldn't mean it. Spinning on her heel, she hurried to the door. Spending more time with him wouldn't be a great idea. Unlike his grandpa, she didn't need any more distractions, especially ones that made her pulse gallop.

And though she hadn't agreed to Mateo doing the roof yet, she had no way of escaping the biggest distraction of them all.

CHAPTER FIVE

NAI STOOD on the porch with Mateo and the parrot in its cage and almost sighed as she considered all she had to juggle.

Aunt Ivy's pets added so many complications.

First, the dogs. She'd have to get them upstairs and make sure the doors stayed locked. When she'd worked in the café in her teens, food hygiene rules meant pets couldn't be allowed in a food service area. She doubted those rules had changed. Besides, she didn't want to imagine what havoc could ensue if they got loose in the bookstore.

"Why on earth would Aunt Ivy get dogs, especially a bigger dog, when she has a café to manage and no yard for them to run in?" she muttered to herself.

"Your aunt is a softie, though she puts up a tough front," Mateo replied as if she'd directed her question to him. His raised-eyebrow glance her way suggested he knew another Macnamara woman who was the same. "Everybody in town knows the story. How she went to the animal shelter to get a cat when her old cat, Sidney, died, on the basis every bookstore needs a cat. And she left with two dogs as well. Heinz and Catsup."

Turning the key in the lock, Nai let her sigh emerge. The chaos here called for it. "She told me she couldn't resist their sad brown eyes."

"Or the cat's green eyes, it seems." Mateo smiled as he opened and held the door for her. That soft, kind smile that used to turn her insides into mush.

Forget used to. Still did.

She slapped herself on the forehead. "The cat! If Fern took the dogs and the parrot, where's the cat?"

"Hello, Ms. Nai," an older voice called from behind her. "I'm Violet."

Nai whirled around. A woman in an amethyst-colored sweater and a matching skirt, walked toward the bookstore, away from a car that nearly matched her outfit. Ivy told her about Violet and her love of all things purple. Even her silver hair had a lilac-toned rinse. A gray cat squirmed in Violet's arms — somehow she'd resisted tinting it as well.

"I've brought Paige back. As many of our customers say, a fitting name for a bookstore cat." The older woman chuckled. "I'm so glad to hear Ivy is recovering."

"Good morning, Violet." Nai reached out to pet the cat's sleek fur. "Thank you for taking care of Paige. Aunt Ivy hopes to be home by the weekend."

Her heart warmed. What would it feel like to be part of a community the way Ivy was here, cared for, missed? Something she'd never experienced.

She suppressed a sigh, then shook the thought away like

raindrops off an umbrella. So many other things to think about. Keeping the dogs under control. Getting Oscar into his regular cage. Making sure the cat didn't go anywhere near the café.

Thankfully, the store and the café were separated by a door. It wouldn't surprise her if the food hygiene rules were broken when Ivy was in charge. But they wouldn't be while she was here, if she could help it.

The place needed a good cleanup. And the sooner she tackled fixing up the downstairs apartment for Ivy, the better.

Barking announced Fern's return with the dogs. Though they were used to living under one roof, they went wild at the sight of the cat. Fern's arms strained as she struggled to hold their leashes.

Mateo stepped over to the young girl. "Let me help you with them."

He took the leashes from her hands, leaned to the dogs, petted them, and whispered something. They stopped barking as if somebody turned off the sound.

Huh. How about that? So the man was a dog whisperer, on top of all his other skills.

"Is it okay with you if I take the dogs upstairs while you attend to the store and the other pets?" He bent and petted Heinz, the smaller dog, again, and the mutt jumped and licked his face.

Air swooshed from her lungs, her shoulders loosening in relief. "Yes, please."

Forget refusing to accept help this time. Her canine experience totaled zero.

She'd need to discuss the pets with Aunt Ivy when she got home. Two energetic dogs and recovery from a serious heart attack didn't seem a wise mix.

Managing the parrot and cat would be enough. She picked up Oscar's small travel cage. Probably just in time, because Violet approached with Paige. The cat opened her eyes and studied the parrot. Then her pink tongue flicked out, licking her lips as if she already anticipated a nice dinner with the parrot on the menu.

Uh-oh. Nai would have to be careful. She'd never want anything to happen to Aunt Ivy's parrot. Her aunt was devoted to the bird, plus the parrot was such a permanent fixture in the store that he even greeted some customers by name.

She glanced at Paige again. The cat had her eyes half-closed now and appeared to ignore Oscar, but Nai didn't trust that look. The sooner she got the parrot safely into his big cage by the store window, the better. And with Oscar on his best behavior, the transfer went smoothly.

As she walked through the store in the daylight, she couldn't help grimacing. The sunshine revealed even more things in need of attention. Not just books stacked haphazardly, but dark spots on the ceiling, dust on the shelves, and, as she suspected, books in the wrong sections. Something needed to be done about the squeaking floor, as well.

Surprisingly, no barking sounded from upstairs. Mateo must still be working his dog-whispering talent. But he wouldn't be with them all day. No doubt the dogs thought it unfair. The cat got to roam the entire building, via the cat-sized pet door upstairs, while they were restricted to the living quarters. She agreed.

Not that she wanted the dogs barking. Or roaming, either. That cat door better *had* be too small for little Heinz to wriggle through, as Aunt Ivy claimed.

"Well, I'll go dust and organize the romance section." Violet blinked at her and placed Paige on the floor.

The cat stretched and walked away with a disdainful air and a twitch of her tail as if she owned the place.

"Didn't you do Romance yesterday?" Fern peered across the bookstore. "It doesn't look too dusty."

Violet blinked again. "I... don't remember. Maybe I did. Oh

dear."

Oh dear.

"You can say that again," Nai muttered, doing her best to keep a straight face. What had she gotten herself into? "How about you dust the shelves in the mystery section?" she said in a louder voice.

Footsteps on the stairs heralded Mateo's return, but she didn't dare glance at him.

"Did you feed Paige?" Fern asked.

Violet looked up and frowned as if trying to remember. "I *think* I did."

The cat meowed something very much like a protest.

Keeping a straight face was getting more and more difficult. "Maybe we should put down her water bowl and some of her crunchies, just in case?"

Showing no surprise at Violet's uncertainty, Fern strolled toward the café. "I'll get something for Paige and for Oscar and start the coffee brewing at the same time. I'll leave a little earlier today, if that's okay. I have a date."

"Oooh. Nice." Violet's smile widened. Then she turned to Nai. "What was I supposed to do, again?"

Nai suppressed a sigh. "Dust. Or whatever you think is necessary."

The way things were going, she'd need to keep an eye on Violet to make sure she didn't wander outside and get lost. And the older woman was still driving? Scary. So she not only needed to take care of Aunt's pets, and Aunt Ivy herself when she returned home, but also care for Aunt Ivy's employees, too.

So far, Fern seemed more capable than she'd expected from Ivy's stories.

So far.

"Aunt Ivy asked me to fix up the downstairs apartment for her. I'll go have a look and see what needs to be done." Her announcement was made to no one in particular.

Nai had fond memories of the little apartment. The way Ivy fixed it up for her with two doors, one into the bookstore and one directly outside, insisting at sixteen she should have her own space and her own front door. Determined to prove she was nothing like Mom, she'd never betrayed her aunt's trust by misbehaving.

Violet, humming away to herself in Cozy Mysteries, gave no sign of hearing her, but Mateo accompanied her across the bookstore to the apartment door.

"You have your hands full, don't you?" he whispered.

"More than I realized." Now Nai understood what Aunt Ivy meant when she admitted she'd hired Violet and Fern because they needed the jobs, not because they were a great help. She grimaced as she opened the door. "You were right. My aunt is a softie who can't pass by a person or a pet in need."

Her shoulders sagged. Had she been one of her aunt's rescue cases, too? She'd surely been in need of rescue. Had Ivy taken her in out of nothing more than pity for her only brother's child?

Her spirits dipped even further when she opened the apartment door. The place didn't just need a cleanup job. Boxes of books stacked everywhere made it impossible to see the furniture.

"Oh dear," she repeated Violet's words.

"You can say that again." Mateo's smile and flicker of a wink made it clear he'd heard her grumble at the older woman's forgetfulness. Time to guard her tongue better. She'd hate for Violet to hear her and be hurt.

Hands on hips, Nai surveyed the room, blinked, and blew out a long breath. "Hoo boy. It's a bigger job than I expected, but it's all got to be cleared. Ivy won't be allowed to use the stairs for a few weeks after she comes home."

"I'm praying for her speedy recovery. I'll be glad to help you with the boxes. And…" Intently focused on her face, his eyes darkened as he stepped toward her. "Though I'm sorry it happened this way, I'm glad you came home. I've missed you all these years."

The air around them thickened, charged with awareness. She should look away, step away. She didn't.

"I missed you, too." More than she wanted to admit.

Arms lifted a little, eyes intent on her face, he took a step nearer. Her heartbeat spiked, and her breath caught in her throat. She should hold back, she should. He'd hurt her so badly in the past.

Instead, she leaned toward him, drawn closer by a connection she couldn't explain. Any moment now, he'd kiss her again. Any moment now, she'd kiss him right back.

And maybe, this time, she wouldn't run away.

CHAPTER SIX

THE TINNY buzz of the apartment doorbell brought her to her senses. A riot of confused emotions filled her. Unsure if she felt relief or regret, she jerked away from Mateo, breaking their connection with an almost tangible snap.

Disappointment and something else flashed in his dark eyes.

"One minute, please," she called to whoever stood outside. Those boxes stacked right in front of the door needed moving before she'd have any hope of opening it even a crack.

Mateo sprang forward, ready to assist her, and she waved him back. "It's okay. I'll manage."

To have any chance of getting her composure back, she needed him as far away as possible. Ideally, the other side of the country, but for now, the other side of the room would do.

Thankfully, he didn't insist on helping or on following her when she threaded through the maze to the door. Her hormones and her heart needed a chance to settle down.

As she hauled the heavy boxes far enough out of the way to open the door, she couldn't imagine who'd rung the doorbell. Customers would use the main front door, not this inconspicuous one at the side of the big old Victorian. Unless Reese had decided to come help without waiting for a reply to her text.

Whoever it was, they had either the best or the worst timing in the world.

Finally, she got the door open. Her childhood friend, Kristina, stood on the doorstep, grinning her delight. Squealing, they hugged. So much for being mature and over Mateo. The years peeled away as if she were a teenager again.

"Nai! I'm so pleased to see you again, though I wish something happier brought you home." Her Latina friend, blessed with clear tanned skin, enviable curves, and the sweetest nature on the planet, stepped back and examined her. "You're looking great, *amiga!*"

As that was self-evidently not true, she could dismiss it as more of Kristina's innate niceness. No need to protest that she looked awful, with bags beneath her eyes, messy hair, no makeup, and slept-in clothes. Kris would argue, and neither of them backed down easily.

Mateo wanted to kiss you again. Despite all that, he must have found you attractive. She stomped on that hopeful thought — fast. His kiss would have been for old times' sake, nothing more.

Pushing Mateo from her mind, she focused on her best girlfriend.

"Same here for you. Wonderful to see you, but I'm so sorry for what you've been through." Though Kris had been devastated by her recent divorce, Nai was only sorry for her friend's pain, not the actual divorce. High time Kris broke free of her mean, cheating, belittling, bully of an ex. Cullen had never been good enough for sweet Kristina.

Things she couldn't say to her friend.

"I'm surviving. Starting to rebuild my life." Kristina glanced at Mateo, who'd stayed where he was across the room rather than interrupt their reunion. For a guy, he'd always been sensitive to things like that. "We can talk about that later."

Nai nodded, getting the message. Whatever Kris wanted to say wasn't getting said in front of her cousin. "Okay."

"Reese will be along any minute, too. We're here to help you get the place ready for Aunt Ivy. The three of us together again." Such a kind and thoughtful friend.

"Aww. You guys." Nai couldn't stop smiling. Pure happiness fountained up in her. She loved her besties from forever ago as if they were sisters. Over the years, they'd caught up when they could, but never all together, not since Kristina's wedding in Portland. Group PMs and Facetime weren't the same.

Plus, they'd chosen the best possible time to distract her from Mateo. She really shouldn't feel so big a sense of loss that their almost-kiss never happened.

Kristina's eyes widened as she scanned the box-crowded apartment. "Wow. I realized you'd have a big task, but not *this* big. Good thing you have Mateo here to help." She smiled, hurried over, and hugged him. "*Hola, primo.*"

Hmm, Mateo. Nai had been trying her best to ignore him, though his presence was kinda hard to ignore. She didn't attempt to follow the cousins' rapid-fire banter. Her Spanish was nowhere near good enough to keep up.

Though maybe she should have tried. The way they both glanced at her and grinned suggested she was the topic of discussion.

Not for much longer. Time to thank him and send him on his way. And as soon as he left, ask Kris if Roman was well enough to take on the roofing job.

At the first lull in their conversation, she broke in. "Thank you for your help this morning, Mateo. But you can see, I have assistance to get the apartment ready for Aunt Ivy. You must be tired after working all night. Isn't it time you went home to sleep?"

He shrugged. "It was a quiet shift. I can catch some sleep later. Call me if you change your mind. Kristina has my number. And the offer about the roof still stands."

Did he and Kris exchange winks? She eyed them suspiciously. Whatever scheme they'd cooked up, they could forget it.

Lifting her chin, she threw her shoulders back. "I'll keep that in mind. Thank you."

Ugh. Her clipped tone sounded way too dismissive.

"Um, would you like a cup of coffee and a brioche in the café before you go? I'm sure Fern's already got the coffee going."

As if coffee and pastry could solve everything…

Though, come to think of it, she did start feeling closer to him yesterday over that cup of hot brew. Until she'd fallen asleep right in front of him and he'd carried her to bed. A hint of memory tugged at her. Being lifted in strong arms and snuggling in against a muscular male chest.

Warmth crept up inside her again, setting her face aflame for the umpteenth time this morning.

If he chose to stay for coffee, she wouldn't be joining him, though her rumbling tummy reminded her she hadn't had breakfast yet.

"It's okay." He raised a hand and shook his head a little. "I need to check on Grandpa, anyway. I don't like leaving him alone too long. But remember, you can call me if you change your mind." Mateo smiled, a sweet warm smile that could melt far harder hearts than hers, and turned to leave.

Exactly what she wanted. Yet it took all her willpower — and her friend's expectant gaze — not to trail him all the way home like a puppy. Following him to his truck was bad enough.

"Thank you." She *did* appreciate him rescuing her from the roof. Though of course, if he hadn't come along and startled her, she probably wouldn't have slipped. But he'd helped with the dogs, too.

And now that he was going, she wanted to keep him here longer. What was wrong with her?

"Once I've checked on Grandpa and run a few errands, I'll come back. Just in case you've changed your mind about me helping with those books."

Stepping back, she pinned on a bright smile. "I won't. You'll be wasting your time."

"Up to you." His confident raised-eyebrow grin suggested he imagined after moving a few boxes she'd beg him for help. Nope. Made her more determined *not* to.

Her back straight and head held high, she strode back into the bookstore. Time to get to work.

Kristina welcomed her back into the store with a slightly worried smile. "Just wondering. There are so many books here already. Where should we move the boxes from the apartment?"

Scrunching up her nose, Nai gave her an apologetic glance. "Uh, sorry. The only place they can go is upstairs."

"Right." Kris eyed the steep staircase and the rickety railing. "Oookay. Good thing Reese is coming to help, too."

Reese.

Her other bestest friend. Her beautiful supermodel friend.

Self-conscious, she ran shaky fingers over her hair. "I just need to go upstairs and check on Aunt Ivy's dogs."

They *were* being suspiciously quiet. And she'd need to make sure they were shut into a spare room while they came and went with the books. If, while she was up there, she brushed her hair and changed her T-shirt, no big deal. Right?

Much as she loved Reese, she always felt inadequate in comparison.

She didn't make it as far as the bedroom. When she opened the door at the top of the stairs, Heinz shot past her. She slammed the door before Catsup could follow and galloped after the little dog. Aunt Ivy would be so upset if Heinz managed to get out onto the street. Mateo's dog-whispering gift would come in handy now.

Once downstairs, Heinz contented himself with barking at Paige and jumping up as if he was on springs to try to reach her.

"Heinz, shush."

Just out of reach, the cat stared down at him from the sales counter, then swiped a casual paw at his nose the next time he jumped.

The swipe connected. With a yelp, Heinz hid behind Nai's legs. Laughing, Kristina handed her one of the leashes hooked over the stair post. With that clipped to his collar and the handle wrapped around her wrist, the little dog wasn't going anywhere. She hoped.

And just in time. Through the glass section of the entrance door, she glimpsed familiar strawberry-blonde hair.

"Phew. Thank you. Now we can let Reese in." Nai flung the door open and wrapped Reese in a hug.

Kristina's enthusiastic squeal rang even louder than Heinz's yapping as she rushed to join them in the group hug. "The trio's together again!"

"For a while, at least." As soon as she could, she'd be out of here. Staying was the last thing on her agenda. Nai cupped her hands around first one friend's face then the other, giving them a gentle shake. "You girls... I should've known to keep silent about needing to rearrange the house. But, oh my, it's so good to see you both again."

"How's Aunt Ivy recovering?" Reese asked.

The grief Nai had managed to push down till now bubbled up. As tears prickled in her eyes, she swallowed hard and then released a heavy breath. "Not that great. Her heart has suffered some permanent damage." Her voice wobbled, small and broken.

Suddenly, she realized how close her beloved aunt had come to leaving this world. Without Ivy, she'd be alone. No living relatives, unless she counted Mom.

Rephrase that. No living relatives on speaking terms with her.

Had God intended this as a wake-up call? A reminder of how short life was, to make them question their priorities? Did He even care at all? Maybe life was what she feared, just randomness, no plan or purpose.

Pathetic thoughts better suited to a pastor or a philosopher than a PA. Thoughts she had no intention of giving more airtime to.

Pulling herself together, she did what she did best. Focused on the practicalities. "So that's why we have a lot to do today." Wobble over, her usual brisk tones returned. "We need to clear out the downstairs apartment and prepare it for Aunt Ivy. It'll be a while before she'll be able to climb the stairs to her bedroom again. Let's get to work."

After locking Heinz and Catsup into Ivy's bedroom and checking both Fern and Violet were managing in the bookstore, she ushered her friends into the book-choked apartment.

Being in that tiny one-roomed space with her friends sparked bittersweet memories. Moving to Aunt Ivy's and getting away from Mom had been the right thing to do, despite the drama Mom created and the battles it took to get here. For the first time in her life, she'd had a sense of home, someplace solid and secure, and even more important, someone who cared for her. As they relocated the stacked boxes, her old photos and high school pennants pinned to the faded pink walls appeared.

Each had a memory involving the girls.

And involving Mateo, too. Thank goodness, when he dropped by again, he'd accepted that when she said she didn't need help, she meant it.

Not that it stopped the girls from teasing her about him.

"Mateo has changed a lot," Kristina chimed as if she'd read Nai's mind. "My cousin grew up nicely. Far from the awkward, bashful teenager he used to be. Tall, muscular, and rather attractive, despite those scars. So, what was that about you falling off the roof?"

Nai suppressed a sigh. Mateo must have told her, and now, the girls wouldn't let it go. No hope for that. In as few words as possible, she told the story.

"Hmmm, so Mateo came to your rescue." Reese strolled to one of the remaining boxes and lifted it. Somehow, Reese even made hauling books around look elegant.

"How romantic." Kristina grinned.

"Romantic or not, I'd prefer to get through the rest of my visit without seeing him again if I can help it. Some things just aren't meant to be." She didn't try to stop the acid edge creeping into her voice. The last thing she needed was her friends playing matchmaker, and she suspected the cousins' Spanish banter could have been setting her up somehow.

Which reminded her, in the storm of hugs and reminiscences, she'd forgotten to ask whether Roman would do the roof. She hoped it only needed patching up. Though what she'd seen before slipping into Mateo's arms suggested the entire roof might need replacement in the near future.

"The roof, could Roman…" Her words trailed off as her friend shook her head.

As she lifted a box, sadness pooled in Kristina's dark eyes. "Sorry, girl. Roman is still out of action after that motorcycle accident. His ankle didn't heal right. I'm sure he'd be happy to help if he could, but I don't see how in his present condition. He's having to turn down even simple decorating jobs."

So, she wasn't left with a lot of choices. Leave the roof to keep leaking till Roman was well enough, or accept Mateo's offer. "I'm so sorry about Roman. I hope he'll recover soon."

A sigh left Kristina's lungs as she walked to the door. "Yeah, me, too."

Reese winked at Nai. "I guess you'll just have to accept help from the handsome Mateo Rodriguez."

"Rub it in, why don't you?" she grumbled. "Maybe I *will* do the repairs myself."

Probably realizing that after her near-miss fall even Ms. Independent might need to be Ms. Realistic, Reese only laughed.

After a full day of lugging heavy boxes upstairs and stacking them in an unused bedroom, the apartment was empty of everything but furniture. Nai flopped against the wall. Her only breaks had been taking the dogs for a couple of very short walks, and the sandwich lunch she and the girls grabbed.

"Phew, we're done with the boxes. Cleaning the place up and making it homelike for Ivy won't be nearly as much work now." She summoned the energy to pull both her friends into a tight hug. "Thank you so much, girls. What would I do without you?"

Reese and Kristina hugged her, then eased out of the embrace. Kristina raised one eyebrow. "Maybe accept help from—"

Nai threw her friend a warning glance, and Kris stopped midsentence. No prizes for guessing who she'd been about to name. She'd already grabbed Nai's phone and added his number to her quick dial list, amid plenty of teasing.

Changing the subject, Nai clapped her hands. "Let's have some coffee and pastries in the café. My treat."

They clustered around a café table, steaming cups of fresh-brewed coffee and a plateful of warm, just-baked brioches in front of them.

"Who'll say grace?" Kristina asked.

Biting her lip, Nai said nothing. She wasn't ready or willing to disclose her lapse in faith to her friends just yet. They'd always held far stronger beliefs. Though she noticed Reese also remained silent.

Kris grabbed both their hands. "Okay, *I'll* say grace."

After her short simple prayer, Nai echoed her amen.

While Kristina and Reese gave every appearance of enjoying their brioche, wolfing them down, she nibbled hers. Despite her hardly eating all day, too many painful memories lingered. The way Mom criticized her for eating anything, even lettuce leaves. And the binge eating that followed once she stopped living with Mom. She never wanted to lose control like that again.

Kristina leaned forward and launched into a long complicated story about a new guy in town she'd met and her scheme to dress as a man because he insisted he wanted her twin brother, not her, to remodel his home.

Crazy!

Almost as crazy as her own idea to climb on the roof and fix it herself.

Still, she agreed to help Kris with her masquerade. One — anything to help her closest friend. And two — she loathed that male chauvinist attitude of thinking only a man could do the job. She'd encountered that way too often in the corporate world. Though she'd offered to make Kristina and Roman a loan to cover his medical bills, her friend, as independent as she was, flatly refused.

Kris wouldn't accept help when she could do it herself.

Nai felt the same. She'd learned to do many things for herself. But much as she hated to admit it, when it came to the roof, she did need to let someone else do the job. And with Roman out of action and the only other home repair and roofing guy in town booked up for weeks ahead as a result, she had no choice. She'd have to phone Mateo tomorrow.

Unlike Kris, who she suspected wanted to do the decorating work for the new guy in town as much for time with him as the money, she'd be having to accept help from the man she least wanted to accept it from. Mateo Rodriguez, always coming to her rescue.

No matter how much she kidded herself otherwise, when she left Chapel Cove this time, she'd be leaving a part of her heart behind.

CHAPTER SEVEN

MATEO SMILED as he guided his truck along the Chapel Cove streets. Home to Abuelo's place after his final night shift for this week. Life was good. Life was very good.

Ever since seeing Naomi again, something warm and sweet glowed deep inside him. Despite her running away after he kissed her for the only time, despite her refusing to date him, despite the way she'd friendzoned him in senior high, she'd stayed in his heart. God blessed him, giving him a second chance to show her he was worth loving.

As he stopped at a red light, his chest tightened. He didn't have long. Though he prayed for Ivy's recovery, Naomi would surely leave as soon as her aunt was well enough.

So, don't let yourself get attracted to her again. The commonsense thought came way too late. Letting Naomi go again wouldn't be easy.

The light turned green, and he moved forward. If only he could move forward with Naomi, too.

She seemed much more confident now, more independent. Maybe *too* independent, if that stunt on the roof was any guide. But a few times, he'd glimpsed the vulnerability he'd seen in her teens, lurking in those hazel eyes, magnified by her thick glasses.

He made a turn. And just like when they'd been teens, she still set his pulse pounding. He'd never forgotten her. And of course, he still remembered kissing her in the rain, the overwhelming wave of awareness in his veins, the sweet taste of her lips, the startled look in her eyes.

Did she remember it, too? He'd come so close to kissing her again, yesterday in the apartment.

His phone rang, and he answered on his hands-free. "Hello, this is Mateo."

"Mateo, it's Nai." She coughed a little. "Well... you were right. Kristina's brother isn't available to do the roof repairs. And I'd like them done before Aunt Ivy comes home. At least, repaired enough to stop the leaks until I can get someone to replace the whole thing. Um...does your offer still stand?"

What? His jaw dropped, and he almost let the steering wheel go. Nai admitting he was right? Nai accepting help?

His help?

"I'll pay for the materials and for your time, of course." Her words rushed out, tripping close together.

His fingers clenched on the steering wheel. So she wasn't *really* asking for help. Not when she reduced it to a financial transaction.

"Are you... are you still there?" Something tensed her voice.

"I'm here. Just shocked you asked me. And it's not a matter of money. I offered to *help* you, not to take your money. Help Ivy and Abuelo, too."

"I don't have any choice other than to ask you. Not only because I don't enjoy waking up to a wet pillow, but also because I can't have Aunt Ivy come home to this sort of worry." The sharpness of her words cut through the cab. When had she become so defensive? "If you can't take care of the roof, I understand. I know you must be tired. Plus, you have another night shift coming up."

Typical Naomi. If she did ever ask for help, she'd always tell the other person all the reasons they shouldn't help her. The girl's mom did a massive number on her self-confidence. "I don't. I have three nights off. Plenty of time."

"Oookay." Sounding doubtful, she stretched the word out.

"I'm on my way home now, but once I've showered and made sure Grandpa has some breakfast, I could come around to measure up for the materials I'll need."

Despite her hesitancy, assisting her with the roof felt right. Not only so he could spend more time with her, though that was a bonus he wouldn't say no to. Many people in Chapel Cove had affection for Ivy, including his grandpa — friendly affection, of course. Doing this roofing job gave him a perfect opportunity to talk Abuelo into getting out of the house to do something beyond succumbing to grief.

And... helping people was what Mateo did. His duty and his obligation. Surely, God's reason for making sure he survived the accident that killed his parents.

After parking near the stone-colored clapboard Cape-Cod-style house with a chimney protruding from its asymmetrical roof, he bounded up the small stairs. Hmm, more cracking and flaking in the paintwork on the white porch. Last year, his grandpa would've already repainted it. This year, Abuelo didn't care.

Sorrow and the desperate need to help the grandfather who'd raised him weighed heavy on Mateo's shoulders. He thought by now, a year after her death, the old man's grief would be lifting. But if anything, it intensified. When Abuela died, his grandpa didn't only lose a beloved wife, he lost his will to live.

As Mateo turned his key and pushed the heavy tan-brown door open, he called out. "Abuelo, it's Mateo. I'm home."

As always, his breath stilled in his chest, and he prayed as he waited for a reply. One day, there would be none.

"In here." His grandpa's voice sounded from the living room.

Mateo forced a smile as he entered the room, cluttered with knickknacks his grandparents had collected over the years. His grandpa sat on the same striped living-room suite he remembered from his childhood, staring at the TV, switched on but with no sound playing. His clothes hung loose on his once burly frame.

"Good morning, Grandpa." Mateo used the Spanish his grandparents always preferred to speak at home.

"What's good about it?" The older man barely glanced away from the news channel.

Mateo didn't let his smile waver. "After we have breakfast, I need your help. Aunt Ivy's house has a roof leak, and I've volunteered to fix it. But I'll need your advice on what to buy and the best way to repair it."

Grandpa's eyes, once so bright, were bleak now. "I don't feel up to going out."

"Come on, please? We can't let Ivy Macnamara come home to a house with buckets in the attic to catch the drips. Not after such a bad heart attack. With Cousin Roman still on crutches, he can't help."

Grandpa's eyes narrowed. Then he sighed. "I guess it won't hurt to look."

"Great." Mateo did a mental fist pump.

Soon they were on the road toward the old Victorian, with Abuelo's ladders and tools in the pickup bed. "Let me tell you what happened at the bookstore yesterday, and you'll know why I'm so keen to help."

Mateo wouldn't be able to protect Naomi's privacy, anyway, since Violet and Fern would gossip with anyone who came into Ivy's on Spruce. By now, all of Chapel Cove likely knew about him catching Naomi when she slipped on the roof.

He made a turn, then glanced at his grandpa.

"Who told you I want to hear it?" Abuelo's white eyebrows drew together, and his shoulders slumped forward.

Concern for the older man constricted Mateo's chest, but he didn't let the remark stop him. Like he hoped, Grandpa listened, though he pretended not to. When Mateo got to the part about her blaming him for her near-fall, Grandpa chuckled.

Thank You, Jesus! He hadn't heard his grandpa laugh in a long time.

Naomi returning could be a good thing in more ways than one, though she probably wouldn't be happy if she found out she was a source of comic relief.

"So Naomi Macnamara is back in town. I remember you used to study with her. I know you liked her." Abuelo's voice became thoughtful with a tinge of sadness. "Maybe this is your second chance. Be grateful for your second chances, grandson. Many people don't have them."

A vise tightened on Mateo's heart as he parked outside the quirky old bookstore and helped his grandpa out of the truck. Both because he hoped not to mess up his second chance with Naomi and because he longed for Abuelo to accept a second chance at living, too.

Squinting in the sunlight, his grandpa peered at the building. Then his focus shifted to the roof. "A lot of work is needed here. But you're right to start with the roof. No point painting trim if the roof isn't sound. Hmm. It's been a while since I last used a ladder."

Mateo stepped between Abuelo and the ladders. He'd claimed to need the old man's help to get him out of the house, but he couldn't let his grandpa attempt to climb to the roof.

"How about I go up and take some photos with my cellphone? Then you can tell me what I need to do. I do the work — you provide your expertise." Supporting his grandpa by the elbow, he walked the older man to the entrance and up the shallow front steps. "Grandpa, you know, Violet is getting rather…" He searched for the right word.

"Forgetful?"

"Yes! Could you help her in the bookstore while I do the roof? Nai was worried about how vague she seemed yesterday. Even if you just sit in the café and check now and then if she's okay."

Grandpa chuckled. "Violet actually used to be very smart. She was a schoolteacher, you know? A knowledgeable lady."

Mateo opened the door and let his grandpa inside. He scanned for Naomi. There, behind the counter, running up a tally for a customer at the cash register. Her cheeks reddened, her unruly dark hair escaping its ponytail, and her lip caught between her teeth, she looked flustered but more in charge than yesterday.

As it had a quarter of a century ago, his pulse skipped at the sight of her.

She glanced up and their eyes met. Raising his hand, he waved hello. A shy smile curved her lips. Then she turned her attention back to Mrs. Naylor.

Fern opened the café door, and the scent of just-brewed coffee and fresh pastries drifted in. His grandpa breathed in deeply. "I guess I could do that. You'll be okay with taking care of the roof?"

"Sure. I'll come to you when I need advice on what to do."

After Mateo settled Abuelo at a small table and bought him a coffee and a sweet bread roll, the older man glanced at other customers with the first spark of interest he'd shown for a while. A little of Mateo's burden lifted.

When he strolled into the bookstore, Naomi was busy with another customer, Melanie from the Pancake Shoppe and her young daughter, in the children's books section. For a moment, he simply watched her. As much as he wanted to wait till Melanie left and talk to Nai, be near her, he had things to do.

Like get on the roof before she changed her mind.

When she looked up, as if aware of his gaze on her, he pointed up. She nodded. Hopefully, she guessed what he meant. After an inspection, he could guestimate how much material to buy.

Minutes later, he had Abuelo's ladders in place. Professional quality, from when his grandpa was the town's handyman. Far better than the rickety old thing Naomi braved yesterday. Plus, from helping Abuelo in his teens, he knew how to use the special roof ladder that hooked over the ridge.

Once on the roof, he examined it, snapping pics with his phone as promised. The damage was worse than he'd thought, but as long as the plywood sheathing under the roof remained sound, he should be able to patch it up.

Making a mental list of all he'd need to buy, Mateo climbed down again and reentered the bookstore. Naomi was nowhere to be seen, and Grandpa leaned on the counter, engrossed in conversation with Violet.

A half-smile tugged at the older man's face while Violet waved her hands in the air. He heard the words *Mateo should marry Naomi*, then a screech, mimicking the parrot. Mateo guessed she was reliving yesterday. To Grandpa's credit, his eyes widened as if he heard the story for the first time.

Well, he *hadn't* heard that part. Mateo had chosen not to include the parrot's words in his retelling.

Hope for his grandpa's healing stirred him. Instead of interrupting, he sent a text to Abuelo's number, telling him what he intended to do, then jumped into his truck and took off for the home renovation store.

It didn't take him much more than twenty minutes to get shingles, nails, and felt paper. Partly, because there was no line at the store. Mostly, because he hurried, longing to get back to the bookstore and see Naomi again.

Only back a day and a half, and yet already, he knew. It'd ache worse than a broken leg when she left.

Chapter Eight

THE SCREECHING and frustrated shrieks reached Nai, even over the vacuum cleaner. Kicking the off switch, she dashed from the apartment into the bookstore. This wasn't just Violet dramatizing a story for Mr. Rodriguez. Those screams sounded real.

Taking advantage of a lull in customers to work on getting the apartment ready for Aunt Ivy's return clearly hadn't been one of her better ideas. With Violet in charge, anything could have happened.

No matter how much she'd tried to prepare herself for anything, the reality left her unsure whether to cry or laugh. The parrot flew circles close to the ceiling while Violet chased him, her purple skirt askew, her silver bun disheveled. Mateo's granddad waved his arms at her and shouted for her to stop, to no avail. The dogs, as if offended about missing all the fun, barked madly upstairs.

Maybe she should simply be glad the shelter hadn't had a python or an iguana as well, the day Aunt Ivy visited.

Spotting a box in Violet's way, Nai called out. "Careful!"

Fear clenched her stomach. If the frail older woman tripped, a fall could be serious.

Somehow, Violet sprang in the air and landed on the other side. "I'll catch you! Just you wait till I do!" she shrieked at the parrot.

Nai rushed in the opposite direction, closing all the doors and windows as fast as she could to prevent Oscar from getting outside and flying off. "Please be careful, Violet."

Maybe if she could bring the bird its favorite food, it would fly down? Aunt Ivy let him out of his cage when she was here alone.

Thwack! Violet knocked down a kid-sized chair in the children's books section, then another one. "I opened the cage to give him fresh water and a little treat, and next thing I knew, he was flying around the ceiling," she panted.

"Aren't you supposed to be dusting, Violet?" Fern appeared from the café, wiping her hands on her apron. Yesterday's hippy chick had morphed into rockabilly today. "What's all the noise ab—?" She glanced up, then stopped midword, eyes wide.

The main door burst open, and Mateo rushed in. With all the noise, he probably thought a murder was in progress.

"Shut the door and lock it," Nai shouted. The last thing she needed was a customer walking into this mess, or worse, holding the door open and letting Oscar escape.

Though, oh boy, was she glad to see Mateo.

As he took in the scene, his jaw slackened. "Whoa."

"No kidding." She thought with longing about her office and the desk where even a single pencil wasn't in the wrong place. Though it had one drawback.

No Mateo.

At a moment like this, she really shouldn't be grateful she'd managed to find flattering black trousers that fit her perfectly, along with some pretty blouses, in Chapel Cove's one women's clothing store. Shouldn't even be thinking it.

"I can catch Oscar." Fern climbed on a chair and swiped at Oscar as he flew past.

The barking increased upstairs.

"Ladies, no offense, but the parrot is getting more and more frightened." Concern creased Mateo's forehead. "You should get down from that chair."

"Violet, Fern, it's okay. Please leave Oscar to me. I don't think the business insurance will cover staff falling off chairs or tripping over boxes while chasing parrots. So I'll catch him. Somehow." Nai eyed the poor thing. How she'd catch the bird she didn't know yet. But the rapid pulsation of his chest, visible through his feathers, suggested he was probably terrified.

Apparently, somebody else shared her intention to catch the parrot. Paige padded along the boxes, then jumped onto the counter, green eyes focused on the bird.

Uh-oh.

Nai edged in the cat's direction, whispering, "I think we need to watch Paige."

Fern climbed off the chair, and Violet stopped running and dropped herself into the nearest armchair, breathing fast. One less worry. Though that rapid breathing might be.

"Ms. Violet, are you all right?" Mateo leaned over her, as caring as always. "Would you like me to bring you some water?"

Recovering her breath, Violet patted his arm. "I'm fine, dear. Thank you, though."

Mr. Rodriguez sat beside her and took her hand, clearly feeling she needed comfort after her ordeal.

Grateful that base was covered, Nai shifted toward Paige, hoping to snatch her before anything else could happen. Paige was overfed, spoiled rotten, and lazy. Surely, she couldn't catch a flying parrot. But still…the cat often managed to climb even the highest bookcases. Best not to take anything for granted. She crept nearer Paige.

Then the bird circled lower, just above Fern's elaborate, fifties-style hairdo. Before Nai could grab Paige, the cat leaped in the air. Oscar screeched louder and flapped his wings frantically.

Thanks be to God, the cat didn't reach the bird. Sadly, she did reach something.

The top of Fern's head.

The parrot, as if surprised by this new development, quieted down, and perched on a bookshelf, head tilted to one side and pupils expanding and contracting as he watched. Fern screeched now as she thrashed around the room. The cat, probably afraid to fall, seemed to sink her claws deeper as she uttered some wails of her own.

"Fern, please stop," Mateo ordered, stepping in front of the girl. His voice held an unmistakable tone of command.

Startled, Fern stopped instead of barreling into him.

One step at a time, he approached Paige, who eyed him with suspicion. Then he snatched the cat and scooped her from Fern's head. Her fifties' hairdo didn't look styled any longer. It looked more a bird's nest, and the parrot eyed it from his bookcase perch. Surely, he couldn't be considering landing there next.

Yes, he could be. No "surely" about *anything* in this place.

Violet glanced up from her chair. "Fern, I think it's safe to say your date hair doesn't look like date hair any longer."

"Oh no!" Fern lifted her hands to feel her hair.

"If a man loves you, he'll love you even on a bad hair day." Mateo smiled reassurance to the younger woman while petting the cat. The standoffish creature purred in his arms.

Nai reached out and took Paige from him. "Fern, why don't you

71

go to the bathroom and freshen up? For now, just cover your hair with a chef's hat. You can leave the café earlier if you need time to restyle your hair before your date."

The fewer people in the room panicking the parrot, the better.

Sitting comfortably in an armchair provided for browsers, Violet rearranged her bun without looking in a mirror. "I don't care if I don't have date hair. Don't need it. I *know* I already look good."

Nai wished she had one ounce of the older woman's confidence.

Still holding the cat, she moved to the apartment door. Paige needed to be out of the way, too. Nai opened the door just wide enough to shove the cat through and shut it before Paige had the chance to dash out again. "We'll have to ignore her caterwauling. She can stay there till Oscar is tucked back in his cage."

"That's next on my list."

Though Mateo's calm voice offered reassuring certainty, Nai placed her hands on her hips and arched her neck. "And *how* do you propose to do that?"

"Let's see. Could be, it won't work because the parrot might smell the cat on me. But it's our best chance to catch him without distressing him with a net, so I'll have to try." He fished something out of his pocket and made a clicking sound.

Huh.

"It's called a clicker. I stopped by the pet store and bought it for you, in case you couldn't find Aunt Ivy's. One of my other cousins used to have a bird, and we trained it to step up onto our arms and do other tricks. Right after a clicking sound, the bird gets a treat."

"I hope my aunt *did* train her parrot." The haphazard way dear Aunt Ivy did everything else didn't instill confidence. But sure, it was worth a try.

He lifted his arm, elbow sticking out. The parrot circled in the air above him, and then… Oscar landed on his arm! Nai released the breath she'd been holding. Was there *anything* Mateo couldn't do?

"Hello there, mister. Great job! You're a smart bird, aren't you, Oscar?"

"Do you have a treat to give him?" Nai moved closer. She should've paid more attention to the parrot's favorite food and stocked up.

"I have some macadamia nuts I brought for him. Oscar used to adore them. His tastes might have changed over the years, but let's try it." He fished a small packet of macadamia nuts out of his jeans pocket with his free hand, then looked at her.

Understanding his dilemma, she took the packet, opened it, and emptied a few nuts into her palm. Hopefully, the bird wouldn't bite her. Ivy warned her he could inflict a nasty nip when he chose.

The parrot picked out a macadamia nut and seemed to like it. Nai would applaud if she didn't have the treats in her hands.

"Now, we move to the cage. You put the nuts in there for him, so he knows there's a treat waiting."

When the cage was within reach, Nai placed the nuts she still held inside it.

"Let's get you back home." Mateo kept talking to the bird as he slowly, very slowly, moved his arm and placed the parrot inside, then closed the door.

"Naomi should marry Mateo. Naomi should marry Mateo," the parrot announced from its perch.

Nai's face flamed. Again. "It's Nai now. I don't know who would have taught him that. Or why."

"Why?" Grinning, Mateo picked up the fallen chairs and the book cart. "Because you should?"

If that was a joke, it wasn't a kind one, and it wasn't like Mateo to be unkind.

She rolled her eyes and huffed before heading to the apartment door to release Paige, whose wails at being locked away from all the fun had escalated. Released from her prison, the cat shot off to crouch on the highest bookcase, glowering at Nai. But at least the noise had stopped.

Thanks to Mateo. He'd come to her rescue so often. From protecting her against playground bullies at school, to stopping her from falling off the roof, to catching Oscar.

But how could she get him to understand that she didn't *need* rescuing, that, unlike her mother, she could handle things on her own? She didn't want to be so desperate for love and attention, so needy, a victim forever searching for a rescuer. She didn't want to come to rely on someone who could let her down again.

She could manage on her own just fine.

Okay, she wasn't managing things all that great right now, but only because her life didn't involve such chaos. Living in a real-life slapstick comedy wasn't nearly as much fun as watching one.

If anyone had filmed the past five minutes, they'd all be finding themselves on *America's Funniest Home Videos*.

The doorbell chimed.

"A customer. We'd better open up again. It's a store, after all." Violet wobbled when she tried to stand.

Nai waved for her to sit again. "Rest a little longer. I'll let the customer in."

Customers. Not one, but three.

She suppressed a grimace and pinned on a welcoming smile instead. None of them seemed to need assistance, each walking straight to a specific section and then studying the shelves.

Phew. Floppy with relief, she wanted to collapse in an armchair herself. What a morning!

How was she going to manage the store, fix up the apartment, make sure Violet didn't fall, comfort Fern that she still looked beautiful before her date, take the dogs for their regular much-needed walks, keep an eye on the cat and parrot, get her work back to her boss, *and* deal with Mateo being here working on the roof? All this after waking up to a bed full of Aunt Ivy's pets and dragging herself to Kristina's before seven to help her friend don a not-entirely-convincing disguise.

Give her the typical hundred-items-daily To Do list she tackled at Ideas and Inventions any day.

She resisted the urge to slide to the floor and leaned on the counter instead. "Oh dear."

"You can say that again." Violet stood, less wobbly this time, and ambled toward the fifty-something woman browsing the romance section. "I'll just see if MaryAnn wants any help choosing her book. We have some lovely new romance releases. Then I'll put that fresh water into the parrot cage."

"No!" Nai and Mateo shot the word out at the same time.

"You attend to the customer." Nai softened her tone, reminding herself Violet meant well. "Mateo and I can attend to Oscar." Her nerves *so* wouldn't survive a repeat performance.

"The time in Chapel Cove is going to be interesting for you, isn't it? You'll be glad to get back to Austin." Mateo's voice brushed her hair. When she glanced up at him behind her, sympathy and a touch of sadness tinged his smile.

Nai winced. "Interesting isn't the word. And yes, I will."

Apart from missing a certain tall, dark, and handsome police officer, who'd somehow taken up permanent residence in her heart.

Who, if she was honest with herself, had never left it.

CHAPTER NINE

MATEO NAILED down the last of the replacement shingles. He'd rather use cedar shingles. Far better quality. But the last roofer had used asphalt, and for a patch-up job, he'd had to go with what was there.

At least Naomi wouldn't need to worry about wet pillows or overflowing attic buckets. His muscles ached, but a good ache, the ache of a job well done. Fatigue reminded him he'd been awake all night.

Naomi was worth it. Or, as he'd have to get used to, Nai now.

While fixing the ridge capping in place, he chuckled.

The open-mouthed and wide-eyed expression on her face as the parrot flapped and screeched and Fern ran around with the cat on her head. Priceless.

Nai was so out of her element.

He'd best not confess that, after she left for college and he waited for his place in the Police Academy, *he'd* taught Oscar to say their names. Best not confess yet, anyway, though he prayed the time would come when he could.

Gathering up his tools, he tucked them into his toolbelt and then climbed down the ladder. Job done.

As he loaded the leftover materials and tools into the back of his truck, she emerged from the bookstore. Or, more accurately, the leashed dogs dragged her from the bookstore. Probably full of pent-up energy after being shut in much of the day.

Fatigue forgotten, he moved to help her with the excited pair. They could walk the dogs together.

"I'm fine." She stopped his words before he could suggest it.

Then not one but two squirrels dashed down from the spruce tree outside Ivy's, running off by different routes.

"No!" Nai yelped, struggling to hold the leads. He reached her too late. The dogs broke free and ran in opposite directions, each chasing one squirrel. Worse, the sudden jerk as they slipped their collars threw Nai to the ground.

Concern squeezed his heart as he bent to offer a hand to help her up. "Are you hurt?"

"I don't think so. But I can't believe I let the dogs get away." She groaned as he pulled her to her feet.

"Blame it on the squirrels. Or on me for distracting you. Okay, I'll go get Catsup, and you try to catch Heinz." Grabbing the larger collar and leash she held, he took off after the bigger and faster dog.

Thankful for his training, he raced after the mutt. Catsup better not think this was a game of chase.

"Got ya!" He grabbed the dog and slipped the collar over his head. "Catsup, sit."

Either from surprise or from some remembered remnants of

training before he landed in the shelter, the dog plopped on his behind.

"Good boy." After tightening the collar a notch, Mateo stooped to pet Catsup on the head, wishing he had a biscuit to reward the dog. "Though not so good boy for running away. Please don't do it again."

Catsup tilted his head, as if considering it, and gave him a couple of loud yips.

"Let's go see if we need to look for your companion, shall we?" Mateo straightened and scanned the surroundings for Nai and Heinz.

Catsup yelped out another bark one could construe as a yes.

There they were! Nai carried Heinz, clearly not trusting the leash any longer. She cradled the little dog in her arms, tenderness softening her face and glowing in her eyes. Like her aunt, Nai put up a tough front but was a softie at heart.

As soon as she looked up from the dog and saw him, her sweet expression fled.

Something inside Mateo shifted. Would he ever be able to persuade her to let her guard down with him again?

Catsup edged closer to Mateo and licked his hand, his tongue rough against Mateo's skin. Offering comfort or asking for the same treatment as Heinz?

"Don't even think it, bud. I'm not going to carry you." Mateo's lips tugged up.

They met Nai and Heinz halfway.

"Thanks." She hugged Heinz closer. "I don't know what's happening lately. I'm not usually this helpless."

"It's a different environment for you. Fish out of water and all that." He glanced at her as she strode beside him. May as well say it. "You know, it's okay to ask for help. None of us can do it on our own. I ask for help all the time, especially from God."

Avoiding his gaze, her glasses screening her eyes, she didn't reply.

So, he'd be the one to do most of the talking. He could handle that.

Though he'd long overcome his boyhood shyness, something about Nai still made him as tongue-tied and awkward as he'd been in his teens. "Let me check on Grandpa. I'm guessing by now he'll be ready to go home. Then how about we take the dogs to the park? They need to run around and get some proper exercise."

She started shaking her head, then stopped midshake. "Okay. Going to the park is a great idea. For the dogs, of course."

The narrow-eyed glance she threw him seemed designed to warn him not to read too much into her agreement.

"Of course. Only for the dogs." He couldn't hide a smile.

He wouldn't mind spending more time with Nai. But after her earlier reaction to his not-really-joking comment that they should get married, wisest not to say so.

"I'll shut these two in the apartment while you drive your granddad home, and I let Fern leave early to get her date hair back." She peeked at him so adorably. "I know you must be exhausted, but would you be okay to wait till after I close the bookstore to take the dogs to the park?"

"No problem." He *was* tired, but not so tired he'd turn down the chance of more time with Nai.

Rather than walking the dogs through the bookstore, Nai headed to the side door leading to the apartment. Mateo used the main entrance. He looked around for Abuelo.

His grandpa and Violet lounged in the armchairs laughing and joking. Even after spending most of the day at the bookstore, rather than being tired, the old man had some of his spark back. He even had more spring in his step, clambering into the truck cab with minimal assistance.

"You can drop me off at the bookstore again tomorrow, if you want. I quite enjoyed helping Violet." Abuelo's tone was airy. Too airy, combined with a mischievous air of suppressed excitement.

Mateo eyed his grandpa, one eyebrow raised in a question mark. "Sure." For now, he didn't have time to investigate why. Not if he hoped to make it to the pet store before it closed on his way back to Ivy's.

God willing, the excitement meant nothing more than an eagerness to see Violet again. Though eccentric and forgetful, the older woman seemed good-hearted.

Everything worked as he hoped, and pet store bag in hand, he arrived at the bookstore just as Nai turned the Open sign over to Closed.

She opened the door before he knocked. "Perfect timing." Loud howls and yips from the apartment told him where the dogs were. "Catsup and Heinz are looking forward to their trip to the park."

Probably not as much as he was.

Even if he'd thought it was wise to tell her that, he didn't get the chance. As soon as she opened the apartment door, the dogs raced out, barking and running enthusiastic circles around them.

"Sit," he commanded, maybe optimistically. It worked. Even Heinz obeyed, quitting the yaps to squat at his feet. "Good dogs." He tugged gently on their ears and gave them a small dog biscuit each.

Nai's lips scrunched to one side, and she frowned. "I don't have much experience with dogs. Well, *zero* experience. I have no idea how to manage them."

"Make sure they know you're the boss and reward good behavior, like I just did." He reached into the bag. "So they don't slip their collars again, I bought these harnesses."

Within a few minutes, he'd fit their harnesses and attached the leads. Again, he kept hold of Catsup. The larger dog might pull too hard for her. Once outdoors, even little Heinz managed to drag her to the pickup in his enthusiasm.

How the dogs knew where to go, he couldn't guess. Some canine sixth sense God blessed them with.

He opened the truck's tailgate and patted the surface. Catsup leaped in. After lifting Heinz, Mateo tied their leashes up secure and short. The last thing he wanted was them getting overexcited enough to jump out of a moving vehicle.

Then, before she could do it for herself, he hurried to open the passenger door for Nai.

"Thank you for everything you're doing for me, Mateo."

Unlike their teenage years, when he'd often been able to guess what she was thinking, it seemed harder now to gauge the emotion lurking in her guarded eyes. Sadness? Regret? Hope?

Or all of them combined?

The drive to the park on the outskirts of town didn't take long. Nowhere in Chapel Cove was far away. Nai stayed silent, her brow creased. The dogs barking in the back more than made up for her quiet.

Once he parked, he opened the door and breathed deeply. The air held the fresh green of spring foliage and grass, plus the salty tang every breeze in Chapel Cove carried. He rushed around the truck to open the door for her.

Of course, she was already climbing out of the vehicle. "It's fine. I'm capable of opening my own doors."

Typical Nai.

No point arguing. He shrugged and vaulted into the truck bed to untie the dogs. "We can set them loose here."

Nai gestured to the vast open field, extending down to the river. "I hope they know to come when called."

He laughed. "Me, too."

She picked up a stick, drew her arm, and threw the stick. Catsup and Heinz sprinted away.

Surprisingly, the little mutt made it to the stick first and returned with it, his tail wagging like a propeller. Then the dogs seemed happy chasing each other.

Mateo gestured at the nearest timber bench. "Would you like to sit?"

In their teens, he'd carved "Mateo + Naomi" on it. It was *their* bench, or at least he'd considered it so. Layers of paint now covered that naïve inscription, just like layers of time, misunderstandings, and hurts covered their budding love.

"Sure." She nodded, but her gaze remained fixed on the dogs.

He shed his jacket and placed it on the bench, and they sat. This park held sweet memories. The place he'd first held her hand. The place he'd first wrapped his arm around her shoulders, too. Each time, it took him days to work up the courage.

He nearly snorted. It was probably going to take him as long to do that now. Maybe longer. While he'd developed confidence he'd lacked as a bashful teenager, Nai had also changed. She'd built a fence around her heart higher than the one around Abuelo's backyard. Career-wise, she'd opened doors for herself. But was she happy?

He hoped so, but somehow, he doubted it.

Not soul-deep happy.

Slowly, very slowly, he reached for her hand. She didn't exactly hold his hand, as he'd hoped, but she didn't pull away, either. He knew not to ask for more, but just leave his hand resting over hers. Nai couldn't be rushed.

Warmth spread through him, rich and sweet as *cajeta*, the caramel sauce his grandmother used to make. "Are you happy in Austin, Nai? And... do you hate being back here?"

Brow furrowed, she didn't reply.

He understood why she wanted to escape Chapel Cove after

high school. Her childhood was more than difficult. Nai never complained, but everybody knew. Nai's mom didn't care who heard her verbal abuse.

He understood her need to take up her college scholarship and achieve all she could. Not surprising success became an important goal for a girl who grew up dirt poor in a dilapidated trailer. Aunt Ivy would've helped, but Nai's mother wouldn't let her.

Like her mom's nastiness, everyone in town knew of her family situation. Another reason pushing her to leave.

What he didn't fully understand was Nai's hurt retreat to friendship at their first setback on the path to a closer relationship, the mess over their junior prom. Back then, he'd let his own injured pride get in the way of setting things right.

"Why does it matter to you?" Her voice was quiet as she watched Catsup's and Heinz's antics. Her fingers twitched beneath his.

Inhaling, he straightened his shoulders. Why was declaring how he felt for her tougher than facing down an armed robber?

Lord, please give me the words and the courage to say them!

Purpose infused him. As Abuelo said, he'd been given a second chance to tell her what he never did before. He'd be crazy not to take it.

"Because you matter to me. You always did. You always will."

There. He'd said it. Even if she left for Austin once Ivy recovered, telling her felt important. Knowing it would be too much too fast for Nai, he somehow resisted the urge to draw her close. Just saying the words was enough.

Enough for now, anyway.

Her hazel eyes widened behind her thick glasses. Her hand shaky, she tucked strands of glossy ebony hair behind her ear. "You never told me."

"I guess I hoped you knew."

Catsup dashed to him. Glancing away from Nai, Mateo ran a hand down the dog's spine and along his tail. Then Heinz yipped and took off to chase a squirrel, and Catsup joined his buddy. The squirrel shot up the tree, and the mutts stayed under it, barking in vain, as if not understanding why the squirrel didn't want to come down to play.

"No, I didn't know." Biting her lip, she looked away. "I don't exactly hate being back. I vowed to never return, but..." She hesitated, and her eyes clouded. "My mom... how things were. Even though she'd moved to Portland, I wanted to get away. Be somewhere no one judged me because of her."

Sensing she hadn't finished yet, he stayed silent.

"But the Cove holds good memories, too. The times I spent with the girls or at Aunt Ivy's. And the time spent with you. Until..." Her words trailed off. Then she shook herself a little. "Forget that. We'll let the past stay in the past."

Until cut him bone deep. He swallowed and gazed out to the river, then returned his focus to Nai. Squeezed her fingers, just slightly. The simple gesture sent a wave of awareness through him.

She pulled her hand away.

"We need to talk about it, Nai, not pretend nothing happened."

"I don't want to talk about it." Her voice held a hint of steel, warning him not to push things any further.

He *did* want to talk about it. He wanted to rewind time, let his hurt feelings go, forgive, and tell her he understood, instead. Except he didn't understand, and if she wouldn't talk about it, he never would.

Help me to, Lord. And please, help Nai.

He'd never meant to stand her up for the junior prom, but a twenty-four-hour tummy bug laid him flat, literally. Of course she'd been hurt.

And he'd been hurt, too, that she could think he'd *choose* to stand her up, deliberately embarrass her in front of their whole class.

When he'd asked her to accompany him, a few weeks after she'd run when he first kissed her, they'd pretended the prom wasn't a date. Just two friends agreeing to hang out with each other. Yet they'd both known it was something more — something new and beautiful they teetered on the edge of.

The angry words they flung at each other the following day ended that. Changed their friendship. Made it distant, wary, untrusting.

He couldn't help hoping they could regain what they'd lost.

Catsup and Heinz left the squirrel alone and ran up to the bench, demanding his attention until three sparrows landed near a piece of bread somebody had left and the dogs were off again in pursuit.

He longed to turn his gaze on Nai, but looking at the dogs was safer. When he looked at her, he needed all his willpower not to kiss her. Time to shift to a less personal topic. "Tell me about your job. I always imagined you'd have a business of your own rather than working for someone else. CEO rather than PA."

Her chin tipped. "I love my job. My role is far more than personal assistant. I've helped build a billion-dollar company. Besides, I can't imagine leaving Jesse, my boss. The guy is a genius, yet sweet and kind. Brilliant when it comes to his ideas and inventions, but for real-life stuff, he'd be lost without me."

She spoke of her boss with such tenderness and admiration. Sharp jealousy stung Mateo. "Do you... Are you..." Ah, he might as well say it rather than let doubts torture him. "Do you... like him?" Hopefully, she'd guess he meant more than mere liking.

To his surprise, Nai laughed. "I like him as a person, but he's more like a younger brother than a boss. We have huge mutual respect and trust, and that's one of the things that makes my job great."

So, she wasn't in love with her "genius" boss. Relief let Mateo breathe again. "Are you seeing anyone?"

She shook her head, sending dark strands flying. "No time to with my job. You?"

"I'm single." He straightened, sat taller as if a boulder rolled off his shoulders. "I imagined you'd be married by now, or at the very least engaged."

"Really?" She groaned. "It's not as if I'm a raving beauty like Reese or Kristina."

Her low self-esteem about her looks pained him with a physical ache. Why couldn't she see herself as he did? He reached for her hand again, and he cradled it in his like something precious. "You're always beautiful to me."

Her lips parted. "I–I didn't know you'd learned to flatter."

"I mean it. When I met you, you were the most beautiful girl I'd ever seen. And until I take my last breath, you'll still be the most beautiful woman to me." Where did those romantic words come from? And yet he meant every one of them. He held her hand a little tighter.

He never wanted to let her go. But he couldn't make her stay, either.

What he *could* do was help her believe she was worthy of love and admiration. Because she truly was.

Her breathing became shallow. "Do you mean it?"

"Of course. I've never lied to you. I never would. Especially about something so important."

For a moment, she gawked at him, a blush coloring her cheeks. Then she leaped to her feet, pulling her hand away again — pulling her heart away as well? "We need to go back. I have work to do. Let's get the dogs."

The mutts were in less of a hurry to leave and took some persuading into the truck.

As Mateo drove to the bookstore, he stole more than a few glances at her profile. Could he trust that God brought Nai back into his life for a reason? That maybe, just maybe, they could get it right this time?

CHAPTER TEN

AS HER ALARM chimed, Nai opened her eyes, groaned, and switched it off. Then she felt her pillow.

Dry.

The way it should be, but she couldn't take a dry bed for granted. Especially since it rained again last night.

No need to climb to the attic to check the buckets. She could trust that, if Mateo told her the roof was repaired, it was repaired. She *did* trust him. At least, when it came to stuff like that she did.

He'd probably want to check the buckets for himself just to be sure. Her pulse quickened a little at the thought of seeing him again.

No, no, no.

Not at the thought of seeing him again. Just at the thought of everything remaining on her To Do list for today. After yesterday's shenanigans, she'd gotten exactly nowhere with cleaning and fixing up the apartment.

Time to get going.

As she stretched, something soft and warm shifted to her right. Paige, taking full advantage of the cat flap in the living quarters' door. Which reminded her, she'd need to fit one in the apartment door, too.

Stretching in the other direction instead, Nai's feet touched something else warm. Heinz. Like yesterday, Catsup dozed peacefully on the rug near the bed.

Kinda cozy to wake up with them here. A nice alternative to sleeping alone. And a way better alternative than Mom's solution. She began to understand why Aunt Ivy chose to bring all the critters home, despite the bookstore being less than suitable accommodations.

Maybe Mateo would help her with them again today.

No doubt about it, he was a good man. He'd worked so hard yesterday, after being on duty the night before. And then he'd helped her even more by taking the dogs to the park.

As she recalled their conversation on that bench, her face heated. Despite the hurts of the past she'd refused to discuss, she'd still longed for him to do more than hold her hand. Like put his arm around her and hold her tight. When he dropped her and the dogs off at the bookstore yesterday, she'd wanted to invite him in for dinner.

Not that she'd be cooking. Her kitchen skills extended to pouring milk onto breakfast cereal and microwaving Lean Cuisine meals. But take-out from Tía Irma's would've worked.

When she tried to scrape up the courage to ask him, the words stuck in her throat.

Wiser *not* to ask him. A good man, yes, but not the man for her.

A man like him deserved better. A familiar chorus of put-downs echoed in her head.

Nai lay still and closed her eyes the way she had in childhood when she didn't want to face Mom's blame game yet. It wasn't her fault that the adorable toddler she'd been grew into an awkward tween and even more awkward teen, complete with buckteeth, unwanted fat, and pimples.

All her fault, according to Mom, for sucking her thumb and sneaking candy. All her fault that, when the modeling work and the TV ads stopped, Mom couldn't keep up the payments on the house and moved them into the trailer park. All her fault that, just by being born, she'd ruined her mother's life.

And she ruined her father's life, too. She'd heard the whispers, that, if he hadn't been forced into marriage at nineteen, he might not have died so young.

No wonder she'd run from Chapel Cove just as soon as she could. Resisting the urge to draw the blanket over her head, Nai pushed back the bedclothes.

None of that was true.

If she told herself often enough, she'd believe it. She wasn't that hurting kid any longer. The braces she'd paid for as soon as she could afford them fixed her teeth. Growing up fixed the acne. A careful diet, discipline, and a busy job fixed the comfort eating.

More than that, she'd made it. Achieved her ambition to make a million dollars. Choosing to take her annual bonus in company shares had been the smartest thing she'd ever done.

Mom lived in Portland now; she lived in Austin. Yet it seemed she carried Mom's taunts with her.

At forty, she shouldn't let childhood stuff affect her. But being back here woke memories she hoped she'd forgotten. The memory of being called ugly, of feeling ugly, and of wanting so badly not to be ugly.

Mateo's kind words yesterday couldn't erase all that.

Time to get out of bed and stop feeling sorry for herself. Time to grow up. Make the bed, brush her teeth, get ready to face whatever her day brought her.

Careful not to disturb Paige and Heinz, she slid into a sitting position. The pets were sleeping so peacefully, bedmaking might need to wait. That would give her a couple of minutes longer to spend getting ready.

Not that she wanted to look prettier for Mateo. Not that she cared what Mateo thought of her. He was a good man. A friend. Nothing more.

As Nai maneuvered her legs out of bed, Paige opened her eyes and stretched. "It was kind of him to drop his life in Portland and return to Chapel Cove to be there for his granddad after his grandma died," Nai said to the cat. "Apparently, he accepted a job much lower in rank."

"Meow." Paige closed her eyes again.

Just great. Nai cringed. She was talking to a cat. Even worse, she was passing Violet's gossip to a cat. No doubt, Paige had heard it all before. But still, what next?

Catsup opened his eyes, leaped to his feet, and let out a few friendly woofs in greeting.

"Good morning, Catsup. Let me go to the bathroom and get dressed, and I'll take you and Heinz outside." Well, she answered her own question. Next came talking to the dogs.

Careful not to wake Heinz, she climbed out of bed. She'd learned yesterday that getting clean and dressed while the yappy mutt bounced around her didn't make a good combination.

Her attempt didn't work. Heinz went from sound asleep to frantic excitement in less than three seconds.

With a disgusted expression, Paige jumped off the bed and stalked away.

In Ivy's bathroom, Nai brushed her teeth, enjoying the minty toothpaste flavor. Maybe she should put on some makeup, in case Mateo decided to stop by. Put on the most flattering of the few outfits she had. And try to style her unstylable hair.

No. How many times did she need to tell herself no?

A quick glance at her watch told her she didn't have much time to walk the dogs before Fern and Violet arrived. Moving fast, she changed into black jeans and a sea-green sweater.

Heinz barked and pranced in excitement as she fastened his harness, while Catsup tried his best to curl up and go back to sleep.

When she passed his cage, Oscar squawked.

"Yes, Oscar, I'll feed you soon. Just let me walk the dogs first."

Cold air greeted her as she stepped out into the Oregon spring morning.

As Catsup whined softly, Nai rubbed her palms over her arms. "Okay, I see your point. You'd rather still be in bed, and so would I. But it could be a while before I can take you outside next."

While Heinz bounded off the porch, Catsup tried to sneak back indoors.

Nai closed the door in front of his nose as the leashes pulled her in two directions. "Oh no you don't. Come on."

After the dogs did their business and she did the cleanup, she took them upstairs and washed her hands. Her phone beeped with an incoming text.

She slid it from her pocket and glanced at the screen.

Her heart beat faster at Mateo's name. Sometime very soon, she needed to stop behaving like a pathetic teen.

Even if she still felt like one around Mateo. She opened the text.

I HOPE YOU'RE HAVING A GREAT MORNING AND THE PETS ARE BEHAVING. HOW'S THE ROOF?

She thought a second, then typed: HOLDING UP. NO LEAKS. THANKS.

Heinz ran to her and yapped.

She stroked his wiry fur. "I know it doesn't sound too romantic. Not that I'm trying to be romantic."

Heinz shook his head and yapped again as if giving her advice. Yep, probably even a real dog was better at this than she was.

A new text chimed, and she hurried to open it.

HAVE A WONDERFUL DAY.

She replied: YOU, TOO.

"Sorry, Heinz. That's as good as it gets with me."

Heinz tilted his head, seemingly at a loss for words. Or at least, for barks.

Her phone rang, and her pulse jumped when *Mateo* showed on the screen again.

Knees wobbling, she sank onto the bed before swiping the screen to answer. "Hello."

Heinz leaped onto the bedspread and snuggled up to her, while Catsup sat beside her and placed his head on her knee. Smart dogs. She needed all the help she could get.

"Hello, Nai." Mateo's voice sounded hoarser than usual. "It might sound silly, but I wanted to hear your voice."

"Yes," she whispered.

"Yes, it sounds silly?" A smile warmed his words.

Great start to the conversation.

She swallowed. "Um...yes. Thanks."

Thanks? What did that mean? Couldn't she at least tell him she liked hearing his voice, too? Things were so much easier in the friendzone. Somehow, since yesterday, it had all changed.

"I wanted to talk to you before I fell asleep. Unless... Do you need my help with anything?"

"No!" He'd helped her too much already. And she wouldn't admit how much she wanted to see him. She would *not*. "Sleep? Wasn't it a night off for you?"

Somehow, she heard his silent shrug. "Well, yes. But one of the

93

guys was sick, so I volunteered to go in."

"Rest today, please."

"I'll try to, if Grandpa will let me. As soon as I wake, he'll want me to drive him to the bookstore. How's your day going so far?" His voice softened.

"It started with me talking to the cat and dogs. Next, I'll be talking to the birds! Oh, wait, I've already talked to the parrot."

His chuckle reverberated down the line. "You're doing the right thing talking to Oscar. Parrots are very social creatures. Call me if you need me. Please."

Then I'd be calling you ten times a day, at least.

She sat up straighter. She'd earned her independence the hard way, and she wasn't about to let it go now. Especially with Mateo.

"Thank you. Sleep well." She disconnected.

Heinz raised his head and grumbled in his throat. Not quite a growl, but surely showing his disagreement.

Her phone rang again, and she couldn't help but smile. She swiped the phone without looking. "Mateo, missing me already?"

There was a pause. "H–hello, Ms. Nai. Sorry to disappoint you, but it's only Fern."

Nai's face burned. "Um, good morning, Fern. Is everything okay?"

"Well, I'm going to be running late this morning. I–I overslept. I'm so so so sorry."

"It's okay." Nai waved away the girl's guilt. "I'll take care of things at the café, and Violet can manage the bookstore."

Hopefully.

"Thank you so much. I'll be there as soon as I can."

Nai rose from the bed. "Time to work, Heinz."

Not for him. The dog stretched and closed his eyes, obviously ready for a power nap.

"Well, okay. Time to work for me. Please behave while I'm

downstairs." She gave him and Catsup a quick pat before washing her hands and rushing downstairs.

In the café, she put on an apron and started on the coffee. While the enticing aroma wafted through the room, she tried to figure out how to use the oven Fern used to bake the pre-prepped pastries.

Nope. Not happening. No instructions anywhere.

She'd drive to Aileen's Pastries and pick up a box of her delicious cakes. They'd have to do until Fern arrived. First, coffee. She poured a mug and lifted it.

"Can I do anything to help you, Ms. Nai? Where's Fern?"

At the unexpected voice behind her, Nai started. Her mug slipped from her hands and landed on the tile with a crash. Thankfully, the hot coffee splashes missed scalding them both.

Turning around, she waved to Violet weakly. "Fern's running late today."

She hadn't heard the front door, and on her crepe-soled shoes, the woman moved quieter than Paige.

"I didn't mean to frighten you. Let me help you clean it up." Violet rushed to her and grimaced when she leaned over.

"It's okay." Nai eased her away. The last thing she needed was the older woman injuring herself. After scooping up the shards in the dustpan, Nai dropped a wad of paper towel on the brown liquid, while wiping down the wall with another wad. At least on the beige tile she didn't need to worry about stains. And the walls needed repainting, anyway.

"I always make things worse when I try to help, don't I?" Violet's skinny shoulders slumped, and sorrow drooped her puckered lips.

Compassion constricted Nai's heart. "You're a great help." Not a lie. More...a kind exaggeration. "This store wouldn't be what it is without you. You add a little..." Nai searched for the word and failed to find it. "Something. A *je ne sais quoi.*"

Violet brightened. "You think so?"

Recalling the scene with the parrot yesterday, Nai nodded with enthusiasm. "I do." She glanced at the kitten-adorned clock on the wall. "Let's have a quiet cup of coffee before the customers arrive."

A smile crinkled the lines around Violet's blue eyes. "I'd love to."

Nai poured two cups of coffee, carried them to the table, and then got a plate with two brioche. She hadn't had breakfast and frail Violet looked as if she could use another few pounds on her bones.

"Sorry, these are yesterday's pastries. I don't know how to work the hot bake oven."

"I'm sure they'll still taste fine." Violet sat, then bowed her head, obviously giving thanks.

A lump thickened Nai's throat. It seemed so easy for other people to find God. But not for her.

Lord, are You there?

No reply. She hadn't expected one.

Violet took a sip of her drink. "I hope Mr. Rodriguez will stop by again today. He was a wonderful help yesterday."

"That would be great, but Mateo needs to rest after his night shift. He'll bring his grandfather in later." Nai forced coffee though her closed-off throat as her cheeks heated. Blushing like a schoolgirl at the mention of Mateo's name. Really?

A knowing smile lifted Violet's lips. "Oh, so you've spoken to Officer Rodriguez already today? Good."

Uh-oh. To make things worse, Nai's face flamed again. Between that and her phone *faux pas* with Fern, by lunchtime, most of Chapel Cove would know Nai Macnamara was falling for Mateo Rodriguez.

Not that it was true, of course. Well, not exactly true, anyway.

Nai glanced at Violet over the rim of her cup. The older woman emanated satisfaction, like Paige if she finally got hold of Oscar.

Oops. She revised her estimate. For everyone to know her secret wouldn't take more than thirty minutes.

Best to turn Violet's attention to something — or somebody — else. "I noticed Mr. Rodriguez Sr. rather enjoyed your company yesterday."

"Me, too. I told him so, too." Violet giggled like a teenage girl, then placed her cup down. "One big advantage of being my age — I can say whatever I want. Do you think it's too late for me?"

Nai's eyes widened. "No. Of course, not."

The older woman gestured at her mauve-colored dress as she munched on a pastry. "Good. One doesn't need to wait until my age to wear purple. Or to give love a second chance."

Nai gulped the rest of her coffee. Did the older woman mean her?

Done with the pastry, Violet pushed to her feet, then patted Nai's hand. "Thank you for talking to me, honey. Lots of people assume I'm rather… absentminded and don't bother."

"I enjoyed talking to you." Shame heated Nai as she washed the cups. She'd been one of those people.

The bell chimed as somebody entered the store. Already? Nai hurried to greet the first customer and then stopped in her tracks. "Good morning, Mr. Rodriguez."

She peered around him, looking for Mateo.

Mateo's granddad shoved his hands in his gray slacks' pockets and shifted from one foot to the other. "Um, Mateo couldn't drive me here till later, so I hopped a ride with a neighbor, instead. I wondered if you needed any help."

Trying not to sag in disappointment, Nai pasted on a smile instead.

"I sure could use your help, Hector." Violet almost sang the words before Nai could reply.

Nai recalled Mateo saying his granddad needed something to pull him out of his grief. Looked like it worked, so she could hardly send the older man away. "Thank you, Mr. Rodriguez. Fern is running late, so I need to pick up some pastries for the café. If you would help Violet in the bookstore, it would be wonderful."

A slow grin spread over the man's face. "I'm sure Mateo would be happy to assist you again today, too, but he needed to sleep."

Nai blinked. "Of course. I didn't ask him to help."

"No. You wouldn't." He studied her as if he could see something in her she couldn't. "He's a good man. He does a lot for a lot of people in this town. You know that, right?"

She nodded. Mateo *was* a good man, but they weren't meant to be. She wasn't the right woman for him. The prom that never happened had simply been a sign of that, stopping things from going any further. Easier to permanently friendzone him, especially with Mom's taunts ringing in her ears.

Except after yesterday, it seemed that friendzone wasn't as permanent as she thought.

She pursed her lips as she showed Mr. Rodriguez how to ring up a tally.

He raked gnarled fingers through his white hair. "I worked at the hardware store before starting my own business. I think I'll manage."

"You're a man of many talents." Violet practically purred, as she rearranged the featured books on a display nearby.

"Thanks." The older man winked at Nai. "It runs in the family."

"Yes, it does." The last thing she needed was another matchmaker, but still, she smiled.

Mr. Rodriguez looked much better than when he and Mateo arrived yesterday. A smile brightened his wrinkled face more than a few times, and the bleakness had lifted from his eyes.

Thank You, Lord.

The prayer appeared in her mind unexpectedly.

As she went through her day, picking up the baked goodies from Aileen's, serving cupcakes and coffee till Fern showed up, then scrubbing out the apartment in between checking on Violet and caring for the animals, her thoughts kept returning to Mateo.

Had he woken up yet? Did he think about her, too?

There was truth to Mr. Rodriguez's words that his grandson was always eager to pitch in and help. Maybe too eager.

A vise tightened around her heart and squeezed painfully. A man like Mateo didn't need to try so hard to earn love. Yet something inside him told him he didn't deserve it. He blamed himself for his parents' death.

She had no idea how she knew that. She simply *did* know.

A memory popped into her mind. A visiting preacher back in her teens, saying that, just like God's grace, love should be given freely, without any conditions. Sometimes the problem wasn't the absence of love or grace. Instead, the problem was the person's ability to receive it.

Maybe before she went back to Austin, she'd tell him that.

Maybe she'd tell herself, too.

CHAPTER ELEVEN

BY THE EVENING, Nai was sure she'd see books or cups of coffee in her sleep. After saying goodbye to Mr. Rodriguez, Violet, and Fern, she had to force herself to keep moving. The bookstore floors needed vacuuming, and chances were she wouldn't feel any more like doing it in the morning.

That task done, she collapsed into one of the armchairs. Her aching legs vibrated from tiredness. And she'd thought her job in Texas was busy. How did people do this every day?

Her fingers itched to call Mateo, but she resisted the itch. Except for that text and phone call, she hadn't had the chance to speak with him the entire day. *Really* speak to him. He'd come in to pick up his grandpa at closing time, of course, and her tummy had performed its usual somersaults at the sight of him. But with everyone else there, they'd hardly spoken beyond hello and goodbye.

She was fine with it. Totally fine. No reason for regret to tighten her stomach. Not at all.

She wasn't going to call him. Nope. It wasn't like she'd hoped he'd call or come to the bookstore when he woke up. If, despite him wanting to talk to her this morning, he didn't want to see more of her, no problem.

Just because her friends' romances seemed to be progressing, no reason her coming back to Chapel Cove would lead to a happy-ever-after. She was glad for her besties. *Genuinely* glad, not just fooling herself. She only wanted the best for her friends.

Kristina had been so hilarious yesterday. First asking her to come over by seven this morning to help the petite adorably feminine Latina to masquerade as a man, so Kris could do the decorating work at Greg's place. Then in the evening phoning for her advice on an "emergency". What to wear to go to the animal shelter as a woman with the guy she'd pretended to be a man with all day. Crazy or what? Maybe the pretense was over, because tonight she had what sounded very much like a date with Greg. Dinner at Tía Irma's with him and his daughter.

Sweet Kristina deserved a man who'd truly love her. Nai only met Cullen once, the day he married Kristina, but she hadn't liked him. Too slick and smooth. Too used to getting his own way, in everything. He'd ogled Reese in a way no married man should. Over the years, he'd turned their bright, confident friend into a bullied shadow of the woman she'd been. The best thing the jerk could have done for Kris was kick her out to start over.

And Reese? Well, Reese looked to be trying that little bit too hard to play down the chance of anything happening with Heath. Only the guy she'd been in love with twenty-two years before, after all.

God willing, before too long, she'd be a bridesmaid at both the girls' weddings.

Her? Nope. No wedding likely. That old joke with her friends that she'd end up like Aunt Ivy, an eccentric spinster book hoarder with loads of pets, might not be too far from the truth, after all.

Though this spell with Ivy's animals made her wonder. Eccentric spinster career woman working sixty-hour weeks and coming home to a serene, spotless, and sterile apartment seemed a far easier option in comparison.

Paige wandered into the room. "If I'm happy being a dedicated career woman, why can't I stop thinking about Mateo? How come it feels like forever since he picked up his grandpa, when it's barely an hour yet?"

So, she was back to talking to the cat. Great. Maybe crazy cat lady *would* be her destiny, after all.

"Meow?" No longer standoffish, Paige jumped onto Nai's lap and got comfortable. The cat closed her eyes and purred.

Nai sighed. Normally, she'd be reaching for a clothes brush to remove the pet hair coating her black jeans. Here, she gave up the battle. The most practical goes-with-everything pants color for her job in Austin was far from practical here.

She gently stroked behind the cat's ears. "Yeah. I know. I survived without talking to him for over two decades. Now I'm missing him after only an hour." Her hand flew to her mouth. Did she say that out loud? "Well, it's not like you're going to tell anyone my secret."

Which most probably wasn't a secret anymore.

"Mateo and Naomi. Mateo and Naomi," Oscar squawked from his cage in the bay window.

"Oscar, do you *have* to say that?"

The bird danced happily, dipping his wings and bobbing his head forward. "Mateo and Naomi should get married."

"Oscar, no. My life is in Austin. Mateo and I are *not* getting married." Like the bird would pay that any attention.

"Getting married, getting married."

"Meow." Paige opened her eyes and tipped her head slightly.

"Right. You never know what that bird might blurt out in the worst moment possible. I'll have to watch what I say around him."

The cat fixed her gaze on Oscar, and her little pink tongue flicked out.

"Yes, he's a blabbermouth. But don't imagine for one minute that means you'll get to eat him."

Paige, as if losing all interest in the conversation since the fun had gone out of it, put her head on her paws and closed her eyes.

Careful not to disturb the cat, Nai fished her cell phone from her jeans pocket and called Aunt Ivy for her daily check-in.

"Hello, dear. How are you? Surviving the chaos? Is everybody still alive?" Her aunt sounded stronger.

Grateful for the spunk in Aunt Ivy's voice, Nai chuckled. "Today wasn't quite so chaotic. Oscar stayed in his cage. Paige didn't decide Fern needed her for a hat. I didn't try climbing on the roof. And yes, everybody is still alive, even Violet. How are you?"

"Much better. With the new medication, those pesky abnormal heartbeats have finally settled down. Dr. Moreno tells me he might release me from the hospital on Saturday."

"Great news!"

But she had a lot to do by Friday evening. She hadn't set foot in the apartment today, let alone done any housework. Paying for a maid service to come in might be the best option, if Chapel Cove had such a thing. She'd check the local paper and the internet tonight, then start phoning first thing in the morning.

"Isn't it?" Satisfaction rang down the line, loud and clear.

"I'll come pick you up, of course."

"Thank you, child. Though are you sure? It's your birthday."

Yep. The big four-oh. She couldn't decide if she felt happy or sad about the rapidly approaching milestone.

"I'm sure Dr. Moreno would gladly keep me in another day if I asked," her aunt continued. "Or I'd drive myself home if they'd let me."

"No way!" The horrified exclamation escaped before Nai could stop it, and she took a deep breath and softened her tone before saying more. As stubborn and independent as she was, Aunt Ivy could easily see no as a reason to go do the opposite. "You won't be covered by your vehicle insurance for the first six weeks, remember. And my birthday's not a big deal. Reese mentioned something about going out for pancakes in the afternoon, but it won't break my heart not to celebrate. Getting you back home is far more important."

"Okay, and thank you. I guess I'll have to let you drive me." Reluctant gratitude sighed through the speakers. "I can't wait to get back there and start taking care of everything again."

Riiiiight. As if Nai would let Ivy move a finger before she fully recovered. She'd make sure the nurses and Dr. Moreno told *her* what the discharge care instructions were, not just her aunt. And no matter how much she wanted to get back to her safe, predictable life, she had no intention of leaving until Lucille returned from Denver and could help in the store.

But she wouldn't tell Aunt Ivy yet. That argument could wait. Once Ivy returned home was soon enough.

Paige lifted her head and meowed. Nai smiled. "Did you hear that? Paige says hi." A few barks reached her from upstairs, and "Ivy! Ivy! Come home soon," from the parrot. That bigmouthed bird really was smart. "Catsup, Heinz, and Oscar say hi, too. Can't wait to see you. I wish I was at the hospital with you."

Her aunt huffed. "Nonsense. No need to smother me with love, child. You're doing exactly what I asked you to do. Taking care of my employees and my pets so I don't have to worry about them.

And I thank you for that."

The warmth in her response radiated clear to Nai's core. "You've done so much for me. It's the least I could do."

"Again, nonsense."

For a few minutes, they chatted about the store and the pets until Nai decided her aunt needed to rest.

After disconnecting, Nai forced herself to get up. "Sorry, Paige." She stroked the cat in apology for disturbing her.

Right before he left, Mateo's granddad, an American history aficionado, had asked her about a book in her aunt's drawer of rare books. One of the earliest Oregon state histories.

Nai hid a smile as she found the small key to the drawer on the key ring her aunt had given her and walked to the cabinet. Was he interested in that book? Or was it a ploy to come back tomorrow to see Violet again? Or maybe both?

Without thinking, she tried the drawer. It opened without her unlocking it.

Uh-oh.

Had Violet or Fern forgotten to lock it? Maybe, like so much else here, the lock didn't work anymore.

Or? All of Chapel Cove knew Ivy had a few rare books and knew where she kept them, too.

Nai shivered. No, she must be worrying about nothing. No one would steal from Aunt Ivy, surely. She pulled the drawer open and blinked. And then blinked again.

When she checked this drawer two days ago, it contained way more books. She drew in a shaky breath.

Okay, don't panic. Maybe those books had sold and been picked up by the buyers. She glanced at the big What's Happening at Ivy's on Spruce announcement board, focusing on the section where Ivy posted a title page photo and information for all her more valuable books. None had been taken down, as they should be when the book sold.

Nai rubbed her forehead.

Think.

She fumbled for her phone and called Fern.

"Um, yeah? Hello, Ms. Nai."

"I'm sorry to bother you after working hours, Fern, but I have a quick question. When was the last time you looked in the rare books' drawer? And what books did you see there?"

"Hmm. Yesterday. One of the customers inquired about a book but decided not to buy, so I returned it." The list of the books Fern rattled back matched the pinboard.

So three titles were missing.

"Do you remember if you locked the drawer after looking there?"

"Of course, I remember." An indignant huff puffed through. "And of course, I did lock it."

"Thank you. Have a good evening." After disconnecting, Nai leaned against the wall. Her knees wobbled too much for her to trust them.

Just fatigue.

The books were missing, and she needed to call the police. Unlike most of the used books in the store, the volumes in the rare books' drawer were valuable. According to the prices on the announcement board, the missing books totaled well over a thousand dollars.

But an official investigation would put suspicion on Violet and Fern. And the stress could interfere with Aunt Ivy's recovery. If possible, she needed it resolved before her aunt came home.

What could she do?

Contact Mateo. Ask him to investigate, unofficially. She didn't have any other choice. Go upstairs, check on the dogs, start a meal microwaving, and then pick up the phone. Her heart gave a little bump.

So much for not calling him.

So much for trying to kid herself she didn't *want* to call him.

Not picking up his phone to call Nai as soon as he woke after napping a few hours stretched Mateo's willpower to the max. He wanted to hear her voice again, wanted to be with her. Wanted it so much he ached.

But something told him he needed to step back. He'd already done plenty to show her he wanted more time with her. Maybe too much. Thanks to his exhaustion, he'd said way more than he intended this morning.

On top of yesterday at the park, too. Nai was smart enough to figure out how he felt for her. He'd leave the next move to her. She had to decide she wanted more time with him.

Chase her, and she'd run.

Rather than visiting the bookstore to check on how things were, he busied himself working on Abuelo's house. Tough going what with his mind circling back to Nai, but he got through a bunch of little jobs the old man insisted he'd do himself, but hadn't.

Then he moved on to weeding Abuela's vegetable garden. Kneeling where she'd knelt, smelling the good rich soil she'd tended, he felt close to her. She'd been a mother to him, not a grandmother, replacing the mother he'd lost so early.

When he collected Abuelo from the bookstore at closing time, he'd ignored his instant physical response to seeing Nai. The rush of hormones speeding his pulse rate. The way his brain emptied of everything but her. The way his shoulders automatically straightened and he stood taller.

And the way his eyes kept going back to her, no matter how

many times he tried to drag his gaze away.

She'd looked so delectable in an emerald green top that brightened the green flecks in her hazel eyes, with dark strands escaped from her ponytail framing her face and pet hair all over her black jeans. He was willing to bet Nai normally never allowed a single hair to drift out of place, and as for pet hair…

He swallowed. Hard to resist his urge to hold her close and kiss her, despite Abuelo, Violet, and Fern being there. He'd hurried his grandpa out of the store, simply to avoid the temptation.

At least, this evening, he'd have a distraction. The guys from the station had a permanent table booked at Tía Irma's for Thursday night. In the meantime, he sat with Abuelo while the old man ate the simple meal Mateo had prepared for him.

"Fine woman, that Naomi Macnamara, don't you think? I wouldn't have minded if you'd spent more time with her when you met me at the bookstore today. I'm amazed she's still single." After forking up a mouthful, the old man chewed thoughtfully and peered at him over his plate of *arroz con huevos*.

Abuelo seemed intent on making sure he couldn't forget Nai.

"I'm amazed, too." Best to keep his reply simple. He couldn't be sure the old man wouldn't repeat whatever he said to Violet, who'd then make sure the whole town knew. Convincing Nai being with him was worth giving up her job and her life in Austin was a tough enough challenge without adding well-meaning gossip to the mix.

Especially when Nai had only been back in town three days. He'd need a lot more time to woo her. The more time he spent with her, the more determined he became.

At least Abuelo had his appetite back. The bookstore visits had done him good. And some teasing in return wouldn't go wrong. "Violet Smith is a single woman, too. I don't mind if you spend more time with her, either."

Abuelo huffed and avoided the subject. "Isn't it time you left for Tía Irma's?"

Laughing, Mateo stood. "It's a little early still, but I can take a hint. I'm going."

No doubt, as soon as he stepped out the front door, Abuelo would have his cellphone out and be texting or talking to Violet, possibly even inviting her around to watch a comedy they'd been discussing when he arrived to collect the old man.

And he really *didn't* mind.

Tía Irma's parking lot was full when he arrived, and Irma stood outside the entrance door comforting a sobbing teenage waitress whose green-streaked hair matched her uniform skirt. No need for his cop Spidey sense to guess something was wrong.

Irma looked up as he approached, and relief filled her gaze. "Mateo. Am I glad to see you. You've done advanced first-aid training. A little girl Linda served just had a bad allergic reaction. Tell her it wasn't her fault. She won't believe me."

"Irma is right." He racked his brains to recall what he'd learned about anaphylaxis and emergency treatment. "If someone is severely allergic, even a single molecule floating in the air can trigger a reaction. Serving the meal doesn't mean anything you did caused it."

"Oookay." Doubt still hooded the girl's red-rimmed eyes, but her sobs reduced to sniffles.

"See? You can trust Officer Rodriguez. We're telling you the truth." Irma patted her arm. "Linda, why not take the rest of the evening off to recover. But please, be sure to come back to work tomorrow. I don't want to lose you over this." She hugged the girl and sent her off.

"What happened?" he asked, once the waitress left to collect her purse and jacket.

Irma sagged against the doorframe. "I don't know, exactly.

Kristina Vela was here with a guy I haven't seen before and his daughter. The girl had a reaction and collapsed. It looked pretty bad. The man gave her a shot. Then they rushed her away."

"The child is okay?" Something like this would devastate kindhearted Kristina, especially with the tough times the Velas had recently.

"The shot seemed to work, thankfully. The little girl was talking again when they left for the medical center." She loosed a long breath. "All we can do now is pray for her."

Before he could reply, his phone rang.

Naomi. His mouth suddenly dried as his heart rate accelerated. His confidence evaporated, slamming him back to a shy teen again.

So much for the evening with the guys as a distraction.

So much for kidding himself he *wanted* a distraction.

Chapter Twelve

SHE SHOULD hang up. She should hang up. She should hang up.

With each unanswered ring of Mateo's phone, the thought pulsed through Nai's brain.

She'd put the call off as long as she could, busying herself upstairs. While feeding the pets, tidying up the living quarters, and deciding what to eat for dinner, she'd avoided it for a good thirty minutes.

When she couldn't put it off any longer, she'd sat at the dining table with her phone in front of her for a few extra minutes before she dialed. And it seemed her tactics to psych herself up for the call were for nothing, anyway, since he wasn't answering.

Then, on the seventh ring, just when she expected the call to go to voicemail, he picked up. "Sorry, Nai. I was with someone and needed to excuse myself first."

Hot jealousy surged through her, surprising in its intensity.

No, no, no. She did *not* feel that way about Mateo. If he was dating someone else, that was fine and dandy. Besides, getting possessive about a guy she hadn't seen for twenty-something years after three days back in town was just plain nuts.

As if he knew what her silence meant, he clarified, "I'm at Tía Irma's, the Mexican restaurant. It opened since you left. The owner wanted my help with something."

"Oh." Her bottled-up breath escaped with a whoosh, and her shoulders sagged with relief she had no right to feel. "Kristina's there tonight with Greg and Chelsea. How's their date look to be progressing?"

He blew into the phone. "Uh, I hate to tell you. Not so good. That's what Irma wanted my help with. The little girl had an allergic reaction to the meal, not long before I got here. They're at the medical center."

"Oh no! Poor Kris. I'll have to call her and make sure she's okay." She hardly ever prayed, but she did now for Chelsea. For all three of them. Kristina and Greg would be terribly worried.

"Before you do, can I check? Did you call because you need my help with something? If you want, I can come around, and we could walk the dogs together? No problem skipping the weekly tacos with the guys." His casual tone sounded as if he didn't care in the slightest what she replied. So casual, it suggested he *did* care.

Maybe, that he cared a lot.

She clamped down hard on her instinctive flare of joy. Just wishful thinking for her to read anything into his words. He couldn't possibly care for her. Not really. Mateo helped everyone. That's all it was. The original all-around good guy, he needed to be needed.

Besides, she'd be leaving Chapel Cove and flying back to

Austin when she could safely leave Aunt Ivy. The last thing she wanted was feelings for Mateo Rodriguez again.

So, if he doesn't care for you and you don't care for him, where's the harm in saying yes?

Logic she couldn't find an argument against.

"Okay." The word felt dragged from her. "I need your advice about something here in the bookstore. And I'd appreciate your help with the dogs. They're due for another walk."

If she could just keep reminding herself she didn't care for him, she *definitely* didn't care, she'd be okay.

"I'll be there soon." Just as she was about to disconnect, he spoke again. "Have you eaten? I could get us some takeout."

"You get something for yourself. I'm fine." So, she wasn't about to admit that after grabbing a brioche for breakfast and more brioche for lunch, dinner would be the frozen 250 calorie diet meal for one circling in the microwave already.

The second he ended the call, she speed-dialed Kristina.

"Hello, *amiga*. I heard what happened at the restaurant. Are you all right?" Concern for her friend tightened her voice.

Kristina snorted. "I'm not the one who nearly went into anaphylactic shock."

"You know what I mean." So, Kris wouldn't see her eyeroll, but she'd surely hear it.

"Chelsea is doing better. She's with the doctor right now." Her friend fell silent for a long moment. "I keep imagining him kissing me. I can't stop thinking about him. I'm falling for him."

Somehow, Nai guessed Kris didn't mean Dr. Johnson. Or even the cute younger doctor she heard had joined the medical center.

To cover up her urge to say "Me, too" about Mateo, she resorted to teasing her friend to cheer her up. "Don't say it in such a tragic voice. It might be a good thing."

Kristina emitted a sound somewhere between a groan and a

sigh. "He's a grieving widower. And I'm burned on men. And Greg is way younger than I am, to top it off!"

"Yeah." Another eyeroll Kris wouldn't see. Though she felt for her friend's heartbreak, all she'd been through, she'd hate to see the girl throw away a chance for a better love, too. "Of all men in Chapel Cove, you had to choose a handsome, muscular, well-off young guy who apparently also has a kind heart. I mean, really, what *do* you see in him?"

And of all the guys in Chapel Cove, *she* had to choose a handsome, muscular, well-respected not-so-young guy who she knew, for a fact, had the kindest heart in the Cove.

Except she hadn't chosen him. Not in the slightest.

She *didn't* care for him, right?

"You're not helping," Kris grumbled. "And then that thing with me being Roman. No, impersonating Roman. Well, you know."

"I know." Nai shook her head at her friend's crazy stunt of pretending to be her own brother. Even with a wig, a fake beard, and a stick-on mustache, Kris hadn't been exactly convincing. Plus, Greg was sure to meet the real Roman sometime. "So, what are you going to do? Stop seeing Greg?"

For Kristina's sake, Nai hoped not. After Cullen, the girl deserved better. And how wonderful if Greg was it.

"Impossible. He just offered me the job to take over his repairs."

Phew! Nai chuckled. "See, you won't have to wear a mustache and beard any longer. Things are already looking up."

"Nai! Gotta go. We'll talk later, okay?"

"Yep, and I'll want to hear all about that kiss."

As she pulled the steaming hot meal from the microwave, Nai hoped Kristina got that kiss. She genuinely did.

But much as she teased her friend and was happy for her friend, she wasn't sure she truly wanted to hear all the romantic details.

She didn't want to *think* about all the romantic details.

Especially with Mateo due to arrive any minute.

After gulping down her meal, she hurried to brush her teeth and attempted to tidy her messy hair. It misbehaved far more in the coastal humidity than it did in Austin. Short of gluing her hair together with hair spray like Violet, she'd have to let it misbehave.

The doorbell rang, and her tummy fluttered. Once again, she had to remind herself. She didn't care for Mateo. He was just an old friend. She wanted to save Aunt Ivy from any unnecessary worry over the missing books. That's all.

It didn't count as lying if she only said it to herself. Didn't it?

She told the excited dogs they'd need to wait and firmly shut the door on them before running downstairs to open the door to Mateo. A smile lit up his eyes as if he was glad she'd interrupted his guys' night out.

He looked better than ever in a heavyweight blue denim shirt and charcoal jeans. His sleeves, rolled back a couple of turns, hinted at his tanned, muscular forearms.

She swallowed. "C–come in."

And try not to drool, girl. Or at least, try not to drool *too* obviously.

"Advice first or dog walking?" As he stepped into the bookstore, frantic yelps echoed down the stairs, and he laughed. "Sounds like Heinz and Catsup know what they prefer."

Nai huffed, directing her eyes toward the ceiling. "I won't be able to hear your advice over their racket, so maybe I can explain the situation and ask your advice as we walk?"

"Sure." He nodded agreement. "There's a cool breeze this evening. You'll need a sweater or a jacket."

Or your arm around me. She almost slapped a hand over her mouth to make sure she didn't say it out loud. Honestly, since being back in the Cove, her thoughts misbehaved even worse than her hair.

Only a few minutes later, the dogs harnessed and leashed, they stood on the porch.

"Boardwalk tonight?" Mateo asked. "I'm guessing you've been too busy to make it down there yet."

She had. And she did love the ocean, especially this time of evening when the sunset glow bathed everything with a special radiance. "Okay."

They headed down Cedar Avenue and through the Cove's main shopping area toward the shore.

"There's a leash-free section of beach now. If we go there, these two can run around as much as they want," Mateo suggested. "Easier for you."

As if in agreement, Heinz tugged harder, doing his best to tow her along. For a small dog, he was strong. Must have some muscles hidden under all that hair. In contrast, Catsup pranced happily beside Mateo but didn't pull.

Mateo eyed the smaller mutt. "Coming back, maybe we should switch dogs. Heinz needs to learn some better leash skills. At least running on the sand should help tire him out."

And get him covered with salt and sand. Oh well, she could rinse both dogs off in the apartment bathroom if needed, so they didn't track sand through the bookstore.

She barely restrained a sigh. "They do need the exercise. I was so busy today, they got far shorter walks than they wanted."

As they came out onto Wharf Road, beside the boardwalk, the sound of the waves breaking on the shore, the squawks of the seagulls, and the tang of salt lacing the air intensified. The brightly lit Ferris wheel still turned in the amusement park beside the tidal estuary. Fishermen still lined the old jetty hoping for a catch.

Those hadn't changed, though so much else had.

The luxury homes across the river were all new, and many of

the stores lining the boardwalk had changed. The amusement park had a new ride, dipping down over the river.

And she'd changed, too.

No longer the girl growing up in squalor, whose Mom was rightly known as trailer trash. She'd proved herself, made her million, would never be trailer trash again.

No longer the shy insecure teen, full of romantic hopes and dreams, the girl who'd been so wounded and vowed to forget those dreams when things went wrong.

At least, she hoped she'd changed.

Or did coming back here mean she hadn't changed at all?

Erasing the thought, she stared out to sea.

Though the boardwalk faced south as much as west, curving around the bay, sunsets viewed from here could be spectacular. Like tonight's. The sky's bright hues reflected in the sea, painting its deep blue green with streaks of pink and orange and purple. The low streaks of clouds above the horizon seemed lined with rose gold.

"What a sunset! Doesn't seeing this make it easy to believe in a Creator God?" Mateo waved out over the sea and nodded in satisfaction, as if God had arranged the beauty just for them.

"Hmm." Best to stay noncommittal. She *did* believe in a Creator God. She simply wasn't quite convinced He believed in her.

She used to love wandering the shorefront with Kristina and Reese around this time of day. They'd buy ice cream cones and lean on the wooden railings and watch the sun slide into the ocean.

And here was the row of tables with chess boards built in, where she and Mateo often came to compete. Amazing that they remained. Her fingers lingered on the worn wooden surfaces as she passed them, roughened by age, wind, and salt spray.

Nostalgia gripped her for the uncomplicated friendship they'd had. So much else in her life had been soured by Mom, but her friendship with the girls and with Mateo had been a constant. Until she hit her teens and her pesky emotions kicked in to spoil things.

"Remember when —" They spoke at once, then laughed. As their eyes met and held, something real and tangible passed between them, almost shimmering in the golden air for an endless moment.

Breathless, she glanced away, gripping the railing.

"Should we let the dogs loose?" Her words emerged way shakier than she wanted.

"Sure. The dog zone is just ahead."

Her only consolation was that he sounded shaky, too.

As they slipped their shoes off, unclipped the dogs' leashes, then stepped down onto the soft dry sand, she knew.

She hadn't changed as much as she hoped. That girl who'd dreamed romantic daydreams about Mateo Rodriguez as she watched the sun set, still did. Still dreamed the same dreams, still felt the same emotions, still hid the same hopes in the harbor of her heart.

And it still couldn't possibly work out. Romantic relationships weren't for her. She had her career, her life in Austin. She and Mateo were headed in different directions. She didn't have his faith, never really had.

That, too, hadn't changed.

Though when Mateo took her hand, enveloped it in his strong warm grip, she wondered.

What was that saying she had as a poster on her bedroom wall when she set her heart on winning a college scholarship? "A ship in harbor is safe, but that's not what a ship is built for."

Could she stop playing it safe, stop hiding in her safe harbor, set sail, and risk heartbreak again? Could they find a way to make it work?

CHAPTER THIRTEEN

THE NEXT afternoon, his heart beating fast, Mateo pulled up outside the bookstore and parked at the curb. Things with Nai were progressing, for sure. She'd actually chosen to call him yesterday. She'd allowed him to hold her hand in their sunset walk on the beach with the dogs. She'd agreed to a meal with him at Tía Irma's tonight.

He knew exactly how he felt for her. Couldn't be more sure. Seeing her again told him why, despite dating other women from time to time when he lived in Portland, he hadn't felt led to get serious about anyone else.

Nai. She'd been hiding in his heart all along. All it took to reactivate those feelings was seeing her again.

But he didn't want to scare her away by taking things too fast. He remembered all too well how she'd scurried away, then become guarded and distant after he kissed her for the first time. Memory swept him. The feel of her sweet lips against his, something he ached to repeat. The blood rushed faster in his veins.

Whoa!

When he'd decided to take things slowly, this wasn't the best memory to focus on.

Swallowing hard, he smoothed his best gray slacks and removed an invisible speck from the sleeve of his carefully ironed shirt. While he wasn't usually a guy to dress up, even for church, he wanted to look his best for Nai.

Knowing her, he'd most likely gone to the effort for nothing. She'd be fine with him wearing jeans and a T-shirt. She'd probably be wearing jeans and a T-shirt herself.

Maybe he'd overdressed. Should he go home and change?

He almost snorted. He had it bad. Even worse than he'd been over Nai in his teens. When he'd had to miss their junior prom, he'd been devastated.

Lord, I need Your help here. You know when it comes to romance, I… well, I don't know what to do. Especially with Nai, when she's so important to me. Please, help me not to mess up.

A little before the bookstore closed at seven, he walked up the crazy-paved path, across the porch, and into the bookstore. Holding hands yesterday, while the dogs chased seagulls along the shore, had wiped all other thoughts from his mind. He'd forgotten to ask about the problem she said she wanted advice on.

Scanning the store, he spotted Nai, talking to a mom and her daughter in the Children's Books section. The mom shifted position, and he recognized her. Melanie from the Pancake Shoppe, back again. Her little girl must love books. She'd been in only a few days ago.

But his attention was all on Nai.

Good thing he *had* dressed up a bit. Instead of jeans and T-shirt,

Nai wore a flowing skirt the color of the sea, shimmering blues and greens, with a pretty green blouse. Her favorite color, and it suited her so well. Her hair was done different, softer. And somehow, she looked even more beautiful than she normally did.

She squatted to the girl's level as the child turned the book pages, and her smile held such kindness, such tenderness, he melted.

Children of our own? I know we're both forty, but if we didn't wait long to get married, could that be possible, Lord?

He reined in that thought before it had any chance to go beyond his silent prayer. Taking things slowly, remember? No matter how much he wanted to rush Nai, he had to hold back.

Though when she stood, turned to face him, and their eyes met, the happiness shining in her gaze made him wonder. Maybe he could rethink the taking-things-slowly part?

Right on cue, the parrot squawked. "Mateo, Mateo. Mateo should marry Naomi."

That glow he saw in Nai's face was a good sign, but he'd best not admit he taught Oscar to say that. Not yet.

Nai ducked her head over the cash register, but not fast enough to hide her endearing blush.

"Clever boy." Mateo stepped to the huge cage filling the bay window, opened the access door, and held out his hand. "Here. I brought you a couple of macadamia nuts."

Oscar took a nut in one clawed foot and bobbed. "Thank you." Not only smart, the bird had manners, too.

As soon as the bell over the entrance door jangled when the customers left, Violet bustled over to Nai. "Your date is here!" she trilled. "Why don't you leave early?"

"No, I'm sure Mateo won't mind waiting a little longer until we close." Nai threw him a glance with a clear message. *Please, don't mind!*

"I'm happy to wait." He leaned against a bookcase. "Grandpa's already left for his veterans' reunion weekend, so I don't have anywhere else I need to be."

Nai's relieved nod showed he'd given the right answer.

"We missed Hector's help in the bookstore today. I hope he'll join us again next week." A hint of coquettishness tipped Violet's hopeful smile.

Abuelo seemed equally taken with Violet, despite her eccentric ways. He'd come a long way in rejoining the world. Last week, he'd been despondent and half-hearted about attending the reunion trip. Today, he'd left filled with excitement over seeing his buddies again.

Easy to reassure the older woman with an honest reply. "I'm sure he will. He enjoyed spending time here."

"Ms. Nai, we can take care of things." Fern walked into the bookstore through the door separating it from the café. That girl must have good hearing, to hear through the door. "Everyone knows the bookstore will be closed tomorrow while you bring home Ms. Ivy, so they'll understand if the store shuts a little early tonight. And Tía Irma's has the best enchiladas ever!"

What Fern had to compare them to he wouldn't try to guess, but he was grateful for her support.

"Well…" Forehead creased in doubt, Nai hesitated. "I guess we could. I walked the dogs early, so it's just cashing up to do."

"Girl, what are you waiting for?" Violet gave Nai a friendly push in the back. "Leave everything to us."

Despite the woman's fragile appearance, the push was strong enough to make Nai stumble forward. He jumped to grasp her upper arms and steady her.

"Thank you, Mateo." A shy smile curved her full lips, and the way she said his name made it sound like music.

Oh, how much he loved that shy smile! But then, he adored so many things about Nai. Her fierce loyalty to the people she loved. Her brilliant mind when it came to math and business. Her humility. And even her awkwardness at times. He'd had to work hard to overcome his shyness, so he could relate.

Her stubborn independence, he wasn't quite so sure he adored, but it was part of who she was, so he just had to roll with it.

And hope he could convince her he was worth letting it go for.

"Okay, we can close early," she said. "But I'll stay to balance the day's receipts."

"Up to you." Fern shrugged. "In that case, do you mind if I go now? I've already closed up in the café." The girl grinned and fluttered her eyelashes. "Gotta get my date hair and my going-out makeup on."

As the changeable girl was in blonde bombshell mode today, and already wore electric-blue eye makeup and long fake eyelashes, he shuddered to think what else she'd add.

Nai looked up from the cash register and smiled. "Sure, you can go."

"So, I'm the only one without a date tonight?" Violet pouted, though her blue eyes twinkled.

He chuckled. Something told him Abuelo was likely to change that soon.

"Mateo and I aren't going on a date, either. We're just…" Nai trailed off, seeming at a loss for how else to explain them having a meal together.

Pulling out the cash drawer, she locked it. "I'll just take this upstairs and get my purse." Her face pinking, she hurried upstairs.

Violet winked at him. "You're doing good so far."

"I need to." He straightened and lowered his voice. "Since Nai came back, I feel sure she's the woman for me. But she can't be rushed, and I don't have a lot of dating experience. In here" — he hit his chest — "I'm still the shy, gawky sixteen-year-old who messed up with her last time."

Violet giggled and leaned closer like a conspirator. "I'll let you in on a little secret. It's like that for everyone. We're all still sixteen inside, especially when it comes to dating. She had her model friend come by earlier to help her get ready. That should tell you something."

It did. Impossible to wipe the grin from his face.

Before he had a chance to reply, the door upstairs creaked open, and Nai dashed down the staircase. "Let's go."

She looked date perfect. Whatever Reese did for her, it worked.

Not that he'd insist this was a date, much as he wanted it to be.

And not that Nai needed makeup or dressing up. He found her beautiful no matter what she wore, and maybe that was what attracted him to her in the first place. No unnecessary words or fake eyelashes when it came to Nai. One hundred percent honest and transparent.

They walked outside, and he opened the truck door for her. This time, she let him.

Soon, he parked outside Tía Irma's. Held not only the truck door open for Nai, but also the restaurant door. He ached to wrap his arm around her shoulders, but now wasn't the time.

Hopefully, soon it would be.

As soon as he opened the door, the rich savory odors of Latin cooking hit him, and he inhaled deeply.

His favorite restaurant because the food and aromas reminded him of family dinners.

Problem was, it reminded him not just of Abuela's cooking, but his mom's. He could barely remember her face by now...he'd been so young when she died. But he couldn't forget the scent or the taste of the beef fajitas with sautéed onions and peppers she'd cooked.

He'd never been able to eat it since. When trying to comfort him not long after his parents died, Abuela cooked him the meal. It choked him.

While they waited to be seated, he pushed out a long low breath and struggled to loosen his tense shoulders. This evening, the memories hit stronger than they'd ever been. Normally all he got was a niggle of grief, easily suppressed.

Must be being here with Nai. Of all his friends, she'd understood. She knew the pain of losing a parent, too. Of only having a few fleeting memories to go on.

"Are you thinking of your mother?" She seemed to read his thoughts.

He winced. "How did you guess?" So much for the lighthearted date-friendly conversation topics he'd researched on the internet.

"You hardly ever mentioned your parents, but when you did, you always had the same sadness in your eyes. And you sighed in that same way, too." Her fingertips brushed his forearm as if to offer support. "Please stop blaming yourself. It's not your fault she and your dad died in the accident."

"I don't know."

Before he could say more, Linda, the young waitress he'd spoken to last night, arrived to lead them to a vacant booth. He fell silent until she handed them the menus and left.

"It feels like my fault. The guilt hits me out of nowhere sometimes, makes it hard to breathe." He sat in silence for a moment, emotions racking him, nails digging into his palms. That pain was a relief, a small respite from the pain inside him.

Finally, words emerged, choked and broken. "Mom died because of me. Why didn't Dad try to pull *her* from the car first, instead?"

Nai placed her hand over his, clenched on the scarred oak table. "Maybe because if he had, all three of you would have died?" Her voice, holding such gentle concern, twisted something deep inside him.

"Maybe." Like his mind had been wiped, he had no memories of the accident, though sometimes he had flashes of fear and pain and flames that might be part of it.

"I know you pray a lot. Your faith is way stronger than mine. So... shouldn't you surrender your guilt to the Lord? Trust Him with it? Let Him heal you?" Her hand squeezed his, then rested on it lightly.

His skin tingled from her touch. She had a point. Was this guilt something he'd held onto, refused to let God take from him? Could be, Nai being back in Chapel Cove was part of His plan in more ways than one.

Lord, help me surrender my guilt to You. Please take it from me. Help me not to grab it back from You. Help me to trust in You, to trust You have a plan and a purpose, even in this.

Nai leaned forward. "You prayed, didn't you? I saw it in your face."

That was another thing about Nai. He never had to explain things to her. "Yes. I'm trying to do what you said."

"I'm glad."

Her hand squeezed his again. Then she jerked it away when the tap of heels on the tiled floor announced Linda's return for their order.

Snatching up the menu, Nai studied it. "I'll have chicken enchiladas. They come with rice and beans, correct?"

The waitress nodded, her green-tinted hair ruffling up and down like Oscar's feathers. "Yes, and a small salad on the side."

He didn't bother looking at the menu. He always ordered the same thing.

"Your usual, Officer Rodriguez?" Linda stood with her pen poised.

Time to try something different. He took a deep breath. "Beef fajitas, please."

The tight band constricting his lungs and closing off his throat every time he thought of his mom loosened a bit. Eating her favorite meal again wasn't disloyal to her memory.

"And an iced tea," he added when he saw the waitress waiting for something.

"Oh, for me, too. Thank you." Nai smiled.

"I'll bring you a pitcher." The girl clattered away from their booth.

While waiting for their food, they talked about what they'd both done in the years since leaving the Cove, painting their lives for each other the way scenes from artisan lives hand-painted the colorful mustard-hued walls. Warmth spread through him as they exchanged glances and soft Tejano music accentuated their stories. He'd always enjoyed her company, right from their first meeting in Sunday school. Now, as an adult, he enjoyed it even more.

But while he appreciated their rediscovered friendship, he wanted more than friendship.

Much more.

The food arrived soon, and just the scent made his mouth water. It was okay to remember Mom. Happy memories. He could stop blaming himself that he'd lived and she'd died.

When the waitress left, he bowed his head and said grace aloud, adding a silent plea that he'd be able to eat the food.

Seconds passed before Nai said a hesitant amen.

She'd had such a difficult childhood, difficult in a very different way from his. At least he'd had Abuelo and Abuela, loving grandparents. In their teens, when a bunch of kids from his class accepted Jesus as Lord at Vacation Bible School, she'd struggled with her faith. Seemed perhaps she still did.

An extra, silent, prayer whispered in his mind. *Lord, please help Nai find her path to You. Show me how to help her know You better.*

He took his time rolling up the meat and veggies with cheese and guacamole. Finally, admitting to himself he was scared, he breathed deep then took a bite of his beef fajita.

Please, don't let me choke.

He didn't. The delicious food went down fine. Instead, as he chewed another mouthful, letting the taste linger in his mouth and in his memory, tears filled his eyes.

Though somehow, he wasn't ashamed for Nai to see them, he mopped them up with his napkin.

When he glanced at her, she'd laid her cutlery down and gazed at him, eyes warm and concerned, brow a little furrowed.

"I don't know if I ever told you, but Mom used to make beef fajitas for me. My favorite meal and hers too," he explained. "This is the first time I've been able to eat them since she died." He drew in another deep breath. "And the first time I've shed tears since she died, as well."

Tears glistened in her eyes too, and her misty smile glowed with a sweet radiance. "I'm glad," she repeated.

Their gazes locked and held. "I am, too. Thank you." Then swallowing, he glanced at his plate.

Utensils clicked against porcelain as they ate. He felt no need to speak. The silence was easy and companionable, not strained.

"Um..." Nai broke the silence first. "Well... as we're talking emotional stuff, it feels time to say I've wanted to tell you something for a while." Behind her ebony-framed glasses, her gaze seemed to question the wisdom of speaking.

His fajita froze midway to his mouth. "Yes?"

Whatever it was, it might not be anything he wanted to hear. Those hazel eyes of hers seemed to see right into his soul.

A slow breath escaped her. "Well... um... I couldn't help noticing something, and maybe it's connected to the guilt you mentioned. While I'm sure everybody appreciates you being so helpful, you don't have to be so eager to assist everyone around you. You were the same in your teens. It's kind of you, but sometimes I wonder if...if you're trying to earn the right to be alive. And trying to earn the right to be loved."

Buying time to answer, he bit off a mouthful of fajita, putting the remainder down and then chewing on beef and peppers while he chewed on her words. He'd become so used to helping others that he didn't ever think about why.

His shoulders rose and fell in a shrug. "You could be right, I guess. Survivor guilt. But what's so bad about wanting to be helpful?"

"There's nothing bad about it. Unless it becomes a compulsion, a need to be needed that turns you into a professional rescuer. The flipside of the way my mom was and maybe still is — a professional victim, looking for a man to rescue her." She swirled her amber-hued drink, ice clinking against the sides in a delicate rhythm that somehow matched her. "You don't seem to recognize you're a good person, one of the best. You don't need to earn the right to exist. You already have that. You don't need to earn anybody's good opinion or love. You already have it."

His fingers wrapped around his cold, smooth glass. "So you're saying..."

She took one more mouthful of her enchilada and then pushed her plate away. "The right to exist and true love are both unconditional. Like God's love. You don't have to keep working so hard to earn it."

Her words touched something deep inside him.

Better if she'd said *she* loved him, of course. Not that he wanted her to love him the way old Mrs. Gibson did because he mowed her lawns for her. He wanted more from Nai.

But still, no matter what, God loved him unconditionally. And he loved God unconditionally, too. Could others love him the same way? Not because of what he did for them, but just because?

Even Nai?

Was his helpfulness even a barrier between them, because of her determination not to be needy like her mom?

Nodding thoughtfully, he finished his last bite of fajita. "You have a point. I'm going to pray about this. Thank you." He waved at the dessert and drinks menu. "Would you like a dessert?"

"Not for me, thank you. Go ahead and have one if you want." She patted her tummy. "The enchilada was delicious, but such a big serving."

She'd only eaten half of it, and it wasn't *that* big a serving. No forgetting the day a bunch of them had been hanging out on the boardwalk eating ice cream. Nai's mom marched right up to her, grabbed her cone out of her hand, threw it in the trash, then berated her, called her all sorts of cruel names, right in front of everyone.

Maybe, in her own way, Nai also still tried to earn the love her mom had never given her.

This might not be the best time to tell her that. It would look too tit-for-tat. But someday, when the time was right, he would. Along with so many other things.

Like telling her he loved her. Always had. And always would.

CHAPTER FOURTEEN

NAI DIDN'T actually believe in that unconditional love she'd mentioned to Mateo.

Well, okay, she did.

Just not for her. But Mateo, sure. No doubting that God, and pretty much everyone who knew him, loved Mateo. He was that sort of guy. There for everyone. Always ready to go the extra mile, to give that bit more. The sort of guy Mom looked for so desperately and never found.

At least he seemed to have listened and considered what she'd said. And maybe lightened up on some of the burden of guilt he carried, too. If *she'd* been able to help *him* for once, she was glad. The guy was so competent, so together...she felt a mess in comparison.

Enough of the deep and meaningful. She wasn't going to admit to the nagging whisper insisting she had her own guilt to surrender to the Lord.

After Linda cleared their plates and Mateo ordered two coffees, he scrunched his face in a pretend grimace. "At the risk of sounding like I haven't listened to anything you just said about me wanting to help too much, I'd like you to allow me to drive to Portland tomorrow when you go to pick up Ivy. Her old beater is fine for you to use around the Cove, but I'd be concerned with you driving all that way in it."

So he'd noticed she returned the rental to the small local agent for the car company.

"I should have kept the rental car, but at that stage, it could have been another two weeks before Ivy was released." Lips pursed, she shook her head. "Trying to be frugal without thinking it right through. I called today about getting it back, but they already booked it to someone else."

"Even if you still had the rental, it's probably wise to have two people in the car. Just in case Ivy... you know."

Thankfully, he didn't say it. His concerned expression said it for him.

Before she even left Austin, she'd consulted Dr. Google on the likely issues facing Aunt Ivy. She'd read some scary statistics about the possibility of another heart attack, or worse, another cardiac arrest. All she could do was hope those statistics were inaccurate and watch the AHA video on how to do CPR on a loop till she felt she could do it if she had to.

And yes, she'd prayed she wouldn't have to, though whether God heard her prayer, she had no idea.

"You're right about that, I guess." Her lips pressed tight together, as if guilty over letting the reluctant words loose. He *was* right. But the whole drive there, they'd be alone in the confined space of his truck. Just being so close to him during the five-minute drive to the restaurant stirred her hyperactive hormones into a frenzy.

Of course! His truck! The perfect excuse. "But your truck won't be suitable to bring her home in. I'll be fine on my own. I'm sure her cardiologist wouldn't release her unless he was confident she was stable." Had she kept the triumph from her voice? Maybe not.

Mateo chuckled. "It just happens that one of my buddies needs a truck this weekend, so we're trading first thing tomorrow morning. He'll have my truck till Sunday night. I'll have his top-of-the-line sedan. Must be a God thing, right?"

Yeah, right. Only if He wanted to push her and Mateo together. If He did, she had a bigger problem than she thought.

"Must be," she muttered.

"What time should I come around to pick you up tomorrow?" Though he surely realized how reluctantly she'd conceded defeat, Mateo did a far better job of keeping any hint of satisfaction from his voice. Maybe she was the only one who saw this as another battle of wills, like their epic chess games and their fierce competition to be the best in their math class.

Counting backward from when the girls wanted to meet at the Pancake Shoppe for her birthday, she allowed a couple of hours to get Ivy safely settled in the apartment, a couple of hours for the inevitable delays at the hospital, and a good three hours for the round trip.

"About ten?"

"Sure. No problem." He smiled his easy smile as if giving up the better part of another day to help her was nothing. "And what was that other issue you wanted advice on?"

She rubbed her chin. "Issue? Advice?" Again, she sounded like Oscar.

The Mateo Effect.

Just being near him turned her mind to cotton candy. Pink,

fluffy, sticky sweet, and dissolved to mush when touched. The sooner she returned to Texas and got her brain back, the better.

"When you phoned yesterday, before we took the dogs to the beach, you said there was an issue at the bookstore you wanted my advice on."

"Oh no! I completely forgot. And it's important, too." Her hand rose to slap her forehead, and she huffed. She was getting as bad as Violet. Was it something in the water here?

Seriously? How could she have forgotten?

Answer: easily.

In the rush of helping Violet and Fern with the bookstore customers, caring for the pets, hiring an emergency maid service to fix up the apartment and clean the bookstore, finding an outfit for Ivy to wear home from the hospital, installing a cat flap in the apartment door for Paige, working remotely for Jesse, catching up with her friends, *and* thinking way too much about Mateo in between being totally distracted by his presence, easy to see how she'd forget.

Just listing it all exhausted her. She needed caffeine.

With perfect timing, Linda set their coffees on the table.

As soon as Linda left, Mateo raised an eyebrow. "And the issue is?"

Patient as always, he didn't rush her. Simply sat waiting for her to speak. His eyes intent and warm in their focus. One more thing she'd always loved about him.

He listened. Really listened.

Sighing, she stirred her coffee. "I discovered some books are missing. Valuable books, worth well over a thousand dollars, kept in a locked drawer. I'd rather not involve the police unless I have to. If it's Violet being absentminded again and she's put them somewhere else, I don't want to embarrass her."

Mateo nodded. "That's kind of you. And from what I see of

Violet, it does seem possible."

"More than possible." Her shudder was only half-pretended. "Violet is a sweetheart, but *so* forgetful. Problem is, I searched all the bookshelves and all the cabinet space, and I can't see that she's mis-shelved them. Seems it's common knowledge where the pricier books are stored, and half the Cove knows where the key is kept."

He nodded. "Lower drawer in the cabinet behind the counter, spare key in a cracked coffee mug filled with elastic bands and paper clips, kept underneath the counter."

Her rueful snort said it all. "Correct. Or at least, it *was* correct. I've moved the key somewhere else now. But how many other folks knew where it used to be?"

"Plenty," he replied to her rhetorical question. "So it's also possible they've been stolen, either by an opportunistic thief or someone who planned this, possibly even a steal-to-order job if the books were really rare. Which, I guess, is why you want my advice?"

"Right. I hoped to get it resolved before Aunt Ivy came back, but things were so busy today it slipped my mind."

And yesterday, once she'd realized she had to phone him about the issue, Mateo and only Mateo had filled her mind.

Not that she dared tell him that. She swung between emotional extremes. Being sure she shouldn't let him imagine anything romantic could develop between them in case her inevitable departure for Austin hurt him. Or being sure there was no harm at all in enjoying his company while she was here because he couldn't possibly care for her deeply and so couldn't be hurt.

"Could we go back to the bookstore and have a look?" He gulped his coffee and waved to the waitress for the bill. "Then I can suggest some strategies. Does the store have CCTV?"

She shook her head and sipped more slowly at her hot coffee.

135

"Nothing like that. The sole security measure is the locked drawer, which may as well have been left open. In fact, it *was* left open. When I noticed the missing books, the drawer was already unlocked."

"Was it?" Mateo seemed interested in that detail, tapping a finger against his mouth.

Forgetting the books, she couldn't seem to drag her focus from his lips, the memory of how they'd felt against hers, the anticipation that maybe, sometime soon, he'd kiss her again.

"Obviously, fingerprinting anyone is out of the question, without opening an official investigation," he mused. "But to catch the person if it happens again, I could install a small motion-activated video camera inside the drawer. It's totally legal."

"Uh, okay."

She should be grateful Mateo had his mind on what was important, rather than the memory of one long-ago kiss. So why did she feel so disappointed? She wasn't her mom, needing a man, lusting after a man, feeling incomplete without a man. Nothing like her mom.

But the longing she felt for Mateo made her feel as if she was.

After he paid and they walked to the truck, he couldn't stop thinking about all Nai said.

Not so much the bookstore thefts. The more personal stuff. She'd always known him better than anyone else, always seen deeper than the surface. Though he ached to bring her close and kiss her senseless, he also loved the fact that she made him think.

And, okay, he also loved the way she made him giddy, just being near her. Nai awoke something in him physically no other woman ever had.

Something was changing inside him. Nai, by her presence and her insight, was helping heal his deepest wounds. Opening him up to let God's healing in. He closed the door behind her, rushed around the vehicle, and climbed into the driver's seat. Then he made the mistake of looking into her eyes.

They'd had such a delicious meal and shared some great memories. And one of the memories they hadn't discussed still made the blood flow faster in his veins so many years later. Their first and only kiss...

He was falling for her again, had already fallen for her. From what she'd said and the warmth and hope glowing in her gaze, he sensed she had feelings for him, too.

Her lips parted, and her beautiful eyes widened. The air charged with awareness. All he needed to do was lean in and lower his mouth to hers, taste her sweet delicious lips again, wrap his arms around her, and pull her close....

He didn't. Instead, he shifted away from her, clicked his seat belt, and sat staring ahead, gripping the steering wheel. As if his hands belonged to someone else, he noticed the knuckles showed white against his tan. That's how much self-control it took not to kiss Nai.

He relaxed his white-knuckle grip and started the engine.

Now wasn't the time. Too much doubt and hesitation had mingled with the invitation in her eyes. He didn't only remember their kiss. He remembered the way she'd pulled back, the fear and confusion on her face.

The same fear and confusion he saw now. Nai wanted him to kiss her. He had no doubt about that. Wanted the kiss just as much as he did.

But if he kissed her now, he'd ruin everything the way the first kiss had. Slam them right back into the awkward self-consciousness that pushed their friendship from deep to something far more superficial, something that never went away. Along with the wounded pride and stupidity after the prom-night disaster that had stopped them from talking about the important things.

Like how they both felt about missing the prom. Like giving their love time and space and encouragement to grow. Like his guilt over his parents, and her issues with her mom.

Instead, she'd retreated into fiercer academic competition than ever, focused everything on winning a college scholarship. Discovered she could fight to become a legally emancipated minor, told her mom she'd start court proceedings if she had to, and moved out of the trailer and in with Ivy. And declared that, like Ivy, she'd stay single, have a career, not marriage.

She'd achieved everything she said she would. Convincing her to give that up to marry him wouldn't be easy.

Tonight was a start. A good start. She'd agreed to him helping her tomorrow with Ivy. Pushing for more was too big a risk, no matter how much he wanted to. The insistent nudge to hold back and slow down felt too much like God's guidance to ignore.

He'd gladly give up a kiss now if being patient gained him a future with Nai. Maybe endless kisses from her, too?

Though he had no idea how to convince her she wanted that future together, too. In only a few weeks, she'd return to Austin. How slow dare he take things? When would be the time to tell her and to show her how he felt?

He just had to trust that, when the time was right, God would let him know and lead the way.

CHAPTER FIFTEEN

HER PHONE'S ringtone woke Nai. Not the alarm, a call. She prised her eyes open. Well, halfway, but that counted, right? Groaning, she fumbled on the nightstand for her cellphone.

Who could be calling this early? Not that she could see what time it was, but her alarm hadn't gone off yet, and she'd set it for an hour earlier than usual.

Then a cold shiver ran down her back. Aunt Ivy? The hospital?

Opening her eyes a smidgen wider, she squinted at the screen. Where were her glasses? The air left her lungs in a sigh of relief when she made out the letter *J*.

Jesse. Her boss.

"Good morning, Jesse. Do you know what time it is here?" Familiarity and years of working for the guy allowed a little bluntness.

A long pause, probably while he either peered at his watch or did the math. Jesse's vision was even worse than hers. Not to mention, his genius rendered him useless at everyday stuff. Like time zones.

"Oh, oops. I forgot you're two hours behind Austin now. I wanted to wish you a happy birthday and ask you how your aunt is doing."

"Thank you. She's much better. I should be able to bring her home this afternoon." Nai shifted a little, disturbing Paige, who stretched but closed her eyes again.

"Glad to hear it." His voice perked up. "Does that mean you'll return soon? I appreciate you doing what you can from there. It helps. But the office isn't the same, the company isn't the same, and even I'm not the same without you here. I didn't realize just what a difference you make."

His praise touched her. She loved Jesse like a younger brother. She loved her job. Feeling the sense of achievement she did at Ideas & Inventions fed something deep inside her.

Torn, she rubbed her eyes. Part of her desperately wanted to be back in her safe familiar world, especially when things with Mateo were drifting into uncharted waters. She'd love to tell Jesse she'd be back at work soon.

But she was always honest with Jesse, and she wasn't going to change now. "My aunt is going to be weak for a while and need help. I have to stay."

"I understand. It's admirable of you to do that for her. I know you'd planned never to return to your hometown. But then, you're a wonderful person."

Her face flamed up at his undeserved praise. "It's not all bad. I've met up with my best friends from school and one old friend who... who... well, who could become more."

No, no, no! Why had she admitted that to Jesse when she didn't even want to admit it to herself? As a distraction, she stroked Paige, burying her fingers in the cat's plush coat.

"I've never heard you speak about anyone like that." For a self-proclaimed geek with no social skills, Jesse was way too perceptive. "Are you falling for him?"

"I don't want to," she whispered as her heart stuttered. "My life in Austin is exactly how I want it."

Time to admit the truth to herself. Maybe she'd fallen in love with Mateo when she was a teen, the moment he'd kissed her in the rain. But she hadn't wanted to admit it then any more than she did now. She'd tucked it deep, deep inside. The thing with the prom, him never explaining, just gave her a convenient hook to hang her backing off onto, so she never had to look at the reasons why.

Jesse had dragged it out to the surface, like a precious pearl in a shell wrested from the ocean floor. She could take that pearl and let it glisten in the sunlight or throw it back in the ocean.

But she couldn't ignore it.

"You're not coming back, are you?" He interrupted her musings.

"Of course, I am!" She sat up as she said the emphatic words, startling Paige into jumping off the bed, barely missing Catsup. The cat hissed as if it was Catsup's fault. His attempt to lick Paige as an apology only seemed to ruin the morning all the more for Paige.

The cat stalked away with a dignified air that said there'd better be a good breakfast to make up for all this.

Holding her phone to her ear, Nai leaped from her bed and rushed to the kitchen before the cat could get even more disgruntled and throw a bigger hissy fit. "I love my job, and I'm good at it. I can't imagine running a bookstore for the rest of my days."

She couldn't imagine letting things develop with Mateo, either, but focusing on the bookstore was way safer.

Hmm… dear Violet's vagueness, the escaping parrot, the leaking roof, and the missing books. And then the need to walk the dogs at least three times a day. "It's total chaos here. I like my life structured and in order. Not turned upside down in a dozen different ways every day."

So why did her heart constrict at the thought of leaving Chapel Cove and Mateo?

She scooped Paige's favorite tuna-flavored food into her bowl. But where was the cat?

On the counter!

"Paige, get down!"

Obeying her for once, the cat jumped to the floor, almost landing in the bowl.

"What *are* you doing?" Nai huffed.

"Huh? Talking to you."

"Oops, sorry." She winced at the surprise in Jesse's voice, then groaned. "I wasn't asking you. I was talking to the cat. I spend my days here talking to animals, chasing dogs, teaching the parrot new words so he doesn't tell everyone who I should marry, supervising a forgetful older staff member, handling customers, climbing on the roof…"

She didn't add walking on the beach holding hands or eating Mexican food with Mateo. Or longing for him to kiss her. Or never being able to stop thinking about him. Or —

"Hold on. Who are you and what did you do with my office manager?" Sadness laced the humor in his words.

"I'm still me. Just me in a different situation."

"Oookay. If you say so." He sighed. "Well, take all the time you need. And if you *do* decide to stay in Oregon, please, will you come back long enough to find me another PA?"

"I have no intention of staying or of leaving you in a bind."

She hoped.

A sweet guy like Jesse deserved more than just a PA. He deserved a soulmate. It wasn't his fault he was geeky and shy around women, and dedicated all his time to hiding out in his workshop. Maybe she could help him, set him up with a partner for this year's charity ball…

Whoa. The matchmaking bug infecting her friends and staff must be contagious. Jesse needed her as his personal assistant, not his personal dating service.

Holding the phone away from her ear, she glanced at the time.

No, no, no! Later than she thought. Later than she'd set the alarm for. Way later.

There really *was* something in the water here! Somehow, she'd set the alarm time but forgotten to set it to ring.

"Sorry, I gotta go. Send me emails for everything you need me to do for you. I have to feed the pets and walk the dogs before we go to pick up Aunt Ivy from the hospital." While she gabbled, she pulled on her jeans.

"We?" The laughter in his voice was real this time.

"Mateo is driving me. But only because it's safer. Aunt Ivy's just been released from the Coronary Care ward."

"Of course it's safer. And that's the only reason. Sure." Jesse's chuckle reverberated down the line. Then his voice grew serious. "Nai, know that I wish you only happiness, whether it's in Texas or in Oregon. You deserve it."

"Thank you, Jesse. Please take care of yourself." Something shifted inside her. Jesse had been pretty much her family for over a decade. She couldn't abandon the poor guy now, could she?

She rolled her eyes at herself. Calling a billionaire "poor" had to be an oxymoron. But undeniably, Jesse needed her.

Could be, when she'd accused Mateo of needing to be needed

last night, she'd really been talking about herself. Had she dealt with the hurt of her all-too-obvious failure to meet Mom's needs by looking for someone whose needs she *could* meet?

Ouch! Her head spun from all these "needs". And from almost admitting she was as needy, too.

If she was, how could she let her job go? Mateo didn't need her. *She* needed *him*.

And she hated that. Hated feeling like Mom.

An hour later, dogs walked, pets fed, herself showered and changed, she hurried downstairs as the chiming doorbell announced a visitor. Her heartbeat did its usual spike at the sight of Mateo. Impossible to kid herself running down the stairs caused it, though she tried.

Her silly heart didn't want to understand this was only for Aunt Ivy's safety. Only because helping people was what Mateo did. No different from all the other people he helped. He had no more personal feelings for her than he did for old Mrs. Gibson or anyone else in Chapel Cove.

Riiiight. And she had no stronger feelings for him than she did for anyone else.

She believed it. Sure she did.

But the spark in Mateo's dark eyes left her wondering if he did. Wondering if, though he hadn't kissed her last night, he'd wanted that kiss just as much as she did.

Maybe she hadn't imagined it, after all.

That only made it harder.

A rush of adrenaline and other hormones flooded Mateo at the sight of Nai. Accompanying her to pick up her aunt was for both her and Ivy's safety and well-being.

And also, no denying it, a good excuse to spend more time with Nai.

Offering her the bouquet he'd asked Sally at the flower shop to make for her, he took a deep breath of the fragrant spring blooms and then forced words from his dry mouth. "Happy birthday."

Nai stared at him as she accepted the flowers. "For me? I assumed they were for Aunt Ivy."

Shaking his head, he bent to pick up the potted indoor ivy Sally suggested he get the older woman. "I see her as more of a potted-plant type. So I got her this as her welcome home gift."

"Ivy for Ivy. She'll like that." Nai chuckled, then raised the flowers to her face. "And... I like these. Thank you."

"You're welcome." Her sweet smile of appreciation as she inhaled the fragrant floral aroma was thanks enough.

"You remembered? Or did the florist suggest these?"

"I remembered you saying how much you liked the perfume of the flowers I'd helped Abuela plant in her garden as bulbs the fall before." Truth was, he remembered everything about Nai. But like kissing her, too soon to tell her that. He smiled. "Okay, I couldn't remember the names. So I pointed to them in the store and asked the florist to make up a bunch of those and those and those."

Nai laughed. "Jonquils." She pointed at a yellow bloom. "Hyacinths." A gentle nudge to a cluster of blue bell-shaped blossoms. "And these are tulips, which don't have a scent but are pretty, so I forgive them for not smelling nice." She touched a larger purple flower.

So he'd got it right. Her approval warmed him even more than her beauty had. He rested a hand on her shoulder and leaned in to drop a quick peck on her cheek. If he kissed her lips instead, he'd probably spontaneously combust.

He hoped he wasn't imagining the flash of disappointment in her eyes as she stared at him, lips parted, bouquet close to her chest, as if she didn't want to let it go.

Then, lowering the flowers to her side, she rushed to speak. "Why don't you find a good place for Ivy's ivy in the apartment, and I'll take these upstairs to put them into water."

"Sure." He eyed her, hoping her shift to a no-nonsense tone didn't mean what he thought it meant.

While she climbed the stairs, he headed for the door leading to the apartment.

Wow. Nai had worked a miracle here. A miracle that doubtless took a lot of hard work.

The room he'd last seen stacked high with boxes somehow transformed into a welcoming homelike space. He felt the soil in the bright spotted planter to ensure it wasn't dry, then placed the potted plant in the middle of the small dining table.

He had a sneaking suspicion that, left to Ivy and Nai, the plant would be dead in a couple of weeks unless he came by to water it. The one time Nai tried to help him in Abuela's garden in their teens, she'd pulled up the good plants and left the weeds.

An extra advantage to the potted plant he hadn't realized when he chose it. An excuse to come by — every single day.

Closing the door behind him, he waited in the bookstore for Nai. Shame the camera he'd ordered to keep watch on the valuable books wasn't due to arrive till Monday or Tuesday. If he'd had it already, he could've set it up now.

Who took the books remained a mystery. The thing with rare books, they were only of value to collectors. He'd mentally run through the usual suspects for thefts and break-ins, and he couldn't imagine any of them having the right contacts.

The Cove wasn't crime-free, but thefts in most places tended more toward things that could be converted to cash. Handbag snatching, pickpocketing, stealing cellphones, laptops, gold jewelry. Not bulky, heavy old books, less likely to find a ready cash buyer.

He couldn't help wondering if Abuelo knew more about the missing books than he let on.

The creak of footsteps on the stairs alerted him to Nai's return, and he turned to smile at her. She was beautiful, though he knew she didn't believe that. And though she smiled, she didn't meet his eyes.

"Let's get going." Again, Ms. Practicality. So his guess about her change in mood had been correct, except the change was even more noticeable now.

Like she'd given herself some sort of talking to while she put the flowers in water and retreated back into her shell. Not just friendzoned. Acquaintance-zoned.

Exactly what he didn't want.

Minutes later, he pulled onto Pacific Avenue, headed out of Chapel Cove. As his buddy's big sedan ate up the miles, Nai remained quiet. She'd always tended to listen more than she spoke, but now their silence became uncomfortable.

He stole a glance at her before returning his attention to the road. Her pink lips pursed, she stared straight ahead. "Nai?"

"I had a call from my boss this morning. He needs me back as soon as Ivy is well enough to leave and she has some help in the bookstore."

The other message she didn't say came through loud and clear. *So we can only be friends.* He winced as he slowed to take a curve.

Best not to reply. Let her talk now that she'd started.

"Some women don't need marriage to make them happy. Look at Aunt Ivy. She's happily stayed single. Well, happily except for the heart-attack part."

Who was she trying to convince? Him or herself?

Her voice dipped. "I'm fine with the way my life is in Austin. Structured, predictable. I like it that way."

Well... he could understand that when every day at the bookstore lurched from one minor disaster to another one step away from disaster. Far from structured and predictable.

"It's great you're happy with your life," he said carefully. "That's what I want for you. To know you're happy."

"I wish that for you, too." Her voice softened. "Very much so. I'm glad we can be friends again."

Friendzoned was far from where he wanted to be with Nai. But dared he hope the strength of her retreat from him mirrored the strength of her feelings for him?

If that was the case, he wouldn't give up wooing her yet. He'd barely begun.

Lord, am I wrong to hope Lucille stays with her daughter for a good long time? Please?

To convince Nai to stay, he'd need all the time and all the help he could get.

CHAPTER SIXTEEN

NAI ALMOST cheered when Mateo pulled the borrowed sedan to the curb outside Ivy's on Spruce. Instead, she contented herself with a relieved sigh.

Despite her initial reluctance, she couldn't help being glad he'd insisted on driving. Worry about Ivy soon erased her intention to stay distant with Mateo. Sitting beside Aunt Ivy in the back seat, she'd watched her aunt's face grow paler and her shoulders slump lower with every mile.

Good thing Dr. Jeff Johnson intended to drop by and check on Ivy this afternoon, or she'd be calling him to request a home visit.

Mateo turned and smiled. "Home again, at last, Ivy."

Aunt Ivy's tight, white-lipped smile in return was less convincing.

"I'm grateful to be home. Thank you. It's been a long week.

149

And now you can go do whatever you usually do on Saturday afternoons." She flapped a dismissive hand at him.

Reassuring. At least whatever pain or fatigue or a mix of both made Aunt Ivy so wan hadn't stopped her forthright habit of speaking her mind.

He chuckled as he opened the car door and swung his legs out. "Okay, Ivy, I will. Once you're safely settled in the apartment. Accepting help doesn't mean you're weak."

Hmm. Her aunt didn't refuse his offered help. As Nai trailed them to the apartment's side entrance, carrying Aunt Ivy's bags, the older woman appeared to lean on his arm. Nai's scanty reassurance vanished faster than dog treats around Heinz.

So unlike her aunt. Maybe borrowing a wheelchair would have been wise.

As she stepped into the apartment, Ivy looked around, smiled, and nodded. "Home. Almost, anyway. You've clearly worked hard, Nai. Thank you."

She had, but Ivy wasn't going to hear her complain. "I had plenty of help."

Naturally, the next thing Ivy wanted was the bathroom.

Nai paced outside the door. What should she do if Ivy collapsed in there? Had Ivy been in there too long already?

She hadn't realized just how nerve-racking this would be. Rather than making things easier, having Ivy home added a new bundle of worries.

Mateo strode to her and took hold of both her hands, effectively stopping her pacing. Stopping her galloping thoughts, too. Despite her best attempts to control them, her fingers trembled in his firm but gentle grip. She let him lead her away from the bathroom door. "Of course you're worried about her. That's natural. But worrying doesn't help. Let's pray, instead."

Biting her lip, she nodded, then closed her eyes. Praying

together felt so vulnerable, so intimate. Especially when he held her hands like that.

"Dear heavenly Father," he said, in a low voice, "thank You for Ivy's recovery so far. Thank You that she's been able to come home from the hospital. Please be with her as she makes a complete recovery. And please also help Nai know Your loving presence as she cares for her aunt and the bookstore. Help her to hand all her worries and concerns over to You rather than carrying them on her own. You tell us that Your yoke is easy and Your burden is light. Thank You for that. We've both shouldered burdens we don't need to. Help us to know we can let You take them from us, Lord. In Jesus's name, we pray, amen."

"Amen," Nai echoed. His prayer touched something deep inside her. That place where she so wanted to believe God could be the good and loving Father she'd never known. Truth was, she *was* tired. Tired of all she carried. So much hurt and guilt.

Could she simply hand them over to Him, the way she'd suggested Mateo should last night?

She opened her eyes and stared straight into his concerned dark gaze. Her breath caught in her throat. They stood so close together, close enough she could feel his warmth, feel his breath soft against her cheek. His hands still clasped hers, reassuring and strong.

Her heartbeat stuttered. She couldn't look away, even if she wanted to. Her body swayed toward him as if drawn by an invisible force. Nearer, nearer, till all he needed to do was lower his head a little and their lips would meet.

Please, Lord, let him kiss me. Then I'll know where I stand with him. Know he feels more than friendship for me, too.

The heartfelt prayer surprised her, probably as much as it would surprise God. Her eyelids fluttered closed in sweet anticipation of a kiss....

The bathroom door opened with a squeak. She and Mateo

sprang apart like naughty kids caught doing something they shouldn't.

Ivy chuckled, and a twinkle lit her gray eyes. "Oops! Did I interrupt a moment? Want me to go back in the bathroom?"

"Of course not. It wasn't a 'moment', at least, not the way you mean. We were praying for your recovery, that's all." Nai's attempt at her usual businesslike tones failed completely when her voice wobbled. "You need to be in bed."

She hurried to her aunt's side. That chuckle sounded more like the old Ivy, and that twinkle looked more like the old Ivy. But she still appeared way too pale and drawn.

The sooner Dr. Jeff arrived the better.

"I'm not ready to go to bed yet." As expected, Ivy protested. "I have to tell the animals I'm home and check the bookstore."

Huh, as if! Nai gave her a narrow-eyed, warning glance. "I was there when the nurse gave you your discharge instructions, remember?"

Aunt Ivy sent her a narrow-eyed glare right back, though Nai sensed her aunt protested only for the sake of it. Like her, Ivy didn't ever relish having to do as she was told. "Okay, I agree to resting *on* the bed for a little while."

"Okay," Nai conceded. That compromise made way more sense than battling to make Aunt Ivy do what she didn't want.

Frantic barking from upstairs suggested the dogs heard Ivy's voice. Squawks of "Ivy, Ivy, Ivy" from the bookstore promised Oscar also recognized her.

"How about I go get the dogs and bring them to you so they can welcome you home?" Mateo walked to the bookstore door and paused with his hand on the handle. "I can bring Oscar's cage in for you, too."

Two boisterous dogs, a noisy parrot, and someone just out of the hospital didn't sound like a good mix, but maybe they'd settle down once they saw her. Nai hoped so, anyway.

"Please do. I've missed them all." Ivy nodded her approval.

When Mateo swung the door wide, Paige stalked through into the apartment as if she'd been sitting on the bookstore side waiting for her human staff to open the door for her, rather than condescending to use the newly installed cat flap.

As soon as Mateo left to fetch the dogs, Nai settled Aunt Ivy on the bed with soft pillows behind her and a pile of books at her elbow. Paige leaped into her rightful place on the older woman's lap, purring furiously when Ivy stroked her.

"Someone's glad to see you home," Nai joked. *She* was glad too, of course, but she and Ivy had never had the kind of relationship where they spoke of their feelings. Maybe it was time to change that. She touched Ivy's hand. "I am, as well."

"Thank you, child. Trusting you to take care of things made all the difference for me." Her aunt's smile held that mischievous gleam again. "I know it wasn't easy for you coming back, but it looks like you've found some benefits."

Nai turned away to fiddle with Ivy's hospital bag. "Mateo and I are just friends, the way we've always been. He's helped me with a few things here, like the roof and the pets. Once you're well enough and Lucille can take over in the bookstore, I'll go back to Austin. I have a life there I've worked hard for."

"You do. But it's your fortieth birthday. A milestone day. Maybe a day to reconsider what you truly want from life?" Aunt Ivy's gentle words dropped into Nai's heart like pebbles into a lake. Small in themselves, but with ripples that spread.

"My life in Austin is exactly what I want."

Her muffled words didn't convince *her*, so she doubted they'd convince Aunt Ivy.

Why did her organized schedule and her immaculate apartment all of a sudden feel cold and lacking? This quirky chaotic bookstore, the people, and the pets — okay, Mateo, too — warmed her heart far more. Though she loved her boss and loved her job and loved knowing she'd achieved so much, when it came to sparking joy, there was no comparison.

Maybe rather than asking herself where *she* wanted to be, it was time to ask God where *He* wanted her to be.

But, the biggest but.

Mateo hadn't kissed her, though she'd given him plenty of opportunities. Was she mistaking his simple gestures of friendship for something more? She needed to be sure. No way could she give up her life in Austin on the crazy hope that maybe he loved her, too.

She wanted to let the past go. Truly, she did. But her fists clenched as her mother's words rang in her head again, as fresh and wounding as they'd been when Mateo stood her up for the prom.

You ruined my life. You're so ugly. Nobody will ever love you. Not even Mateo with his scars. Look, doesn't this prove it?

Hard to believe Mateo would want to hurt her like that, give Mom such a weapon against her. But he'd been angry, refused to talk, refused to tell her why. What else could she think?

If only he'd give her the proof she needed. The proof Mom hadn't been right.

The clatter of claws on the bookstore's wood flooring warned her the dogs were on their way. Mateo, as well. She pushed her hurtful thoughts back down. Way down deep.

Thankfully, Ivy didn't press her with more questions.

Both dogs rushed into the apartment. Heinz jumped straight on the bed and licked Ivy's face, earning a hiss and a sideswipe from Paige. Far better behaved, Catsup sat beside the bed, one paw raised to shake hands.

"Maybe I should have leashed them." Mateo grimaced an

apology.

"Not at all. This is the best welcome home." Laughing, Aunt Ivy fussed over Heinz with one hand while she took Catsup's paw with the other. "My lovely furbabies."

"Okay, guys, she knows you're happy she's home. Let's settle down now. Especially you, Muttley." Nai scooped up Heinz and deposited him at the end of the bed, well away from Paige.

To her surprise, he quieted down, making himself comfortable at Ivy's feet. Catsup curled up on the mat beside the bed. Looked like she'd lost her sleeping companions. She should feel glad to have her bed to herself again.

At least Aunt Ivy's color had brightened, and that shrunken, suddenly-old look that worried Nai had lifted. Ivy brightened even more when Mateo heaved Oscar's huge cage through the doorway and somehow managed to balance it on the far-too-small nightstand beside her so she could open the cage door and scratch the bird's brightly feathered chest.

"Thank you." Ivy smiled. "My favorite people and my animals all in one room. Just the way I like it."

The doorbell rang, the side entrance directly into the one-room apartment.

"That will be Dr. Jeff. He said he planned to visit." While Mateo placed the cage on the coffee table so Ivy and Oscar could see and talk to each other, Nai hurried to open the door.

To her surprise, her aunt's cheeks had pinked. "And here's another of my favorite people."

So, did Ivy have a thing for the doctor? Maybe she wasn't as dedicated to staying single as it seemed.

Smiling widely, peering around her to see Ivy and holding a generous multicolored bouquet of roses, complete with a crystal vase, the stocky sixty-something doctor stood on the doorstep. So could be, this wasn't the medical checkup Nai had assumed, either.

"Please, Doctor, come in." Standing back, she waved Dr. Johnson into the room.

One of her certainties turned topsy-turvy. Of course, she hadn't remained single solely because of her aunt's influence. But Ivy had encouraged her to seek academic and professional achievement. Ivy had been her role model in her determination not to be like Mom.

And now Ivy blushed over a bunch of flowers and smiled up at the doctor, almost shyly?

No. That couldn't be right. She must just be imagining it. The effect of too much Mateo.

Confirming that, Ivy shifted back to her usual no-nonsense self. "Jeff, please tell Naomi that she doesn't need to fuss over me. She should know by now that I'm a tough old bird. It takes more than a little thing like this to kill me."

He snorted. "You made it through this 'little thing' this time, but I'd rather you didn't do it again. Your heart might be tough enough, but *my* heart won't handle it." Laughing, the doctor tapped his chest.

Despite his joking manner, sadness darkened his eyes. Was he recalling how close to death Ivy had skated when she collapsed in church?

Nai's phone beeped in the back pocket of her jeans.

"Sorry." Apologizing to the room in general, she pulled out the phone and glanced at the screen.

A text from Kristina.

Uh-oh. She'd forgotten. The girls had invited her to celebrate her fortieth birthday at the Pancake Shoppe on the boardwalk.

Torn, she read the reminder about the get-together and slipped her phone back in her pocket. She didn't want to leave her aunt alone so soon after bringing her home. She wasn't sure it was *wise* to leave her alone. She didn't feel too much like celebrating.

But it wasn't right to cancel on the girls, either.

Ivy peered at her, eyes bright. "A birthday invitation?"

"Yes." No point trying to pretend otherwise. "Reese and Kristina want me to meet them at the Pancake Shoppe. But I feel I should stay here with you."

"*I'll* stay with Ivy." The doctor was quick to offer. "Hudson is covering the on-call again this weekend, so I don't have anywhere else I need to be."

"I'm not a child. I don't need a babysitter," Ivy protested.

"Humor us, Ivy, so Nai can go out without worrying about you," Dr. Jeff put in, smiling. "Besides, maybe I'd enjoy a few quiet hours in your company."

"Quiet, with these guys here?" Despite her joke, Ivy blushed and pretended to focus on petting the cat.

Nai eyed the doctor, then nodded. If she couldn't leave Aunt Ivy with him, who could she leave her with? "Okay, I'll go. I'll just walk the dogs first."

Clearly hearing the word *walk* both dogs jumped up, wagging their tails.

"I'm happy to walk the dogs." Mateo, who'd stood silently leaning against the wall, straightened. "Grandpa's away for the weekend, so I don't need to rush home to check on him. And my shift doesn't start till eleven."

Nai gaped at him. "You didn't tell me you had to work tonight. Shouldn't you be sleeping? Go home. I'll walk the dogs."

Heinz and Catsup stayed sitting at his feet, gazing up at him in total hero worship. He laughed. "Seems these guys have made up their minds." He glanced out the window at the late-afternoon light. "It's early enough. I can walk them and still get a nap before my shift begins."

Accepting help doesn't mean you're weak. The words Mateo said to Ivy earlier echoed in her head.

She raised her hands in defeat. "Okay. I give in. I'll text the girls to let them know I'll be there soon."

Five minutes later, after she'd readied herself while Mateo harnessed the dogs, they stood on the sidewalk outside the bookstore, leaving Ivy engrossed in an argument with the doctor about a book adaptation. Mateo held the leashes one in each hand, resisting the dogs' attempts to tug him away. Nai jiggled the keys to Aunt Ivy's old wreck of a car. Though neither of them spoke, neither seemed in a hurry to leave.

She tucked the car keys in her purse. "I–I think I'll walk down to the boardwalk. It will still be light by the time I need to walk home." Would he guess her unspoken invitation? *Walk with me?*

"I can take the dogs that way. You okay if I walk with you?" His eyes, intent on her, seemed to ask a far more important question.

One she wasn't sure she knew the answer to. Ducking her head, she glanced away. "Uh… sure."

They walked in silence and reached the Pancake Shoppe too soon. She spotted Reese and Kristina sitting at a window table the same time they spotted her and began waving madly.

Outside the door, Nai stood gazing at him, heart racing. "Thank you, Mateo. I appreciate your help."

Gathering the leashes into one hand, he touched her cheek with the other. "You're welcome, Nai. Anytime. Happy birthday."

Such formal, polite words when the feelings rioting inside her were anything but polite. She held her breath, sure her eyes implored him to kiss her.

And still, he didn't.

"See you, Nai." And he walked away.

Probably a good thing with Reese and Kris watching. What she felt for him now was far too new and fragile and confused to stand up to her friends' inevitable teasing.

She entered the restaurant, inhaling the delicious aromas of pancakes, applesauce, and coffee. Her gaze roamed over families with kids, groups of friends, and a couple with shiny gold wedding rings glinting on their hands, their heads so close. As close as hers and Mateo's used to be when they studied together.

Could she imagine a future with him?

Oh yes, she could, complicated though leaving her life in Austin and moving to the Cove would be. But the gap between imagining and doing was canyon sized. And it took two to make a relationship.

Whether Mateo felt the same, she just didn't know.

CHAPTER SEVENTEEN

NAI SURPRISED herself by enjoying the church service on Sunday morning. Then when the pastor announced the fellowship time afterward and requested everyone to mingle, she cringed. In her teens, so painfully shy with everyone but her close friends, she'd tended to hide behind Reese and Kristina, both so much more confident and outgoing.

Well, as she'd slipped into the pew beside them just before the service started, maybe she could do the same today.

Or maybe not. She stared as Reese turned away from them to hug Kristina's brother, Roman. The hug showed way more enthusiasm than Roman probably expected. Certainly way more than *she'd* expected. Maybe she'd been wrong about Reese and Heath?

Nope. A glance toward the pulpit showed Heath headed their way. So he might have had more than a little to do with Reese's hug. Especially when the second Heath pivoted on his heel and strode away, she let Roman go and hugged Kristina instead.

Nai stifled a chuckle. Next thing Reese knew, she'd have Roman asking her out.

"I didn't expect to see you in church, Nai." Kristina's voice interrupted her thoughts. "Who's looking after Aunt Ivy?"

"Dr. Johnson," she replied. "After I got home last night — and by the way, girls, thank you so much for spoiling me on my birthday yesterday — he insisted on coming back this morning so I could go to church and give God thanks for saving Aunt Ivy's life. There was no reasoning with him that I'd already done so."

So, maybe that was a small exaggeration. She hadn't precisely thanked God in so many words. Not officially. But He knew she was grateful, right?

"We enjoyed 'spoiling you' yesterday. Those pancakes were yummy." Kristina chuckled. "Thank the doctor from me when you see him, for making it possible for you to leave Aunt Ivy."

"I will. Anyway, when he came back again this morning, I figured I might as well humor the man and give him the time with my aunt. She does seem to enjoy his company. He's good for her, I think."

Grinning, Reese flickered a wink. "He is. And, he more than enjoys her company. He admitted he loved her when we went to the hospital to visit Ivy, the day of her heart attack."

Nai detected the hint of sadness shadowing her friend's humor. But Reese wouldn't appreciate her drawing attention to it. Heath Brock had been part of that "we".

"He did?" Hmm. So her guess when the doctor arrived at the apartment had been right.

"He did." Reese's smile and nod held a world of meaning. "Well, to us, not to her. He's too chicken to declare himself yet."

Nai didn't attempt to restrain her disbelieving snort. She'd surely just imagined her aunt's girlish shyness when the doctor arrived with flowers. "The guy's an optimist. Aunt Ivy enjoys his company, but she's always assured me she intends to stay permanently single. No man can come between her and her pets and her books. As far as I know, she's never had a boyfriend or dated anyone."

Reese blinked. "But... she almost married Heath's Uncle Trafford five years ago."

It was Nai's turn to blink. More than blink. Her jaw dropped so hard she consciously had to close her mouth and swallow before she could speak. "What?"

"I hear they were as good as engaged, and then he fell ill. You didn't know?" Her friend eyed her, genuine concern shining in her eyes.

Nai rubbed her forehead. "I knew she grieved his death. But more than that?" Mouth pursed, she shook her head. "Aunt Ivy never let on that he was more than a good friend."

One of her certainties in life just crumbled.

Had she only imagined Aunt Ivy as a happily single woman who wasn't simply marking time while waiting for marriage? The polar opposite of Mom, so desperate for male support and attention. Ivy's encouragement spurred Nai to work hard for her scholarship, to get through business school, to find a job she could devote herself to and excel in. Her aunt had been her role model for as long as she could remember.

And it seemed her image of her aunt was totally wrong.

Plus, if Ivy had come close to marrying Trafford Brock, it stung more than a little that she'd never mentioned it.

Not wanting any more of her illusions shattered just yet, she moved away from her friends. The pastor's request not to stick with friends and family, and speak to other people instead, gave her the ideal excuse.

A lot of them, she'd already seen during the week at the bookstore. Like widowed Melanie, who ran the Pancake Shoppe with her mother-in-law and had served her and the girls some wonderful food last night. Relaxed and easy, Nai enjoyed catching up with Mel and a few other folks, too.

Seemed Mateo was now the only person she remained shy with. That frustrating beyond-the-ordinary shyness and self-consciousness had kicked in as soon as teenage hormones gave her a changed awareness of the boy who'd been a lifelong friend, and she hadn't lost it yet.

Or lost the awareness.

Thankfully, his family usually worshiped at a different church, plus he'd probably be sleeping after working last night. So, she didn't have the Mateo Effect to contend with this morning.

Phew!

When Melanie scooted off to get her daughter from Sunday school, Nai stayed chatting with Mel's friend Jeannie, who'd inherited one of the orchards up the river and supplied the Shoppe with apple products, as well as selling at Chapel Cove's farmers' market.

Hmm. That set Nai's business antennae twitching. One of her case studies in business school had been helping a chef friend get her specialty food products into upmarket stores. Maybe she could help Jeannie do the same. And the farmers' market wasn't only for foodstuff. A weekly stall there could help Ivy's on Spruce clear some of the huge backlog of used books.

If she was staying here, she could—

Nai chopped the thought off short. Lots of things she *could* do. Except she wasn't staying. She belonged back in Austin, not here in the Cove.

Didn't she?

A glance at her watch reminded her she really should get home to Aunt Ivy. Excusing herself, she hurried back to her seat. The same pew she'd always sat in, ever since she started attending this church at twelve.

Very little had changed. The old wooden pews now had some padding, upholstery on the seats and backs. Stained glass filled the long narrow windows behind the pulpit. Though the modern church was beautiful in its own way, she'd always had far more of a sense of spiritual things in the old chapel, up on the headland.

In her teens, when she used to daydream about marrying Mateo, those daydreams often included a wedding there.

Huh? Where had that crazy memory come from?

Reaching under the pew to grab her purse and then slinging it over her shoulder, Nai found Reese and Kris. "I'd better get home. Not that I don't trust the doctor to take care of Ivy, but her dogs are due for another walk. How about we have another girls' night out on Tuesday evening for your birthday, Reese? We could go to that fancy seafood restaurant on the boardwalk. My treat, I insist."

Unlike her to splurge on a meal. Usually, she preferred frugality. But with Kris and Reese both being taken for a ride financially as well as emotionally by their exes, the seafood place was probably well outside their budgets. She could afford it.

Silly of her, but she preferred not to go back to Tía Irma's. Too many memories of Mateo intruded there.

"Sure," Kristina answered. "I'd like that. It's very generous."

"Sounds great." Reese's response was slower, more hesitant. Could be, she hoped Heath would ask her out instead.

"Excellent." Nai kept her smile sunny and her tone breezy. "So if we don't see each other before then, seven on Tuesday." With a wave, she moved to leave.

Ever perceptive to her feelings, Kristina gave her a quick hug first.

The drive back to the bookstore took only a few minutes, and she parked behind the doctor's black sedan. Rather than head straight for the apartment, she entered via the bookstore and ran upstairs. Wise to change out of the best black pants and teal green ballet flats she'd worn for church. Jeans and sneakers were far better suited to walk the dogs in.

Her knock on the apartment door received an almost immediate reply.

"Come in." Ivy's voice, bright and chirpy. Seemed the doctor really *was* good for her.

Ivy sat in the electrically powered recliner Nai had the local furniture store deliver, the doctor in a dining chair beside her, watching a historical drama on Netflix.

"I'm home from church," Nai said, then felt idiotic for stating something so obvious.

The dogs, who'd been sound asleep when she opened the door, leaped up and barked as soon as they heard her voice, wagging their tails furiously. Those mutts had an instinct for knowing when it was walk time.

Well, their leads and harnesses in her hand probably gave them a clue, too.

The doctor chuckled and rose to his feet. "Someone thinks they should go for a W-A-L-K!" He spelled it out, letter by letter. So he'd been around the pair enough to guess the W-word would send them into even more of a frenzy. "Two someones. Want me to take them out?"

Nai *did*, so she could ask Aunt Ivy about Trafford Brock and find out what Ivy felt for the doctor. But if Jeff did have a thing for Ivy — and a certain glow in his gaze when it rested on her aunt suggested he *did* — then he deserved as much time with her as he could get.

Unlike Reese with her "chicken" comment, Nai understood him being reluctant to declare himself. If Ivy didn't return his warmer emotions, it could ruin their friendship, as well as make their professional relationship strained.

Didn't she feel that way about Mateo, except with her life in Austin and their history as added complications?

"It's fine." Smiling, she waved Jeff back to his seat beside Ivy. "Stay with Aunt Ivy, please. Looks like you're both having fun there. And after my pancake dinner last night, I need all the exercise I can get."

Aunt Ivy huffed. "You two! Neither of you letting me do more than brush my teeth on my own! I'm not helpless. I should be out walking my dogs."

Since brushing her teeth this morning left Ivy exhausted and needing to lie down, Nai didn't want to think what walking a boisterous dog like Heinz would do. But arguing with Aunt Ivy? As pointless as arguing with Heinz.

Ivy would match her in stubbornness, dig her heels in, and argue just for the sake of it. Nai hoped she wasn't as difficult, but guessed she probably was.

"I know. But humor us, okay?" she asked, as she harnessed Heinz. The little dog bounced in excitement, making it take twice as long as it should to get him buckled into the bright blue webbing. "Remember what the cardiac nurse told you before you left the hospital? You need a slow, gradual increase in exercise to give your heart muscle the best chance of getting strong again. Too much too soon will reduce your chance of recovery."

Ivy shook her head. "Naomi Macnamara, don't try to tell me you wouldn't be exactly the same. I know for a fact you are every bit as stubborn. And every bit as independent."

A little too close to what she'd just been thinking. Ouch!

"I—"

"Whether Nai would be the same if this happened to her is irrelevant," Jeff cut in before she could say more. "She hasn't had a major heart attack. You have." Emphasizing his words with a waggled finger, the doctor shot his gaze to the ceiling as if asking God for patience. "Made worse by the fact you refused to seek attention sooner. I expected you'd be a difficult candidate for cardiac rehab."

He raised a hand to forestall Ivy's protests. "Let me finish. Here's how it works. You forgo a little independence now, so you get back to being as independent as possible faster."

Lips twisted to one side, Ivy matched his eyeroll and spread her hands. "Okay, I give in. With you both ganging up on me, what chance do I have?"

Laughing, Dr. Jeff turned his raised hand to Nai for a high five. "Finally, the woman sees sense!"

Nai liked the doctor. No doubt Ivy would lead him on a merry dance, and she still hadn't gotten her head around the need to shift her mental image of Ivy from a resolutely single woman to a woman open to romantic relationships. But she couldn't help hoping he did manage to woo her aunt.

The walk in the refreshing spring air gave her time to reflect on the ways she was like Ivy. Behaving just as stubbornly about aspects of her life.

Her insistence she'd be returning to Texas to stay, for example? Her insistence on playing it safe, not risking Mateo knowing what she felt?

Time to admit it. She missed him. Today was the first day she hadn't seen him at least once since being back in the Cove. Only a week, yet it felt so much longer. It felt like a lifetime.

Oh, he'd texted this morning after his shift to check Ivy was fine, and she'd wished him sweet dreams. Maybe he'd text later and offer to help with the dogs this evening.

Or maybe, to prove to herself that she wasn't toxically independent, she'd text him, instead. To prove that she wasn't even more of a chicken than the doctor. Worse, a chicken who flapped her wings and clucked loudly to tell the world she wasn't a chicken.

She pulled out her phone, but her hands shook too much to thumb-type a message.

This wasn't such a big deal. She was totally overreacting. It didn't have to mean anything more than proving a point to herself. They were good friends. Nothing more.

And since it didn't mean anything more, no harm leaving it till tomorrow.

As she tucked her phone back into her pocket, all she could hear was clucking.

CHAPTER EIGHTEEN

ON MONDAY morning, Mateo came home after his night shift unsure whether to hope Abuelo wanted to visit the bookstore again today or hope he didn't.

The old man's near-daily visits last week gave him the excuse to see Nai, sure. But loving her as he did, staying where she seemed to want him, safely friendzoned, became harder by the day. Things weren't progressing, no matter what he did for her.

Maybe things weren't *ever* going to progress. He knew better than to rush her, but not rushing her wasn't getting him anywhere, either. Of course, it *had* only been a week. But after twenty-something years waiting for a girl, a guy got kinda impatient.

His grandpa had come home from his veterans' weekend tired but cheerful last night, so he half expected the old man might still be in bed. Instead, he sat at the kitchen table, reading the newspaper.

"*Nieto*, I'm worried about you. You've got to tell me what's wrong." Putting his paper aside, Abuelo gestured for Mateo to sit.

Was he that obvious?

"Nothing is wrong." Mateo pulled out a chair and sat opposite his grandpa.

The older man waggled a finger at him. "Don't lie to me. I could see it on your face when you were a little boy, and I can see it now. It's about Naomi Macnamara, isn't it?"

Mateo stared at his grandpa. No point trying to deny it. "How did you know?"

"I'm not a cop like you, but I can put two and two together. And I may be old, but I remember things well enough." The old man tapped his white-haired head. "I remember how upset you were when you couldn't go to the prom with her. And when she went away to college before you went to the Police Academy. It has to be about her. Did you two have a falling out?"

"No. It's just...we don't seem to get beyond being friends. And it's great. Being friends with Nai is great." Mateo did his best to keep any bitterness out of his voice.

"But you want more, right?" Nodding, Abuelo leaned closer across the table, forehead creased in concern.

"I want to be with her for the rest of my life. I love her. But it doesn't matter."

"What?" Jerking back in his chair, his grandpa bellowed, "How can love not matter?"

"It matters. Of course, it matters." Propping his head in his hands, Mateo loosed a long breath, almost a sigh, pathetic as a lovestruck teen. "She only wants friendship from me. She told me so."

"Hmmm." Abuelo rubbed his forehead. "That doesn't sound right to me. I've been in the bookstore and seen the way she looks at you. And I remember when you were teens and studied here, how she blushed a little when your eyes would meet, how tender her smile would become when she thought you weren't looking. I'm sure of it. Naomi has strong feelings for you, too."

Hope flickered inside Mateo. "So why would she say she wants to stay friends?"

His lips turning down, his grandpa spread his hands wide. "You know what her mom was like, the terrible things she said to her daughter. Things like telling her she was ugly and no man would ever love her."

Anger surged through Mateo, and his hands formed fists, clenched on the table in front of him. He barely restrained the urge to thump the table. "I know. But that's ridiculous. Nai is lovely. How could she believe such lies? And I still don't understand how a mother could say such cruel things to her own daughter."

Abuelo shrugged. "Suzanna had disappointments in her life, and they changed her. Something a long life taught me about human nature — those who've been badly hurt often seek to hurt others. She hurt herself just as much with the things she did. I suspect she repeated those words to Naomi so often that, eventually, the girl believed them."

"But...Nai's forty." A fist pressed against his forehead, Mateo shook his head. "Would she still believe things her mom said so long ago?"

"You're forty, as well." The old man snorted, but kindness softened his dark eyes. "And don't you still believe it was your fault your parents died? Even though nobody *ever* said that to you — in fact, your abuela and I were careful to say the opposite."

He'd never guessed his grandpa saw so much, knew him so well. If only someday he could be half as wise. "I did," Mateo admitted. "Still do, a little. But Nai talked to me about it on Friday, made me see it, made me realize I needed to hand it over to the

Lord."

"Good." Releasing a deep, satisfied exhale, Abuelo nodded. "Now I know she loves you, if she not only realized but also cared enough to say that to you."

That flicker of hope strengthened, became a flame.

"But…" It seemed Abuelo wasn't finished. The old man trailed off and eyed him as if pondering the wisdom of what he intended to say. "Okay, I'm going to ask you. Do you have a similar belief to Naomi? A belief no woman would love you? Is that what's holding you back from telling her how you feel?"

Mateo's hand rose to cover his scarred cheek, the hardened flesh uneven under his fingers. He closed his eyes and sucked a breath through his teeth, a knife twisting in his heart.

Is it, Lord? I know You love me. But can I believe Nai might love me, too? Love me because I'm me, not just because of what I do for her?

His prayer echoed the words she'd said to him last week, during their dinner at Tía Irma's. Simply asking the question opened the possibility of healing, let God into that dark unexplored corner of his heart.

"Maybe." Determination rushed through Mateo, and he straightened his spine. "So, what should I do?"

"Be patient and persistent. But make sure she knows you're serious. Do you know that it took me three months, twenty days, and three hours before your grandmother gave me a chance?"

Mateo laughed. "Not that you were counting or anything."

"Oh, believe me, I counted even the minutes with that girl. And at first, she wouldn't as much as glance at me. Had I given up trying with her, your father wouldn't have existed. And you wouldn't have existed, either."

"That's a strong point. But with Nai…it's been far more than three months. Our entire lives."

His grandpa leaned forward. "I'm guessing she's not a girl who can be pushed into letting things happen fast. But you need to show her how you feel. Show her she's lovable. Make a grand gesture."

"I walk the dogs for her every day. I brought her flowers and took her to dinner, and—"

"I said a grand gesture." Grandpa sighed out exasperation. "Dog walking and flowers and dinner are all good, but they aren't enough. You have to convince her of your love. That you mean business. That she means more to you than anyone else does. That you're so much in love with her you want to spend a lifetime together."

Mateo gulped. When he was so shy with her that even holding her hand was a big thing, how could he possibly do that?

Lord, tell me what to do. Please?

Suddenly, it was all clear. He lifted his head, new hope infusing him. Nai didn't see the things he did to help her as signs of love because they were things he could do for anyone. Things he *did* do for others.

Abuelo was right. The grand gesture had to be something he'd do only for her and no one else.

"I'll buy an engagement ring and propose. Do it properly, go all out on the romance." Mateo pulled his shoulders back. He couldn't let her leave Chapel Cove and lose her again without trying everything he could.

"You got it." The older man smiled. "Now I can see you inherited some traits from me."

"I won't be able to go to Portland to buy a ring till Friday morning once I've finished work. But I'll propose on Friday night. Ask her out to dinner to that fancy place on the boardwalk, and we can watch the sunset and the waves. Nai always loved that. Then I'll do the whole thing, even get down on one knee." Mateo grinned. The more he thought about it, the more Abuelo's idea excited him. "She'll have to know I'm serious about her then."

"That's my boy." Abuelo reached across the table and gave him a hearty slap on the shoulder. Hearty enough to rock him in his seat. His grin widened. So the old man wasn't as frail as he'd feared.

Thank You, Lord! Some hope with Nai, and less need to worry about Abuelo. A double blessing.

He drew in a deep breath and answered a question that hadn't been asked. "In the meantime, I'll just keep doing what I'm doing. Help her, give her what little signs I can, but not try to rush her. Even the grand gesture won't pressure her. I won't push for an answer straight away. But by Friday, she'll know for sure how I feel for her. She'll know for sure I love her."

As anticipation bubbled in his belly and chest like shook-up soda, he smiled. Friday couldn't come soon enough.

Nai parked Ivy's old beater outside the bookstore and rested her head on the steering wheel for a moment as emotions battled in her. Relief that the emergency Kristina asked her to help with, Greg's missing daughter, was safely resolved. Worry about leaving Ivy and the bookstore.

Please, let Ivy be okay. Please, let all the pets be okay. Please, let the bookstore be okay.

Very much like a prayer, though she didn't want to admit to that.

Raising her head, she looked at the building. The bookstore was still standing. No flames of smoke suggesting a fire. No ambulance parked outside. All good signs.

Still, trepidation tensed her tummy as she walked up the crazy-paved path. Leaving Aunt Ivy and the bookstore with Fern in charge had been more than a little concerning. Especially when, after their Saturday closure, the store had been busier than usual today. Plus, Ivy seemed a little more breathless.

But when Kristina called her with an emergency that really *was* an emergency, not a "What should I wear for tonight's date?" emergency, what else could she do? At least she was back in time to close up for the evening. And if Ivy seemed worse, Dr. Jeff had assured her she could call him anytime and he'd visit. He'd even given her his personal cellphone number.

Convincing Ivy she needed a doctor's visit might be a harder task, of course.

She swung the bookstore door open to see floral arrangements on every available surface. Her eyes widened.

Violet, together with Mr. Rodriguez, was deep in animated conversation with Mrs. Kapinsky, an older customer, who already clutched a brown paper bag bearing the bookstore's tree and ivy logo.

And Fern, who'd chosen a gothic look today, with a flowing black dress, heavy black lace-up boots, and even heavier black eye makeup and lipstick, stood at the cash register. The clatter of the printer suggested she'd already set the machine doing the tally for today.

Fern glanced up as the bell over the door jingled, her brow furrowed. "How is the little girl? Is she safe? I'm hoping you being back already means they found her."

Nai smiled. "She is. And they did. Kristina found her, safe and well." She didn't add that she'd watched her friend confront one of her biggest fears to do it.

So, she might be a chicken. Well, no "might" about it. But Kris definitely wasn't. Compared to what Kris did today, what was phoning Mateo?

Um... still a big deal. Just not a big deal involving any risk of broken bones.

Only a broken heart.

Still, her friend's courage challenged her. Maybe it was time to face her own fear.

Maybe. Later.

"Phew! Good news." Fern's creased bow relaxed. Smiling, she waved a hand at the bouquets surrounding her. Enough to stock a florist shop. "If you think this is a lot of flowers, wait till you go in the apartment. I guess you figured that Sally did her delivery while you were out. Almost everyone in town sent Ms. Ivy flowers."

Nai returned her smile. "Looks like it. I'll just go check on Aunt Ivy. Then I can take over for you."

A sag of the girl's shoulders and a downward curve to her dark-lipsticked mouth suggested disappointment. Because Fern wanted to put a hand in the till, or because she had ambitions to do more than pour coffee and plate up pastries?

Nai eyed her. Her business instincts told her Fern's flakiness extended only to her appearance. The girl was ready to take on more responsibility. But the mystery of the stolen books still hadn't been resolved.

She made a snap decision. Easy to check the accounting later, and the missing books gave her the perfect excuse to call Mateo, to ask when he'd install the hidden camera.

"Unless you're happy to finish doing the tally for me, of course."

Beaming, Fern nodded. "I'd like to. *Really* like to. Next semester, I want to sign up for the business course at Cove College. It's evening classes, so I'd keep working, too." She pulled the tally sheets from the printer and threw Nai an uncertain glance. "Actually, hearing about everything you achieved made me realize maybe I could do more, too. Even have a business of my own one day."

Her cheeks heating, Nai ducked her head. "That's one of the nicest compliments anyone's ever given me." Well, nicest compliments she could believe, anyway. The memory of Mateo telling her she was beautiful at the riverside park warmed her face to flaming. Unsure what to say next, she scurried to the apartment door and knocked. "I'll check on Ivy."

"Come in."

Nai scraped her instant frown from her face and replaced it with a cheery smile. Ivy's voice sounded weaker and breathier than she'd like, but she didn't want to show too much concern. She opened the door, and her jaw dropped. Fern hadn't exaggerated about the flowers.

"I know, isn't it crazy? Good thing I don't have hay fever." Ivy chuckled, correctly guessing why she'd stopped and stared. "Now, if only they'd spent the money on books for me, instead." She spoke slowly, stopping to puff a breath every few words. Far more breathless than she'd been.

Though her aunt would hate her fussing. Nai had to. That worrying breathlessness. "What was your weight this morning?"

The cardiac nurse had been insistent. Daily weigh-ins, at the same time every day, as any sudden gain meant fluid retention, a serious complication of Ivy's heart damage.

Ivy's furtive glance toward the bathroom and twitched lips told Nai all she needed to know. Today's weigh-in hadn't happened. She huffed out a frustrated breath. Hopefully, trusting Fern with the cash tally would work out better than trusting Ivy to follow her home care instructions.

Shaking her head, Nai stepped closer to her aunt. At least the woman had her feet up. She could be grateful for that. "Let me look at your hands, please."

Her aunt tucked her hands under Paige, who gave a protesting meow and jumped from her lap. "Traitor! You're supposed to be on my side," Ivy puffed.

A glimpse of her hands was enough. The obvious swelling on either side of the opal ring Ivy wore on her right hand sent Nai reaching for her cellphone. She speed-dialed the doctor on his private number.

Ignoring Ivy insisting she was fine, Nai explained her aunt's symptoms. Five minutes later, Dr. Jeff rang the doorbell and hurried into the apartment. His narrow-eyed, assessing gaze turned into an impatient eyeroll as he pulled his stethoscope from his medical bag.

"Ivy Macnamara, do you want me to send you back to the hospital, or will you show some common sense and follow doctor's orders?" His voice held all the exasperation Nai had struggled to keep from her own.

While he examined Ivy, Nai hurried into the bookstore to let Fern and Violet know the doctor had arrived, so they could safely leave now. Hearing Mateo's voice had nothing to do with it.

Well, not much, anyway. Except that he reassured her by his simple presence.

Nothing to do with it, apart from that teensy detail.

CHAPTER NINETEEN

MATEO'S SMILE as he turned to her warmed Nai all the way through. Somehow, just by him being there, all her worries shrank to a more manageable size.

"How's Aunt Ivy?" His face and voice held such caring.

Face scrunched, Nai spread her hands. "I don't know yet. Dr. Jeff is with her now. Last I heard, he threatened to send her back to the hospital." She loosed a long heavy breath. "I hope it doesn't come to that."

"Oh no. We'll pray for her." Violet grabbed Mr. Hector Rodriguez's hand along with Mateo's, and they all bowed their heads to pray silently.

Mateo took her hand in a firm encouraging clasp, and Fern reached for her other hand. A sense of connection and belonging she'd never felt before soaked into Nai's heart. A sense that, no matter what, she had support.

Her brain failed to form a coherent prayer for Aunt Ivy. The only words echoing over and over in her mind were *Thank You. Thank You.*

Maybe that was enough. Maybe that was all He needed to hear her say.

When Violet and Hector murmured amen, she echoed them and opened her eyes. A new awareness of peace, that had somehow always been there without her realizing it, lay soft and gentle on her heart.

Fern let her left hand go, but Mateo retained her right hand in his clasp. She didn't try to loosen her grip or pull away. Holding his hand felt so perfect, so reassuring, so meant to be.

"Violet, would you drive Grandpa home, please, so I can stay with Nai?"

No need for Nai to ask the question trembling on her lips. No need for him to ask if she wanted him to stay. The relief sweeping her at his words left her needing to cling to his hand even harder.

"Of course." Violet didn't hesitate before agreeing.

"The tally is all correct. What else can I do to help?" Fern added.

"Thank you. Thank you all. Nothing more." There wasn't. Nothing more Mateo could do, either, apart from simply being here. "I'll text you when I have a better idea how Ivy is."

After a flurry of hugs, they left, and she locked the entrance door behind them. Mateo grabbed her hand again in a warm blessing of a clasp.

Perfect timing, as the doctor opened the apartment door and poked his head out. "You can come back in, Nai." His gaze dropped to their joined hands. "Mateo, too, though I'll check that with Ivy first."

"Mateo can come in." Ivy's quieter words floated through the opening.

Dr. Jeff sat at the small apartment dining table, hands steepled in front of his mouth. Nai and Mateo perched side-by-side on Ivy's bed. She clutched his hand like a lifeline.

As if realizing this wasn't the time to be boisterous, Heinz contented himself with jumping on the bed beside Mateo rather than giving his usual exuberant welcome, and Catsup took up station at his feet.

Lowering his hands, the doctor spoke. "I've already explained all this to Ivy, but it's important you know, too. I've called your aunt's cardiologist, drawn some labs, and prescribed her an additional medication. When you called me, Nai, I had an idea what she'd most likely need." A small white medicine box sat on the low coffee table beside Aunt Ivy's recliner. Eyebrow raised, the doctor frowned at his patient and waggled a finger. "Medication I want to see you take — right now."

He leaned forward to pop two pills from their foil strip and handed them to her, along with a glass half-filled with water. Reluctantly, Ivy swallowed the tablets.

"Good girl." Jeff nodded. "Sense from you, at last." The love glowing in his eyes contradicted his acerbic tone.

"Huh! What choice do I have?" Ivy shook her head and turned to Nai. "He threatened me with going back to the hospital if I didn't."

"That or the local hospice, yes."

"No!" The word tore through Nai. "Hospice. Isn't that where you send people to… to… you know…" Unable to say it, she shivered. Mateo squeezed her hand, support and caring flowing from him.

"Don't worry. I'm not saying Ivy's condition is terminal. She's not our usual hospice patient." The doctor gave her a reassuring smile. "But as she's flatly refused to take my advice to let Dr.

Moreno readmit her to the Portland hospital, it's a good thing I can admit patients with specific chronic conditions to the hospice for symptom control."

Nai nodded thoughtfully. So Aunt Ivy had a chronic condition now. That must have been what the cardiologist hinted at when he mentioned her heart problem could be controlled, but was unlikely to resolve completely.

"I hope it won't be necessary," Jeff continued. "The problem is fluid collecting in Ivy's lungs, meaning her heart needs to work harder, and making her short of breath. The medication will remove the extra fluid from her system by encouraging her kidneys to work harder instead."

"In other words, I'll be in and out of the bathroom all night."

Nai almost laughed at Ivy's twisted lips. Her aunt's sour tone still came through loud and clear, despite her breathlessness.

"Right. That's exactly what I want." Smiling, the doctor nodded. "Or at least, for the next few hours. And if you're *not* in and out of the bathroom, I want to know about it. Nai, don't hesitate to call me. The medication should do the trick, but any concerns, just call."

"I will. I'll call you straight away if I'm concerned." Well, not quite the truth. Nai was concerned right now, despite the doctor's reassurance.

He glanced around the flower-crowded room, and his forehead furrowed. "Speaking of the hospice, I'm about to go there now for my evening rounds. Want me to take some of these arrangements there?"

"Please." Her head cocked to one side, her eyes brightening, Ivy gave a wobbly, relieved smile. "I didn't want to say anything to Sally, but so many displays make the place look like a funeral parlor. I'm not quite ready to die yet."

Nai snorted. Trust Ivy to say what none of them dared to.

Loosing her grip on Mateo's hand, she stood and began removing the cards from the arrangements so she could write thank-you notes. He moved to the other side of the room and did the same.

She turned at the whir of the recliner.

Ivy had lowered the footrest and tilted the chair to help her to stand. "The med is working." Her eye-roll showed her opinion. "Niagara Falls, eat your heart out."

Nai hurried to her side. That Ivy accepted her offered arm to support her to the bathroom was confirmation enough. She still had cause to be concerned. Though her aunt's breathlessly delivered joke held reassurance.

When Aunt Ivy lost her sass, that's when she'd *really* have to worry.

"Good." Dr. Jeff chuckled. "Niagara Falls is exactly what we want. While you're in there, we'll load some of these arrangements into my car."

Reluctant to leave Ivy, Nai stationed herself outside the bathroom door while the men carted several loads of flowers out of the apartment.

When the room looked less like a mausoleum, the doctor shook Nai's hand. "You did right to call me, I'll come back to check on her again later, but I'm confident I'll find her much improved." Smiling reassurance, he left.

Mateo stayed. "Want me to walk the dogs, so you can remain here with Ivy?"

Alone with him, Nai bit her lip as tears welled in her eyes. All she could manage was a wordless nod. He strode to her and wrapped strong arms around her. Rubbing her eyes and sniffing, she melted into his comforting embrace and rested her head on his shoulder. She hiccupped back sobs.

What would she do without his support?

Accepting what he offered didn't make her weak or make her

like Mom.

She hoped.

One thing for sure. Leaving him when she returned to Texas would wrench her heart in two.

Could she find a way to stay? Could she take the risk of letting Mateo know how she felt? Could she let love make her brave, like Kristina had today?

She didn't know. She just didn't know.

Next morning, Nai groped for her beeping phone and switched the alarm off, fast, to avoid waking Ivy. Ivy stirred but didn't wake.

Good. Time to grab a quick shower before ensuring Aunt Ivy took her morning meds as prescribed, which Dr. Jeff warned would trigger another round of bathroom visits. She'd have to get by on less than four hours sleep, but the convalescent needed more. Stretching, she lowered the recliner and stood, then walked to the older woman's bedside.

She'd propped Ivy up on three pillows, as Dr. Jeff recommended, but sometime in the last few hours, Ivy had slipped down. Thankfully, her breathing sounded way easier. All those bathroom visits last night had done the job. When the doctor had returned around eleven p.m. for a follow-up visit, his satisfied nod showed she hadn't imagined her aunt's improvement.

Her phone vibrated in her jeans pocket. Mateo.

She smiled as she opened his text message.

HOW'S IVY? AND HOW ARE YOU? WANT ME TO WALK THE DOGS?

He'd been such a help last night, staying a couple of hours after the doctor left, until she felt confident of Aunt Ivy's improvement. Texting her to check things were okay was good. Offering to come back to walk the dogs again as soon as he finished his shift was even better.

Somehow, accepting help from Mateo felt less of a mark of shame, less a sign of failure on her part. It wasn't the same as the way her mom clung to guys. Not one bit the same.

If she kept repeating that to herself, she'd believe it.

SHE'S SLEEPING NOW. I'M SURVIVING. YES, PLEASE!

For the rest of the day, she didn't intend on going farther than the bookstore door and the upstairs living quarters. Her aunt needed watching. Much as she hated to, she'd need to cancel dinner with the girls tonight. Unless maybe Mateo would sit with Aunt Ivy?

While she waited for his reply, she folded the quilt she'd covered herself with for her brief fully dressed doze.

TWENTY MINUTES TIME, OKAY?

A wide yawn escaped her. She really wasn't cut out for these sleepless nights. Rather than typing more, she sent him a smiley face. Time to go shower and change before he got here.

Before she made it into the upstairs bathroom, her phone vibrated again. Reese, this time.

WOULD YOU HATE ME VERY MUCH IF I CANCELED OUR PLANS FOR TONIGHT?

Phew! Saved from being the bad guy and having to cancel, when she'd offered to treat her friends. Talk about perfect timing! Nai detoured to the kitchen and voice-typed a reply while preparing the pets' breakfasts.

WOULD YOU HATE ME VERY MUCH IF I SAID CANCELING WOULD BE A BLESSING?! ;) AUNT IVY HAD A DIFFICULT NIGHT. ALL I WANT TO DO TONIGHT IS CRAWL INTO BED EARLY. BUT WHAT'S THE REASON YOU NEED TO CANCEL? OH, BY THE WAY, HAPPY BIRTHDAY AND WELCOME TO THE FORTIES CLUB.

Reese typed back.

LOL, KRIS AND NAI, THANKS FOR THE WELCOME, I THINK. HEATH

SENT ME FORTY ROSES THIS MORNING AND AN INVITATION TO DINNER. I THINK I SHOULD ACCEPT. I'VE ALREADY TURNED HIM DOWN TWICE—HE'S HOPING FOR THIRD TIME LUCKY. DON'T WANT TO DISAPPOINT THE MAN.

Nai laughed. Both her friends' romances seemed to be progressing well. She'd get to wear those poufy bridesmaid dresses for her besties yet.

SQUEEE! LUCKY GIRL. AND GIVE THE GUY A BREAK, PLEEESE. HE'S ONLY BEEN WAITING A LIFETIME FOR YOU.

Just like she'd been waiting a lifetime for Mateo.

And maybe, he'd been waiting a lifetime for her, too.

Dared she hope that someday she'd also get to inflict ugly dresses on her friends? Something she'd never ever seriously hoped for before. Never ever believed could happen to her. Told herself she never ever wanted.

Things had changed so much in just a week. Out of the blue, now she *did* want it. She wanted it more than she'd ever wanted anything in her life.

Could be, though, she'd done too good a job of friendzoning Mateo. Could be, friendzoned was all he wanted. She shouldn't read more than friendship into his helpfulness.

Even his hug last night. Something he'd probably offer anyone in the same situation in need of comfort. He still hadn't done anything she could say for sure he wouldn't do for anyone else.

She couldn't see much positive in Aunt Ivy developing complications. She'd need to let Jesse know she'd be here in the Cove for longer, possibly much longer. And that meant maybe one tiny glimmer of a good thing.

More time with Mateo. More time, God willing, for him to fall in love with her. The way she'd fallen in love with him.

Chapter Twenty

MATEO DIDN'T mind in the slightest missing sleep for Nai. He'd missed sleep before for far lesser causes. Right after his shift finished, he stopped by to walk the dogs for her.

Though she'd showered and changed and looked as beautiful as ever, the dark shadows circling her eyes bothered him. Somehow, he restrained his urge to hug and kiss her, to kiss those dark circles away. Praise God, she reported Ivy looked and sounded much better. He prayed both women would get a regular night's sleep tonight.

Violet, who'd stayed a few hours with Abuelo last evening while he'd stayed with Nai, picked the old man up that morning for his now-routine day in the bookstore. They pulled up outside the bookstore in Violet's violet car at the same time as he returned with the two dogs, who should be far better behaved after a long

187

run.

Nai met all three of them on the bookstore porch.

"Mr. Rodriguez!" Nai smiled a genuinely welcoming smile as she hugged both Violet and Abuelo. "You know, if you keep coming every day, I'll need to add you to the payroll."

"Hector *is* a huge help to me," Violet purred.

Mateo wasn't so sure. He loved his grandfather dearly, but he hadn't seen much sign of any help, apart from helping Violet gossip with customers. Maybe that was the help Nai meant. At least with Grandpa here, she didn't need to worry so much about Violet.

He noticed Nai didn't answer Violet's comment, just smiled and waved the older man and woman into the store.

"I'll take the dogs around to the side entrance," she said. "Aunt Ivy is awake now but staying in bed a while longer yet, at least till Dr. Jeff comes to check on her."

He nodded as he passed the leashes to her. "Wise move. Are you okay if I come back later this afternoon? I can walk the dogs again. Plus, that camera I ordered is arriving today. I'll be able to install it for you."

"Thank you." She hesitated. "Please, don't say anything to Aunt Ivy about the books. I haven't told her yet." Her chin jutted, and her manner became defensive. "I won't lie to her, of course. But I'm just waiting for the best time to tell her."

"It's okay." If she thought he was going to judge her for that, well, he wasn't. "Have any more books disappeared?"

Nai blinked. "Do you know, I haven't looked? I've had so many other things on my mind...." A hint of heightened color graced her cheeks.

Could be, she meant nothing more than Ivy and yesterday's drama with the missing child. Could be, that blush meant her "other things" also included him. A guy could hope, right?

"Gotta scoot," she said and darted off around the side of the building with the dogs, without meeting his eyes or giving him a chance to reply.

As he hopped into his truck, he chuckled. It probably wasn't only wishful thinking to imagine her reaction was a good sign. A very good sign.

Friday, and the grand gesture Abuelo recommended, couldn't come soon enough.

For the first time, he considered the option that felt impossibly improbable. Nai might say yes. If she did, he'd be the most thankful and blessed man on the planet. Maybe it wasn't as impossible as he thought, after all.

Later that day, after the Amazon delivery woke him, he returned to the bookstore to walk the dogs again and install the camera. He opened the door, then stopped dead. Standing at the counter, Nai leaned toward a tall handsome guy, smiling at him, whispering something to him. Her hand lay on his arm.

Jealousy shafted through Mateo. Sharp and painful, it clenched his gut, shocking in its intensity. His hand lifted to cover the left side of his face, the scars his beard didn't fully conceal resting puckered and distorted beneath his fingers.

Then he recognized the little girl beside the guy, the same one whose missing person's flyer he'd taken down from the patrol house bulletin board last night, as she'd been found safe and well within a few hours. She'd worn pink in that photo, while today her overalls and hair ribbons were a shade of purple Violet would be proud of.

And he heard the guy's reply to whatever Nai had whispered. "Kristina has friends as amazing as she is."

The relief that rocked him left him limp. This must be the man Nai mentioned Kristina dating. And the little girl must be the one who had the bad reaction in Tía Irma's last week. It all fell into place now.

As the other guy left the store, Mateo walked in.

Nai, crouched beside the child, looked up and smiled. He surely didn't imagine something more than her ordinary smile in the warm glow of gladness shining in her eyes.

"Mateo!" Her voice covered him like a caramel-coated embrace. "Chelsea, I want you to meet my friend Mateo. He's a policeman. He's also Kristina's cousin."

Surveying him with serious eyes that seemed to X-ray his soul, the little girl nodded. "Mommy Kristina. Daddy's going to marry her, I hope, so she'll be my mommy for real. My first mommy is in Heaven with Jesus. Are you going to marry Miss Nai?"

If he'd thought Nai blushed this morning, he hadn't seen anything compared to the red-rose color now flooding her cheeks. "Of course he isn't."

"That depends on Miss Nai." He replied at the same time. Eyebrow raised, he said nothing more, simply gave Nai a look.

She refused to meet his gaze. "Just go into the apartment to get the dogs, Mateo. Aunt Ivy is up and dressed now. Let's go find you that apple juice and brioche, Chelsea." Nai hustled the child through to the café.

Laughing, he let her go and went to walk the dogs.

When he returned with a pair of happy but tired mutts, Chelsea and Nai were in the apartment, talking to Oscar and Ivy. He kept the dogs leashed, in case the girl was scared of dogs. If Heinz got excited, he could easily knock over a child.

Something sweetly warm and caring in Nai's face as she bent talking to Chelsea told him that, despite her own terrible mom, Nai would make a wonderful mother.

Until she'd come home to the Cove, he'd never considered his lack of children an issue. But now? A pang of loss shot through him as he imagined the delight of having a daughter of their own, a serious little girl with jet-black hair and a sunshiney smile just like Nai's, dressed in cute purple overalls like Chelsea's.

A child who might never be born.

If only they'd tried harder when they had the chance, made things work when they were in their teens, they could have had a passel of children by now. Even if he could persuade Nai to marry him almost immediately, at forty, best they could hope for was one.

Swallowing a sigh, he put any hope for children in God's hands.

Maybe that longing he'd never felt before explained why Ivy was so attached to the pets she called her furbabies. Though that should be featherbaby, in Oscar's case.

Oscar let out a screech. "Mateo should marry Nai."

He laughed. "Hey, smart bird, Oscar. And she didn't even have to say 'It's Nai now' this time."

The narrowed-eyed glance she threw him held a warning. "If I find out who taught him that, I'll... I'll... I don't know what, but it won't be pretty!" She turned to her aunt. "Aunt Ivy, you must know."

Ivy mimed zipping her lips. "I'm calling the Fifth on that one."

She knew as well as he did who was responsible.

No trace of breathlessness marred her words today, and Mateo sent up a prayer of thanksgiving.

"Mateo should marry Nai," Oscar repeated.

Delighted, Chelsea clapped her hands. "Can we teach the parrot to say 'Daddy should marry Mommy Kristina'? That would be fun for Daddy to come back and hear."

Sure, kid, you can teach him that. It only took about three hundred repetitions to teach Oscar to say "Mateo should marry

Naomi".

Mateo hoped he was at least as smart as the bird. Smart enough not to admit to being the perp.

Not yet, anyway. Once he and Nai were safely married would be soon enough.

"I think Aunt Ivy needs to rest now, Chelsea. You can teach that to Oscar another time." As Chelsea's lower lip started to jut, Nai added, "Let's go see if we have more elephant books. You haven't finished reading the first one, yet."

Pout forgotten, Chelsea jumped up. "Yes, please! More ephalants." In her excitement, she garbled the word. "Thank you for letting me talk to your parrot, Miss Ivy."

Every inch the gracious hostess, even from her sickbed, Ivy smiled. "It's been a pleasure, Chelsea." As soon as Nai and the little girl left the apartment, she flopped back against the pillows and rolled her eyes. "Phew! A sweet child, but I'd forgotten how exhausting children can be."

"Can I do anything for you, Ivy?" He studied her, as unobtrusively as he could. She didn't sound as breathless as yesterday, but he wasn't sure what other signs to look for.

Rolling her eyes, she waved him away. "Don't you start fussing over me, too! Between Nai and Jeff, I'm already getting more than enough of that. Just unharness the dogs and let them come over here, then shut the door so I can rest."

"Can do."

When he ambled into the bookstore and headed for the cabinet housing the rare books, Nai's lovely voice floating through from the children's section formed a powerful distraction. Mateo struggled to keep his mind on installing the motion-activated camera in the rare books' drawer.

Finally, the camera was in place and working. He tested it, and sure enough, photos of his own ugly mug appeared in the phone app he'd downloaded. To finish the job, he plastered a large red-and-white "Security monitored" sticker onto the front of the drawer before locking it.

His grandpa and Violet both watched him work. "You know, I don't think there will be any more problems with missing books," Abuelo said.

The glance the older couple exchanged twitched Mateo's cop Spidey sense. The one that already told him they knew more about the books than they let on. He eyed them, one brow raised. "You think so, huh?"

"I *know* so." Violet grimaced and bit her lip after she uttered the words, and he was sure she'd intended to slap her hand over her mouth before she changed direction and scratched her head instead.

Throwing her a clearly reproachful look, Abuelo jumped in to give her a cover story. "Of course. I mean, look at that big warning label. Who's going to mess with that?"

With Nai within earshot, Mateo decided not to pursue it. Not now, anyway. "If the missing books turn up within a week or so, don't you think that would be the best possible resolution to the problem? No need to cause Nai or Ivy any worry."

Violet and Abuelo glanced at each other again and nodded.

"It would be best, yes." The old man managed to contrive an innocent I-know-nothing expression. "Maybe they'll turn out to have been in the bookstore all along. Just... mislaid."

"Let's hope so."

Mateo had no need to say more. Without a doubt, those books would reappear. *Why* they'd cooked up this stunt between them was a question for another day.

Now, he could lounge in an armchair and relax until Abuelo was ready to go home. Listen to the sweet music of Nai's voice as she read aloud to Chelsea. With her voice washing over him, he couldn't think of anywhere else he'd rather be.

Except maybe standing with Nai in front of the preacher, exchanging their marriage vows.

Someday, God willing.

Someday soon.

Someday very soon.

CHAPTER TWENTY-ONE

NAI DIDN'T quite restrain her groan when she struggled out of sleep to pick up the ringing phone on Wednesday. The one day she'd promised herself a sleep in, and it wasn't going to happen. When she heard what Roman Vela called about, she didn't bother holding back her groan. She'd hoped that text from Kristina last night was a joke.

Seemed it wasn't.

"How can she cancel her birthday? What happened?" Things seemed to be going so well for her bestie and Greg yesterday. If she left a guy like him to go back to Cullen? Ugh!

Roman didn't know any details of his sister's problem, or if he did, he wasn't saying. He just said Kris was upset and he wanted her and Reese to go to Kris, find out what the problem was, and talk her through it.

"You girls have been friends forever. If anyone can help her, it will be you guys."

Nai grimaced. Probably correct.

"I need to check on Aunt Ivy." She'd face a tough choice if her aunt and her best friend *both* needed her.

Clutching her phone, Nai scooted downstairs to peek in on Aunt Ivy. Still sleeping peacefully. Surrounded by her pets. Her breathing easy, slow and relaxed. Phew!

Dr. Jeff had been pleased with her aunt's response to the new med, but had given her what he called a "come to Jesus" talking-to when he visited after office hours yesterday. Reminded her how near death she'd skated and explained again why each of her medications was necessary and important.

He clearly knew Ivy well enough to guess that, at the first sign of feeling better, she'd start skipping doses. Time to wake her soon, make sure she took her morning meds.

Nai stepped back into the bookstore and closed the door. No need to wake Ivy before she had to. "Okay, I'll be there, and I'll pick Reese up on the way."

She'd just scrambled out of a quick shower and was pulling on her jeans when Reese rang. They worked out the timing.

Didn't give her long, but she could do it.

Arrange cover for the bookstore. Get dressed. Check her emails for anything super-urgent from Jesse. Wake Ivy and help her with all she needed to start her day. Eat a bowl of skim-milk oatmeal down in the apartment with Ivy to make sure Ivy ate something healthier than leftover brioche. Walk the dogs. Collect Reese. Go to Aileen's for the chocolate melt cake Kris loved. Drive to Kris's. Drag her friend out of whatever the crisis was.

Nowhere near as easy as the original idea to have coffee and brioche in the café. But still, doable. No time to think about Mateo.

Except that she already was. Rushing out to Kris's meant she wouldn't be here when he dropped his granddad off at the bookstore. Maybe insisting last night that he didn't need to swing by and walk the dogs as soon as he left the patrol house this morning, as he'd offered, hadn't been one of her smartest ideas.

Time to admit it — she missed him already.

But she didn't feel ready to backtrack and ask him for help, either.

Not yet.

The trickiest part was how to keep the bookstore running, without Ivy insisting on getting back to work. If Kris really had a crisis, it might keep her away the best part of the day. Certainly all morning. She wouldn't call Mateo. He'd say yes, of course, but he needed his sleep.

Fern?

Maybe. The girl had wacky dress sense, but she seemed smart. And she seemed willing to learn. Nai picked up her phone again.

"Fern? Sorry to call you so early, but I have a favor to ask you. Would you be able to take charge at the bookstore this morning? Open up, take care of the cash register, keep an eye on Violet and on Aunt Ivy. And do you know someone else who could help out in the café so you can focus on the other stuff?"

Silence echoed down the line for a moment. Then excited words burst out. "Wow! You're trusting me with the store? That's awesome! Thank you! And yes, I know someone. My friend Cas is between jobs, and she has barista experience. She did a week in Starbucks. I can show her how to work the quick-bake machine easily enough."

Riiiight. "Between jobs" and "a week in Starbucks" wasn't exactly reassuring. But what choice did she have?

"Sounds great."

So her voice had a hollow ring? This wasn't the time to micromanage, much as she wanted to. She had too much else to do in too little time.

It all got done. Just.

And over cake and coffee at Kristina's with Reese and Roman, between them all they came up with some practical solutions to help her beat Cullen's dirty tactics. Honestly, she didn't have words bad enough to describe that man! Not ones she could say to her friends, anyhow.

Seeing Kristina's misery brighten into hope was reward enough. Her friend deserved only joy from now on, and anything she could do to help that happen, she'd do.

In midconversation, Kris slapped her forehead. "Girls, remember, today is the day we were going to dig out the treasures we hid at thirteen, after we made our list of things to do before forty." She turned to her twin. "Sorry, us girls only."

They found a garden trowel in the toolshed and bundled into Ivy's old beater for the drive up to Chapel Point. After some friendly argument about the tin's location, they took turns digging. They all agreed that Reese, who'd had the idea, provided the tin, and buried it, should do the ceremonial opening.

Kneeling beside the shallow hole where she'd buried her beautiful biscuit tin so long ago, Reese lifted the treasure chest and set it down on the small pile of dug-up soil. The tin didn't look pretty anymore after twenty-seven years in the earth, the colorful images once adorning it replaced with rust.

The tin didn't matter. Only the contents counted.

Reese lifted the lid and reached inside for the Ziploc bags containing their treasures, before handing them around. Nai clutched hers and said nothing. She still wasn't sure she felt ready to show the girls the contents. The others stayed silent for a long, solemn moment, too. For each of them, the tin meant all their dearest teenage hopes and dreams.

Some they'd achieved. Others, maybe the most important ones, they hadn't. At least, she hadn't.

Or hadn't *yet*.

Reese broke the silence first, excusing herself to call Heath Brock to pick her up here. She'd decided to move into his Uncle Trafford's house. And more, it seemed things were seriously progressing between her and Heath. As soon as he arrived and jumped out of his red pickup, the hunky youth pastor drew her into a hug and kissed her — a proper kiss — right there in front of them.

Nai smiled, glad for her friend. At least one of their love lives was going right. The anti-Cullen tactics they'd worked out for Kristina should make it possible for her to be with Greg.

And that left only her.

After dropping Kristina off with a quick hug, Nai drove back to the bookstore and hurried inside. The usual welcoming scent of books, coffee, and freshly baked pastries greeted her. Presumably in honor of being in charge today, Fern had dressed more conventionally in a black pencil skirt and businesslike jacket.

Almost more conventionally. Her huge clompy ankle boots complete with silver spikes added that unique Fern touch she'd come to expect.

Fern grinned as Nai strode to the counter. "The bookstore's fine. Ms. Ivy's fine. The café's fine. I can't tell you how happy I am that you left me in charge!" Excitement and grateful pride bubbled from the girl.

"And I'm happy you were able to take charge. Thank you!" Nai meant it. She gave the girl a quick hug. "If your friend is willing to stay in the café, are you okay to stay in charge the rest of the day?"

"For sure!" Fern's ecstatic grin grew even wider.

Not only would that give Nai the chance to catch up on a lot, the girl seemed to thrive on the added responsibility.

Nai was used to being the boss. Really, ninety-nine times out of a hundred, she even bossed *her* boss. But maybe delegating wasn't a sign of failure on her part. Maybe, instead, it could be a gift both to her and the other person.

A huge paradigm shift to make.

Like shifting from seeing Aunt Ivy as committed to staying single. Reese's mention of Trafford Brock, who she claimed Ivy had almost married, set Nai wondering again. Mainly, wondering why it bothered her so much. Because she'd chosen Ivy as a role model, then found she'd modeled herself on mistaken ideas?

After knocking softly on the apartment door, she went through to check on Ivy. Dr. Jeff and her aunt sat together at the dining table, one of the huge jigsaw puzzles Ivy loved to do taking up the entire small table. A sunset seascape, very like the ones from Chapel Point. The remains of sandwiches from the town sandwich bar lay on a plate beside them.

No hint of anything more than companionable friendship in their placid smiles as they looked up at her.

The doctor stood, then bent to kiss Ivy's cheek. "Time I got back to my office, Ivy. Hello, Nai. I hope your friend's birthday breakfast went well."

"It did, thanks." Nai peeked at Ivy's medication box. Good, she'd taken her midday pills. Not surprising, with Jeff there. "Don't leave on my account."

Shaking his head, he smiled and tapped his watch. "I'm not. I did a home visit nearby, so thought I'd drop in to have lunch with Ivy. My afternoon appointments start soon." With a pat for Paige and each of the dogs, and a farewell for Oscar, he left.

Alone with her aunt, Nai gave her an assessing gaze. Were she and the doctor more than friends? "I like Dr. Jeff."

Aunt Ivy chuckled. "I do, too, child. But please, don't go getting ideas of a romance between us, like young Reese and Heath imagine. It's all poppycock. We're just friends. His wife and I were friends, too, right up to Betsy's death."

Poppycock. One of those good old-fashioned English words Ivy picked up from the British cozies she read. In this case, Nai wasn't too sure. She eyed her aunt.

"Reese told me you came close to marrying Trafford Brock. Is that true? You never told me." She blurted the words out, then wished she hadn't. They sounded so petulant.

Lips pursed and brow furrowed, Ivy patted the dining chair the doctor had vacated. "Please, child, sit."

Nai did, then gazed expectantly at her aunt. She had no doubt Aunt Ivy would tell her the truth.

"Yes, I did." Ivy heaved a deep breath. "Trafford and I became close over a number of years, after being friends since childhood. Then, when we'd finally decided to get married, he was diagnosed with a serious illness. He insisted we wait. Turned out, we didn't have time to wait."

Tears gleamed in the older woman's eyes.

Nai reached out and rested her hand over her aunt's. "I'm sorry, Auntie. I didn't mean to bring it up and upset you. It's just... I always thought you didn't want marriage."

Aunt Ivy nodded. "I know." She studied Nai, lips downturned, sadness clouding her eyes. "And it concerns me that perhaps you saw me as someone to pattern your life after, that I'm the reason you never married."

Biting a thumbnail, Nai glanced away. "It's not your fault. But yes, I did take you as a role model for a woman who could be happy alone, who didn't need a man."

Again, Ivy loosed a heavy sigh. "Unlike your poor mother, so desperately needy. Not good for you to grow up with that."

Her aunt brought up what Nai hadn't wanted to mention. Hunching her shoulders, she folded herself over the painful twist in her gut. "I never wanted to be like Mom."

"And she knew it." Ivy tsked. "That's partly why she was so hard on you. Not that there's any excuse for how she was."

"N–no." Nai covered her mouth with one hand. She couldn't bring herself to look up, to meet her aunt's eyes. Too ashamed of the hurt Ivy would see lurking in her own.

"Please, Naomi Jane, don't be so determined to not be like her that you decide never to need *any* man. I worry about you, child."

Emotion trembled in Aunt Ivy's voice, more emotion than her aunt had ever revealed to her. Swallowing, Nai raised her head and met her aunt's anxious gaze.

"I'm happy being single, yes," her aunt continued. "But that doesn't mean I've closed my heart to the possibility of something else. We're designed for partnership. Poor Suzanna did it the wrong way. Desperate for a man, any man, thinking sex was the way to find intimacy. But her mistakes don't make love and intimacy in marriage wrong. I'd hate to see you throw away an opportunity for real love."

Nai bent her head over clasped hands. "Mateo?" Her whisper was barely audible.

"Mateo." Aunt Ivy nodded, certainty echoing in her single word. "He's a good man. Give him a chance. Please?"

"I... I... don't know how he feels about me." Nai rubbed her stinging eyes, wishing she didn't feel so much like that uncertain teen again.

"Just give him the chance to tell you, Nai. Just give him a chance."

Yes, she did need to. She knew it. But with fear ricocheting inside her, she didn't know how.

She simply didn't know how.

CHAPTER TWENTY-TWO

LORD, PLEASE, will You make Kristina strong today? Please, will You give her the strength to face down Cullen and win?

Nai still wasn't praying. Not *really* praying, the way Mateo did. But as she unpacked a box of brightly colored children's books and arranged them on the lowest, kid-height shelves in that section, her words to God felt a lot like a prayer.

It's only because I care for Kris. She deserves love, so much!

Like she needed an excuse to justify praying.

Maybe she did. She didn't get a sense of God's presence. None of the spiritual experiences other people talked about. For all she knew, He wasn't listening, and He didn't care. She'd only gone to church on Sunday to make Aunt Ivy happy.

Still, she wanted to do *something* to help Kristina. Something more than just cheering her bestie on and encouraging her to go for it. Of course, she'd already done that, yesterday, when they'd discussed what Kris intended to do.

Digging up that tin spurred both Reese and Kristina to make changes. Do what they could to pursue their buried dreams.

Her dreams? Those, she wasn't so sure about. Not yet, anyway.

Last book shelved, she stood back to admire the display and gave a satisfied nod. The children's area looked so much more friendly and welcoming now.

The entire bookstore did.

Francine, from the maid service she'd hired to clean the apartment, made a big difference already in just an hour a day after the store closed.

Aunt Ivy might insist she'd take over again as soon as Dr. Jeff let her, but from the state of the place when Nai arrived, cleaning clearly wasn't Ivy's forte. Or Violet's, either. Sweet and kind though the older woman was, her idea of dusting was waving a cloth at the shelves, as she did now.

Anyway, Nai paid the housekeeper, and she had every intention of keeping Francine on after her return to Austin. No matter what Ivy thought. Quirky was one thing. Ivy's on Spruce had always been quirky — that was part of its charm. But unhygienic and unsafe took quirky several steps too far.

The jangle of the bell announced a customer. Nai finished flattening the book box for recycling and tucked it out of sight behind the counter. She looked up with a smile, ready to help if needed.

The pretty, thirty-something woman who entered the store headed straight for the Crime and Suspense section, flicking her dark hair back behind one shoulder as she bent to examine what they had under authors from R to Z. She pulled out a paperback with a blood-splattered knife filling the cover and opened it.

Nai restrained a shudder. Not her preference in books, but to each their own.

Busying herself on the store computer, she scrolled through a greeting card supplier's online catalog. A couple of stands of attractive cards and wrapping paper would make a good addition to the store, considering how many people came in to buy books as gifts. She glanced up from the screen to check on the customer, but the browsing woman didn't appear in need of any assistance.

Violet, bustling over from her favorite spot in the Romance section with a book in her hand, apparently didn't think so. The cover showed a couple running together from a burning building. "Ms. Julia, what about this one? It's a new romantic suspense with very good reviews."

The woman's brows snapped together, and she waved Violet away. "No! I've told you so many times, Violet. Just plain suspense books, not romantic suspense. No romance. None. Zip. Zilch. Please!"

She shoved the book she held back on the shelf and stomped out of the bookstore. Despite her frown and her vehement tone, the emotion shadowing her eyes looked as if it held as much grief as anger.

No doubt, there was a story there.

And equally without doubt, Nai knew that, once she'd soothed Violet's distress over being rebuffed, she'd hear all about it. Whether she wanted to or not.

Face buried in her hands, the older woman flopped against a bookcase. "Why can't I remember? Stupid, stupid, stupid." Her skinny frame shook.

Nai hurried to her and placed a hopefully comforting arm around Violet's trembling shoulders. "You meant well."

She *had* meant well, even if the result was the opposite.

Violet lowered her hands to reveal a tear-stained face and sniffled, before ferreting in the pocket of her lilac skirt for a handkerchief. "I hate upsetting anyone. And it seems I've upset Ms. Julia every time she comes in here. No romance. No romance." She pounded a fist against her forehead with each repetition. "No ro—"

Grabbing her fist, Nai prevented the older woman from pounding one more time. Violet needed all the brain cells she had, and giving herself a concussion was hardly going to help matters. "Please don't do that, Violet."

Violet stopped. "I wish I knew what made Ms. Julia so set against romance. Then I might remember not to offer her those books."

So for once, the unofficial Cove news service didn't know?

"No one knows anything much about her, really. She's a real estate agent, moved to Chapel Cove over a year ago." As if Nai asked the question out loud, Violet replied. "She's good at her job, I hear, but keeps to herself. I mean, she's been here a whole year, and I know next-to-nothing about her!"

That must be a first for Violet, judging by the baffled note in her voice.

"No husband or children," the older woman continued. "No dating, either. Such a shame. We have some nice single men in town I could set her up with, and she's such a pretty girl, too. But I have to remember, no romance for her."

Nai hesitated, knowing she needed to word things carefully to avoid upsetting the older woman again. "Uh, I've noticed something. Every woman who comes into the store, you offer a romance novel. Maybe all you need to remember is to ask them what they're looking for *before* you offer. Some women do want romance, but not every woman."

Shaking her purple-tinted head, Violet eyed her skeptically. "Women who don't want romance? In my experience, that means just one of two things. A broken heart or playing it safe to avoid one. And falling in love is the best cure for that."

Could Violet be right? If she'd been asked the question in Austin, Nai would have been adamant the romance-mad older woman was wrong, wrong — *wrong!*

She didn't need romance.

Didn't need a man in her life.

Didn't need marriage.

Romance was for weak women, not a strong woman like her.

But after ten days back in Chapel Cove, seeing Mateo almost every day, she knew those were lies she'd told herself. Only her fear talking.

Soon, she'd be ready to take the risk of chasing her dream, too. Ready to open her heart and be vulnerable. Ready to let Mateo know how she felt about him, risking that he might not feel the same. Maybe even tomorrow night, after they had dinner together.

Violet's theory might not be right for every woman, but it was for her.

It took coming home to make her realize the truth.

Staying safe and avoiding hurt carried too high a price tag when it meant giving up her chance for love.

Especially Mateo's love.

As soon as Mateo slid from sleep into half-drowsy wakefulness on Thursday afternoon, he checked his phone for messages.

Among the clutter of bank account balance reminders and requests to change shifts at the station, he spotted a text that woke him all the way up. Nai. Asking for help with the dogs, asking if he'd help her take them to Riverside Park after the bookstore closed.

Nai, asking for his help?

Part of him wanted to jump out of bed and sing Hallelujah. Part of him told him he was being ridiculous.

He steeled himself not to read more into the text than it meant. Nai asking for help was a huge step forward for her. But it didn't mean she wanted more than his help.

Of course, he replied with a yes.

As soon as he rang the bookstore doorbell, she swung the door open and emerged with the dogs already harnessed and attached to their leashes.

"I hope you had enough sleep. And I hope you don't mind me asking you to walk the dogs with me." Nai peeked at him through her lashes in a way that, with any other woman, he'd consider flirting. When it came to Nai, he couldn't guess. All he knew was it made his heart flip over.

Even though Nai flirting with him seemed as unlikely as excitable Heinz refusing to go for a walk.

Not much chance of that. The little dog bounced and managed to drag her toward the pickup in his enthusiasm. Again, he wondered how the dog knew to head for his truck and not the street.

"No problem." Mateo smiled. "You know I mean it when I say call me any time you need help."

And I'm happy for any excuse to have more time with you. He didn't say it, though maybe he should.

No matter what choice he made, either option held a risk. Stay silent out of fear of how Nai might react, and he risked losing her. Speak too soon out of fear of losing her, and he risked her retreating, the way she had in their teens. Or the way she had after their almost-kiss at Tía Irma's.

His prayers for God to guide him hadn't provided any clear answer so far. Normally, he tended to treat that as being told to wait.

The grand gesture he intended for tomorrow might not exactly count as waiting.

He opened the truck's flatbed for Catsup and patted the surface. The bigger dog leaped in. As before, he lifted Heinz, then tied their leashes up securely.

"Thank you." Nai's genuinely sweet smile held extra gratitude. And was he imagining it, or did it also hold something more? "It's just…I want them really tired out so they behave better with Ivy. She's doing better now, but when Heinz does his overexcited thing with her, I worry he'll tire her out."

"Wise idea. That little mutt is one of the most energetic dogs I've known." Before she could insist she wanted to do it for herself, he hurried to open the passenger door for Nai. Instead of arguing she was perfectly capable, as she did last time, she let him.

"I hope so." She grinned as she fastened her seat belt. "I have more confidence with handling them now, but I'm not sure I could manage to get both of them back on their leashes if I let them off."

The drive to the park on the outskirts of town didn't take long. Even though it had grown a lot over the years, Chapel Cove remained a small-town.

Nai stayed silent, a slight smile lifting her lips while her brow remained creased a little. Something was bothering her. He hoped she'd trust him enough to share what it was.

Once he parked the truck, he opened the door and inhaled. He loved the scent of the riverside park. The air everywhere in Chapel Cove carried a sharp tang of the sea, but here, especially in spring, it mingled with a scent reminding him more of Abuela's garden, the green freshness of growing things.

He rushed around the truck to open the door for Nai. Again, she let him.

He eyed her. So unlike her. Was she unwell?

She looked well. Beautifully well, with color blooming in her lovely cheeks.

He jumped into the back of the truck to untie the dogs. "There you are, guys, go for it."

Nai laughed as the pair of mutts charged around the vast open field in front of them, extending down to the river. "They'd better come back when you call them. They still don't for me!"

"Keep trying. One day, they will." Good advice. And nothing like the same situation, but how he hoped that one day Nai would come to him, willingly and joyfully.

Catsup and Heinz gamboled around them, demanding their attention. He stroked Heinz while Nai stroked Catsup until the dogs got bored and charged off across the field again, little Heinz leading the way.

A shy smile curving her lips, Nai walked to the nearest wooden bench. *Their* bench, though she'd probably forgotten that.

Unerringly, despite the many layers of paint now covering it, her fingers drifted to the words he'd carved into the wood in their teens and followed their lines. So, she hadn't forgotten.

Hope took root in his heart and sprouted, like a cutting from a willow tree. The willows along the riverbank dropped their leaves every year, spent the winter bare, yet now showed bright fresh green again. Maybe, like the trees, their love might get a second chance.

He stripped off his jacket and placed it on the bench. "Want to sit down?"

"Sure." She nodded, but her gaze remained fixed on the dogs.

Too fixed on the dogs. As the wild-rose pink deepened in her cheeks, he knew she was as aware as he was of what names were carved here.

"Mateo and Naomi." He breathed the words, and she nodded.

While the dogs galloped around the park, he did what he'd done when they'd sat here all those years before. He slipped his arm around her shoulder and pulled her closer. She didn't exactly reciprocate, kept her hands in her lap. But she didn't pull away. She didn't go rigid as she had the first time, either. Instead, she seemed to subtly lean into his embrace.

Could be, that was wishful thinking. But he didn't think it was.

Warmth spread through him at her nearness, and his arm around her tightened. They sat in silence as the dogs galloped around, chasing everything from leaves to sparrows.

A sweet, companionable silence, not an uncomfortable one.

When he brought her here last week, he'd confessed that she mattered to him. She said she hadn't known. How could she not have guessed when he'd done everything he could to make it clear to her?

Had he? Had he really?

No, he hadn't. He only thought he had.

He'd done everything he could to protect himself from more hurt. Retreated. Gone silent. Refused to explain. No wonder Abuelo suggested the grand gesture. Making sure she really *did* know this time.

After the mess of the prom, which was neither his fault nor hers — or maybe both of their faults — they'd retreated into hurt pride. Neither had been willing to admit to how they'd felt. So, after their initial argument, they'd pretended nothing happened. Pretended it didn't make a difference.

Yet, of course, it did. He'd felt Nai back away from what had been beginning to grow between them. That simply made him *more* determined not to explain, so he backed away, too. And they'd never managed to find their way back from it. Even now, twenty-four years later, by not talking, they both still behaved like the hurting sixteen-year-olds they'd been.

He needed Nai to know the truth.

"Remember last week, when I told you that you were

beautiful?" Emotion rasped in his voice.

Looking down at her hands resting folded in her lap, she nodded.

"You're beautiful, inside and out, Nai. You're worth loving. I mean it. I know you think I don't, but I promise you, I do." His arm around her shoulders pulled her a little closer.

Her head lifted. For a moment, she simply stared at him, biting her lip, an even more vivid blush coloring her cheeks. "You didn't stand me up for the prom, did you?" Her words emerged small and quiet and hesitant, yet full of hope.

He shook his head. "No. I was sick, horribly sick. I wanted to go to the prom with you so badly, but I could barely get out of bed to make it to the bathroom. My grandmother called and left a message with your mom."

"Oh." A long sigh escaped her. "I'm sorry." Her hand crept out to rest on his knee, warm and vital and setting his senses tingling. "But you never told me."

"You believed your mom's lies and believed I would stand you up." His hand covered hers and clasped it. "That hurt my pride. I was a fool not to speak, but kids that age tend to be foolish."

"I'm sorry," she said again. He didn't imagine the tears glistening in her eyes as she raised her face to him and met his steady gaze. "I was so disappointed, you see. And... and afraid to let you know how I felt. It felt...too vulnerable. I should have known you wouldn't stand me up on purpose."

Oh, his brave Nai. He could guess how much it cost her to admit that. "Never. I hope I'll never let you down again."

It would be so easy to kiss her now, and he longed to, so much. Taste the sweetness of her lips again. This time, he sensed it, she wouldn't run away. And yet, he knew, he'd be a fool to rush her. Slowly, so slowly with Nai. His head lowered to hers, nearer, nearer—

Then something hurtled into their legs at high speed, startling them into jumping apart. Nervous laughter escaped from them both.

Heinz, with terrible canine timing.

The moment was well and truly broken. Nai slid along the bench, putting some distance between them.

The two dogs cavorted around them, then dashed to sit at the base of a nearby tree, waiting hopefully for a squirrel to appear. After less than a minute, they gave up waiting and settled for chasing each other again.

Even if his grand gesture flopped miserably, he wouldn't give up on waiting for Nai.

CHAPTER TWENTY-THREE

COLD RUSHED down Nai's spine as she rang up the tally for another bookstore customer and she shivered. No reason for her inexplicable feeling of dread.

What was that funny old thing Ivy used to say? A goose walked over her grave?

Business in the store boomed. Probably due to Aunt Ivy's presence, though she'd insisted Ivy rest in the armchair, a little like a queen holding court, rather than working the counter.

No need, now they had Fern spending most of her time in the bookstore between supervising Cas out in the café.

So many people stopped by to ask how Ivy was doing. While they were in the store, most also purchased something. The time Nai spent organizing the place so customers could find a book in the correct section and adding a few new genre-themed displays helped, too.

Violet was less forgetful today, and actually did what she was asked to do. Okay, most of the time. Nai stole a glance at the older woman who chatted on the phone, eyes wide, instead of shelving the just-arrived mysteries.

Oh well. Being more useful most of the time was way better than none of the time.

And... she'd see Mateo this evening. Everything between them felt special, hovering on the edge of something amazing. He'd called her a few hours earlier, asking if she'd have dinner with him. Not Tía Irma's this time, but the upscale seafood restaurant on the boardwalk.

Anticipation tingled through her as she carried another box of books into the Mystery section.

As she started placing the books where they belonged, keeping the authors in alphabetical order, she breathed in the fresh clean new-book smell. Could she admit that working here gave her a totally different job satisfaction from working for Jesse in Austin?

If only that nagging sense of something wrong would go away.

"Ms. Nai, did you hear what happened?" Violet's voice sounded behind her.

Nai straightened and whirled around. She still hadn't become accustomed to the woman walking so silently.

"What happened?" Nai didn't know why they needed the local news station when Violet, with Fern's help, somehow managed to know all that was happening in Chapel Cove and shared it generously.

Nai shouldn't be complaining. People visited the store for just-brewed coffee with a soft pastry and a side of fresh gossip, and walked away with a recently released book.

Violet and Fern were way more valuable to Ivy's on Spruce than she'd thought.

The concern shadowing the older woman's pale eyes this time put Nai on guard.

"Well?" She shot Violet an expectant look.

"It could be a good thing you don't know," she muttered under her breath.

"Something with Aunt Ivy?" Nai's gut tightened. But she could hear her aunt chatting with a customer, her voice cheerful. "Or the pets?"

"Oh no, they're doing great." Violet shook her head.

Nai quirked an eyebrow. "Don't worry. I don't need to know everything that's going on in town. I have to finish this. And we've got a customer needing help." She gestured toward the teenager waiting at the counter with a popular young adult novel.

"Well, okay." Violet hurried to the counter.

Nai did a mental headshake as she resumed filling the shelf. She had more important things to do than exchange gossip with Violet. Like deciding what to wear to dinner with Mateo. She'd need Kristina's and Reese's help with this, for sure. Probably, she'd need to buy a whole new outfit. Nothing she had with her was remotely suitable.

She hadn't expected to be dating. Nai nearly snorted. Dating, her?

But no doubt about it. Tonight *was* a date. Mateo had been clear. The knowledge warmed her, and she wanted to look her best.

Heart aflutter like the heroines in the Regency romances she'd just shelved, she bent for another mystery in the box.

"Miss Nai, I *have* to tell you this."

Nai cringed at Violet's shrill voice behind her. That silent tread. As soon as possible, she'd give the older woman some slightly squeaky shoes as a present.

As Nai swiveled to face Violet, her lips softened into a smile at the genuine concern deepening the woman's wrinkles. Somehow, she'd gotten attached to Violet during the past two weeks. Yes, the woman was absentminded and flaky, sometimes more of a burden than a help. But Violet was kind, lonely, and becoming the grandmother Nai had never known.

People were more important than checking off things on To Do lists.

"Okay. What's going on?" Nai managed a hopefully understanding smile. Telling people stories was important to Violet. She owed it to the woman to listen.

"There was a shootout in Portland. At a jewelry store." Violet visibly swallowed.

So this wasn't even about their little town, though compassion squeezed Nai's chest for the people involved. "Sorry to hear that. Was anybody hurt?"

Violet flopped against the wall. "An armed robber and..."

"Well?" Nai wasn't sure whether Violet had forgotten part of the story and needed a refresher or was dragging her feet.

"A police officer." Violet blinked.

"Oh no. Must be devastating for his family and friends."

Violet's head bobbed up and down. "It is." Tears appeared in her eyes. So kind to feel this deeply for a person she didn't know.

"I feel selfish saying this, but I'm glad Mateo doesn't work in Portland anymore." Nai's stomach dipped. She'd be terrified for him every time he went to work.

"The police officer wasn't on duty. He went there to buy a ring. An engagement ring for the woman he loves, even though he didn't know if she'd say yes."

Nai surrendered to curiosity. "How do you know this?"

"Well—"

"Where are the romances?" a fifty-something woman interrupted Violet.

Nai pointed her in the right direction and offered a few

recommendations. "We just received these, the latest romances from Alexa Verde, a very popular author. She writes about small towns just like ours. I hope you'll love them."

"Thank you. I'll take this one and browse some more, too." The woman peered at the shelves.

Violet's jaw twitched. "Ms. Nai, I know the police officer. He told his grandfather about the engagement ring, and his grandfather told me.

Nai's chest clenched harder. Mateo?

Surely not. Mateo's granddad couldn't be the only older man Violet talked to in town. Besides, why would Mateo be buying an engagement ring? No, no, no. He couldn't be the person shot in Portland today. He couldn't.

But as tears stung her eyes, she knew. He was.

She clutched the book tighter in her hands. "Do *I* know that police officer?"

Please say no. Please say no. Please say no.

"Well…" Violet shifted from one foot to the other.

Was she trying to remember or prolonging the torture?

Fern ran in from the café. "Mateo got shot in Portland."

The book dropped from Nai's hands and thudded on the floor. She nearly followed it as her knees buckled. Only grabbing the bookshelf stopped her from collapsing. "Wh–what?"

"I was trying to break it to her gently." Violet sent the young girl a reproachful look.

For a moment, Nai couldn't breathe, couldn't see, couldn't talk. Then she managed to draw in a shaky breath and focused on Fern, obviously a better source of information. "How badly is he hurt?"

Because she refused to think, much less say it out loud, that he could be dead.

Not Mateo. Please, God, no!

Unlike Violet, Fern answered fast. "From what I heard from a customer, Mateo was wounded and taken by an ambulance to a Portland hospital. That's all I know. Honest."

Wounded. Not dead. Thank You. Thank You. Thank You!

Somewhere through Nai's mental fog, rational thought trickled in. As much as she wanted to fall apart, she had to stay together.

She threw Violet a questioning glance.

The older woman lifted her hands as if in surrender. "That's all I know, too." Then her face crumbled. "Poor Mateo! And his grandfather is so upset, poor Hector."

It would be easy to join her in wailing. Instead, Nai pulled her shoulders back. "I have to go to him. Fern, I need you to manage the bookstore." She raised a hand to forestall Aunt Ivy's inevitable offer to help. "Without letting Aunt Ivy lift a finger."

"Sure." Fern didn't hesitate.

Violet, on the other hand, shook her head. "I'm sure Mr. Rodriguez will want to go to the hospital. I don't think he should be driving himself at his age."

As Nai bolted to the living quarters to grab her purse, she drew another deep breath — this time for patience. Couldn't Violet ever get directly to the point? "Call him and tell him we'll pick him up on the way. You're welcome to come, too. Moral support for Mr. Rodriguez."

It was more for Violet's sake than anyone else's, but the woman didn't need to know that.

While Nai dashed downstairs, her purse hanging on her shoulder, she stopped in her tracks. "What about Aunt Ivy and the pets?"

"I'll help Ms. Ivy and phone Dr. Johnson, if needed. My boyfriend can walk the dogs. He loves dogs." Fern didn't even blink. "We're a community here. We'll manage."

"Thank you." Nai hugged Fern, kissed Aunt Ivy on the cheek, and ran for the door.

If the bookstore was still standing and everyone was fine when Nai got back, Fern was getting a handsome raise.

"Take my car. It's way better than Ivy's old wreck. But please, you drive." Violet panted beside Nai as they hurried out the door. Despite her age, that woman could move fast.

Violet proved herself even more valuable by giving directions to the Rodriguez house. The older man stood at the front door, his hands shaking so badly he couldn't place the key into the lock.

Nai jumped from the car and sprinted to the porch. She touched his wrinkled hand. "Let me help, please."

"Thank you." He let the keys go. The despair in his bleak eyes nearly broke her. She steeled herself against the feeling as she locked the door, then helped him to the car and into the rear passenger seat. Taking her responsibility of moral support seriously, Violet slipped in beside him.

Nai slammed the driver's door with more force than she'd intended.

"Buckle up." She started the engine and pushed the car right to the speed limit as she took off.

"I'm praying," Mateo's granddad said.

"Me, too." Violet chimed in.

A hard lump formed in Nai's throat. She wanted so badly to say, "Me, three," but she couldn't push the words through her closed-off throat.

Her stomach cramped when she pulled onto Pacific Avenue. She couldn't imagine losing Mateo. She just couldn't.

Her hands shook. To stop them, she tightened her fingers around the steering wheel as she passed a black truck, then a crimson-red van. Probably the same red as the blood running from Mateo's wound…

The car jerked, and she straightened it.

"Maybe…I should do the driving?" Violet suggested.

"I'm fine." Nai resisted the urge to grind her teeth. She had to keep it together. She was responsible for her passengers.

Mateo's kind eyes appeared in front of her, and his laughter rang in her ears.

Tears burned behind her eyes, but she kept them at bay. Impossible to drive through a curtain of tears. She changed lanes to pass a fourteen-wheeler.

He meant so much to her. More than she'd ever realized. More than she'd ever wanted to admit, even to herself. And if he'd bought the ring for her, that meant... That meant he had stronger feelings for her, too.

The feelings a man had for the woman he wanted to marry.

The lump in her throat grew bigger. She floored the gas pedal, charged past the fourteen-wheeler, and moved into her lane again.

Violet cleared her throat in the backseat. "Ms. Nai, I've lived a long and mostly happy life, and I'm grateful for it. But I don't want to die yet, especially now that I've found such a great man. Would you mind slowing down?"

"Yes, okay." Nai eased up on the accelerator. If she'd been alone in her own car, that gas pedal would still be flat to the floor.

The road to Portland seemed so much longer than she remembered, even longer than that nightmare trip back to the Cove in the rain, or bringing Ivy home so weak and pale. Finally, she drew up outside the hospital entrance.

She glanced back at Mateo's granddad and Violet, who held hands. "This way you'll have to walk less."

"Good idea." Violet sprang from the car, again surprising Nai with her agility.

Mateo's granddad was far slower leaving the vehicle, but soon, Nai circled the parking lot for a vacant spot. She pulled Violet's sedan into the first space she saw, turned off the engine, leaped out of the vehicle, and dashed to the entrance.

Easy to spot Violet's purple hair in the waiting area. She and Mateo's granddad sat in plastic chairs near the wall. Violet held his hand and whispered something to him. Gratitude that Mr. Rodriguez had someone to comfort him warmed Nai.

But… did they know how Mateo was? Surely, they would've asked. And if the news was bad, surely Violet would be crying. She wasn't.

Heartened by the thought, Nai rushed to the couple.

Slightly out of breath, she sank into the chair beside Violet. "Any news?"

Violet peered up at her. "He's still in surgery. Good thing Hector is here. They didn't want to give me any info." Her nose wrinkled in indignation.

No doubt, highly unusual for Violet not to ferret out the information. If the circumstances were different, a half-smile would tug on Nai's lips.

Instead, she hid her face in her hands.

When was the last time she'd tried to hide from the world this way? Probably in her teens, when her mother was busy finding fault with her.

Maybe that kept Nai away from God all these years. Hard to understand how a kind, merciful God could let Mom treat her that way. It wasn't her fault that her father's family hadn't wanted to accept her mom. Or that her father died soon after doing the right thing and marrying her mother. Or that Nai had grown from a cute toddler into an awkward, unattractive teenager. It wasn't her fault that she'd ruined her mother's life by her mere existence.

And now Mateo lay injured because he'd done what he'd considered his duty.

Why, God? Why?

Everything inside her shook, and her throat constricted.

Somebody touched her hand. Kristina squatted in front of her, and Reese stood nearby. Empathy shone in her friends' eyes.

"It's going to be all right. We're here for you," Kristina whispered. "And for Mateo. A lot of prayers are rising in Chapel Cove. You don't realize just how many people care for you both."

"Here, too." Mr. Rodriguez waved around the full waiting area.

Roman hunched near his crutches, Aileen from the pastry shop, and many others. Men and women in police uniform stood in clusters, concern crumpling their faces.

"We've all been praying for Mateo," Roman said. "And for you, worrying you might lose the person you love." His gaze flicked to Aileen. She paled, and her freckles became more pronounced.

"Nai, it's probably premature to say, but I was looking forward to accepting you in the family as my granddaughter." Mateo's granddad wrapped his gnarled hand around Violet's shoulder.

The older woman leaned into him.

Tears filled Nai's eyes. These were *her* people. Even the ones she didn't know. Maybe she hadn't had the best family in the world while growing up, but God had given her a new family. Not blood-related. But a real, true, caring family, there for her if she wanted to accept it.

She'd gotten what she'd asked for — a successful career and a sense of accomplishment. But God, in His endless wisdom and mercy, had also given her what she hadn't dared to ask for, didn't think she deserved.

A wonderful community of loving people, who, like Mateo, accepted her just the way she was. Her lack of beauty never bothered them, and they saw her the way she wanted to be seen.

At last, she felt what she'd always wanted to feel. Cared for. Cherished.

She looked at the floor-to-ceiling windows, then walked to them. When she came close to the window, sunlight filtered through the clouds, illuminating a simple truth inside her.

Like Mateo said, she was worthy of love. She didn't need to reject it.

For so long, she'd rejected God's love, and still, God had given her so much. She'd been looking for security that doesn't exist, instead of stepping out in faith and taking the risk of trusting.

Both with Mateo and with God.

As she stared at the sunshine, words formed in her mind.

Lord, please forgive me for staying away from You all these years. Thank You for not giving up on me and for drawing me near to You again. Thank You for the gifts You've given me, the ones I didn't even see. Please, please, please guide the surgeons and the nurses and everyone else involved in Mateo's care. And please help him recover as soon as possible. I ask in Jesus's name, amen.

The tight band constricting her chest didn't let go completely, but she could breathe again.

God was good. He'd always been good. And finally, she could believe it.

CHAPTER TWENTY-FOUR

SOMEONE TOUCHED Nai's shoulder. When she turned around, she wasn't surprised to see Kristina and Reese again.

"I just prayed," she told the girls.

"I'm so happy for you." Kristina drew her into a warm hug, and Reese draped her arms around them both. Her friends understood the significance. Whatever happened from now on, her life would never be the same.

Tears stung Nai's eyes again, and this time, she let them slip.

Kristina reached into her purse and passed her a pack of tissues. "Here. And... we'll always be there for you. You know that, right?"

Nai nodded as she wiped her eyes. One good thing about minimal makeup, no need to worry about mascara rivers on her cheeks. She hadn't cried in such a long time, but the tears she shed now somehow softened the lump in her throat.

"Would you like some coffee?" Reese glanced to the coffee concession on their right. "I doubt it's as good as Ivy's, but still…"

Nai wasn't in the mood for coffee and wasn't sure she'd be able to swallow. But her friends seemed so eager to help that she nodded. "Thank you. Coffee would be good. I'll see if Hector and Violet need anything."

She walked toward the older couple, questions whirling in her mind.

How long would it be before they'd know how Mateo was?

If today had gone the way it was supposed to and he'd asked her to marry him, what would she answer?

Not a trace of doubt clouded her mind. Yes and yes and yes, a lifetime's worth of yes. She loved the man. Always had and always would. She'd be happy to spend a lifetime with him. Of course, that was if—

No, no thinking like that.

She hiked her chin as she approached Mateo's granddad and Violet. "Would you like coffee or something to eat?"

"No, we're good," the elderly couple answered in unison.

They already thought and talked in sync. Something shifted inside Nai as she sank into the vacant chair.

"Uh, we have a confession to make." Mr. Rodriguez shuffled his feet and wouldn't meet her eyes. Violet blushed.

"Hmm?" Nai eyed them. She wouldn't be the least surprised if they confessed to being engaged already.

"You know those missing books?"

The books? Nai nodded.

"We took them. They're safe. Just hidden. Uh… we wanted to give an extra reason for you and Mateo to spend more time together."

Nai choked out a laugh. "You… you didn't need to. We

managed to spend plenty of time together, anyway."

"You care about my grandson, don't you?" Mateo's granddad whispered as he leaned in her direction.

"I love him," Nai said simply.

God willing, she'd get the chance to tell him so.

Several hours, many prayers, and two cups of coffee later, a man in moss-green scrubs stepped into the waiting area. "Family of Mateo Rodriguez?"

"We're his friends." Those in uniform leaped to their feet.

Nai's hand shot up. "Here's his granddad, and I'm... I'm... I'm his fiancée."

What did she just say? But she was too desperate for news about Mateo to correct herself.

"You go, girl." Kristina winked at her as they crowded the man in scrubs.

"Technically, that wasn't a lie," Violet whispered, thankfully, not loud enough for the surgeon to hear. "He was buying a ring and was going to propose, so you're as good as engaged."

Nai wasn't so sure about that. Mateo hadn't actually asked her yet.

Lines of tiredness marred the surgeon's forehead. "The surgery was long, but successful. He's stable. The bullet didn't hit any vital organs, and given time, he should make a full recovery."

As a cheer went up from Mateo's fellow officers, the surgeon kept talking about risks and rehab, but Nai barely heard any more after "full recovery". She slumped into the nearest chair.

Mateo made it through.

Thank You, Lord. Thank You! Thank You!

The adrenaline fueling her ebbed away, leaving fatigue in its place. But she could breathe fully again.

"Family members only will be able to see him soon." The surgeon turned and went back through the double doors into the OR.

A wave of relief swamped Nai. She hugged her friends, then Mateo's granddad. Happy tears streamed down his wrinkled face. Hers, too.

Were all her dreams about to come true, even the ones she didn't know she had?

For the first time in years, her life wasn't planned and structured, and it didn't matter a bit.

Mateo survived. That's all that mattered. That, and nothing else.

Her heart thrumming, Nai edged toward Mateo's bed, the disinfectant hospital odors tickling her nose. From what she'd understood from the doctor, the main dangers were past. So why was her pulse pounding a staccato beat?

Lying with his eyes closed, he looked washed out. A bandage covered one shoulder and much of his chest. IV tubes ran from his arms, while other tubes emerged from his chest. Her hand rose to cover her mouth, and she stifled a sob.

His eyes opened, and she straightened her back, pasting on a smile. He was alive, awake, and would be completely well soon. She drew a deep breath as she stepped closer.

He grinned at her, his smile just a tad loopy. Whatever painkillers they'd given him probably hadn't worn off yet. "The nurse told me my fiancée was about to visit. So, you're my fiancée now, huh?"

How did she get herself in this predicament? Her face flaming, Nai ducked her head and shifted from one foot to the other. "Well,

I knew they wouldn't let me see you if I wasn't a family member. And I, um, wanted to see you very much."

His grin widened. The effect of seeing her, and not just pain meds, she hoped. "You wanted to see me very much," he repeated, dragging the words out.

She dropped herself into the nearest chair. "If you keep teasing me, I'll leave. Your grandpa gave up his right to see you first after the surgery to give us some privacy, and you —"

"I love you."

Now she *really* hoped that wasn't drugs talking. "Are... are you sure?"

His expression grew serious. "I've been sure for over two decades. I was so sure that I nearly bought you a ring."

She froze. "Nearly?" Her voice squeaked. Had he changed his mind about proposing to her at the last minute?

"The robbery kind of got in the way." A muscle moved in his jaw. "If I could move right now and had that ring, I'd be on my knee proposing. I intended to do that tonight. So you didn't lie when you said you were my fiancée. Provided you say yes, of course."

Nai wanted to shout yes, scream yes, jump up and down waving her arms yes. But her feelings so overwhelmed her that she couldn't move her tongue, let alone her arms and legs. All she could do was nod.

A shadow passed over his face. "Of course, knowing your practical side, I probably should've asked about some things first. And I was going to, honest, before proposing. I know you won't be ready to say yes yet. I know, once Ivy is better, you'll return to Austin. I know you love your job and you're great at it. It matters to me that you're happy. I thought about it a lot. I probably could find a job with the Austin Police Department. But I don't want to leave my grandpa yet."

She nodded. "Of course not. And now there's Violet, too. From the look of it, they're going to be a package deal from now on."

Her mind whirled. She'd thought she'd had her life figured out, and now everything was turning upside down again.

And she was fine with it.

Lord, where are You leading me?

"Yes, and Violet." Mateo smiled. "With God's guidance, we'll figure it out. Maybe my grandpa and Violet will agree to stay in Austin for a few months until you're sure of what you want. Or maybe—"

"I'm sure of what I want already. I love you."

His eyes widened. "I've never had surgery before. Or the kinds of drugs they've given me. Did you just say what I thought you said, or are the meds giving me hallucinations?"

She'd been hiding from love long enough.

Thank You, Lord, for giving me Mateo and for him not giving up on me.

Nai snatched his hand. "It's not a hallucination. I love you, I love you, I love you. I think I fell in love with you when you kissed me in the rain, but I couldn't admit it. And then when you couldn't come to the junior prom and it hurt so much, I figured I was like my mother, desperate for love she'd never get. And she told me so many times I wasn't worthy of love. It seemed there was no point trying. I ran away. From her and from any hint of being like her. But also from what might have happened with you."

"Nai, you're worthy to be loved and cherished. Haven't I told you? You're amazing." He laced his fingers through hers.

Just his touch sent a tidal wave of sweet sensation through her. "I tried to run away from God, too. But God gave me the most incredible gift. His love."

"I've been praying for you to accept Jesus back into your life," he whispered.

"I have. I'm sorry it took you getting wounded for me to realize all the blessings that were right in front of me. And…" She looked into his eyes. "I've realized I do love Chapel Cove. I never thought I'd say it, but I enjoy running the bookstore and taking care of the pets. I want to spend more time with Aunt Ivy, even when she gets better. I enjoy chatting with Violet and your granddad. Old people have so much wisdom."

"They certainly do." Hope flashed in his eyes. "Does it mean that—"

"I'll need to go back to Texas for a couple of months, to find a replacement to help Jesse. I'll probably have to travel to Austin a few times a year. I'll take care of whatever I can long-distance in between. But yes, I want to move back to Chapel Cove. Permanently."

The joy sparking through her like Fourth of July fireworks told her she'd made the right decision.

His eyes lit up. "That's great. But what I wanted to ask is, does it mean you'll marry me?"

"Didn't I tell you?" She laughed. "Of course, I'll marry you."

"I love you so much." He attempted to sit up to hug her.

She gently pressed on the unbandaged part of his chest with her free hand. "I don't think you should try too hard to move yet."

A shame, when she wanted to kiss him so much. Warmth rose inside her as realization struck.

She didn't need to keep waiting for him to kiss her. *She* could kiss *him*. He'd taken the initiative the first time. Now, it was her turn to be brave.

"Stay right where you are."

Carefully, she leaned over him, making sure not to touch any of the tubes. She brushed her lips against his, shy and tentative. His hand rose to her back, holding her close, and the kiss became far less tentative. Emotion flooded her, wilder and sweeter than

231

anything she'd ever known.

Trying to get even closer to her, Mateo shifted, and she felt him flinch. Pulling away, she placed a gentle finger on his lips.

"No more kisses yet. I can't wait for you to recover fully. I'll help you to get there, in any way I can."

Regret tightened his mouth. "I feel bad you'll have to. I know you have a lot on your plate, and this" — he gestured at the IVs — "wasn't in your plans."

"Neither was love or marriage. God gives us much better things than we could ever plan for ourselves." She traced the outline of his face with her fingertips. A wave of tenderness rippled through her. How could she have stayed away from this wonderful man for so long?

She'd be a bride at forty, and she couldn't be happier about it.

"If only I had that ring," he mused. "As soon as I'm well enough…"

Of course. How could she have forgotten? "I have a ring." She almost sang the words. Grabbing her purse, she fished around till she found it. "Recognize this?"

He squinted at the pretend diamond ring she held out to him. "You kept it? The same ring?"

"I kept it." Tearing up again with joy, she smiled. "When we were thirteen, Kris, Reese, and I put a couple of treasures each in a tin and buried it, to dig up when we were forty. They were supposed to show what we wanted to achieve in life. We dug them up on Wednesday. This was one of mine. Want to give it to me again?"

The toy ring designed for a child wouldn't fit on her ring finger, so he slid it onto her little finger, instead. "Does this mean we've been engaged since we were eight? It's high time we got married, girl!"

"I agree. As soon as we can."

Somebody cleared his throat behind her. She glanced back. Mateo's granddad.

"Sorry I've taken so long." She'd been so wrapped up in her own happiness, she'd forgotten about the others, waiting outside.

"Oh, please. Take all the time you need. I couldn't help overhearing. Welcome to the family."

Her heart opening to the kindly older man, she walked into his inviting arms. "Thank you, Mr. Rodriguez."

"Grandpa, please." He hugged her gently, then let her go. "It's a dream come true for me to gain a granddaughter, especially one like you."

She looked at Mateo, then his granddad, and thought about all that waited for her back in Chapel Cove. Her dreams had come true, too, even the dreams she never knew she had.

Thank You, Lord. Thank You so much.

Kristina had been right all those years before, when she said we should never limit our dreams because God has many, many more wonderful things for us.

He did. And she couldn't wait to discover them with Mateo at her side.

EPILOGUE

Two months later…

NAI SURVEYED the crowded tables at Tía Irma's. The service at the church had been beautiful and spiritual, and she'd spent most of it silently thanking God. And now, their reception, blessed with wonderful food and even more wonderful guests to share it with.

"Even after saying I do, I have difficulty believing I'm finally your wife," she whispered to Mateo, who sat beside her at the head table.

He clasped her hand and brought it to his lips, kissing it. "It took us so long, and I'm so amazingly happy, that I have a difficult time believing you're my wife at last, too."

A delicious frisson of sensation spread through her. Maybe they could've gotten married at eighteen if they'd been brave enough to admit their feelings to each other. Or maybe their relationship wouldn't have worked out then. They'd needed to understand some things to be able to open their hearts to love.

Big things.

Important things.

Things they understood and had worked through now.

Kristina and Reese waved at her. She waved and smiled back. How wonderful that their childhood trio had all found their loves and happiness back in Chapel Cove, even at forty. She grinned at Mateo's granddad and Violet, who had eyes only for each other. And another smile for Aunt Ivy, seated beside Dr. Jeff, happily munching on fajitas, no cheese and no sour cream, doctor's orders.

Nai's heart warmed as she gazed at the people she loved.

"I'm happy your aunt recovered from her heart attack so well." Mateo refilled her half-full glass, as well as his own. "Do you think she and Jeff will ever admit their feelings to each other?"

"I hope so." Nai chuckled. "If they don't, maybe we need to talk with them. Remind them how long shyness kept us apart."

Her gaze moved to the next table. Fern and her boyfriend, a geeky computer science student wearing glasses and a slightly wrinkled gray suit. It must be true that opposites attract. Yet the mismatched pair were clearly in love.

"We made it here at last. And it was worth the wait."

"Worth every minute." Nai grinned.

In typical Ivy's on Spruce form, the journey to their wedding had been a chaotic one.

First, Mateo's recovery from the gunshot wound.

Then, no sooner had he gotten back on his feet than she'd needed to return to Austin. She'd spent most of their engagement there, setting up systems so she could work remotely and finding a good assistant to take over what she couldn't handle from the Cove. The first girl set her sights on marrying a billionaire, and tried to maneuver Jesse into a compromising position. But the second, Lauren, was just the right girl for him.

Things didn't go any better in the Cove after she left Austin and came home. The restaurant's ovens had broken down and were repaired just in time. Plus, another bride had booked the same date. Nai offering to pay for the other couple to enjoy a far more expensive reception at the seafood restaurant solved that problem. The order for the cake was misplaced by the big Portland baker they'd commissioned, and they'd had to beg Aileen to make one. Violet had food poisoning. Oscar flew out of the bookstore and returned unharmed after a long tedious search. Nai's wedding dress arrived with a broken zipper. Once that was fixed, the train had torn off when Violet, recovered from her food poisoning and eager to help as honorary grandmother-of-the-bride, accidentally stepped on it.

Nai and Mateo weathered it with patience, though it took a lot of prayer to *stay* patient. With God's help, they'd trusted the result would be more than worth it. And spending time together, even amidst all the chaos, was precious.

Mateo ducked his head for a moment, then peeked up at her. "Nai, before things go any further, I have a confession to make."

"Uh-uh." But he looked so much like an adorable little boy with his hand in the cookie jar that it couldn't be anything important. Besides, if it was, he would have told her sooner. She'd learned to trust.

"You know how you always wondered who taught Oscar to say 'Mateo and Nai should get married'?"

She smiled, guessing what came next. "I wonder who that could have been."

He nodded. "You guessed right. It was me."

Impossible not to laugh. "Of course. Who else could it have been?"

"You know, I'm so happy that I want everybody to be happy and in love." Mateo's gaze flicked to Roman, who no longer needed his crutches.

Joy expanded in Nai's chest. "Me, too."

She studied Roman. While Kristina's twin had dated extensively, he didn't bring a date to the wedding. Neither had Aileen. Despite claiming she didn't make wedding cakes — *ever* — she'd created the most delicious and gorgeous wedding cake, at the last minute. She'd even decorated her gorgeous creation with a miniature copy of Ivy's on Spruce bookstore and a myriad of tiny books.

Maybe it was Nai's turn to play matchmaker. She had high hopes for Jesse and Lauren, so why not this pair? She caught Kristina's eye and telegraphed her thoughts with her gaze. Kristina nodded. Like many times before, they understood each other without words.

So many other singles here deserved love, too. Hudson Brock, the new doctor. Widowed Melanie from the Pancake Shoppe. Olivia, the school bully who'd grown into a completely different woman. Sally, the florist. Others, too.

Roman stood and tapped his glass for silence. When the room quieted, he pulled the cloth from a large trolley behind him.

"Mateo and Nai got married. Mateo and Nai got married." Oscar bobbed his head as he joyfully squawked from his cage on the trolley.

Everyone erupted into laughter.

"Now, seriously, I do have a few more words to say as we toast the bride and groom." Roman lifted his glass filled with sparkling apple juice. "As I look at many happy faces here, I want to give thanks to the Lord for all His wonderful gifts. Mateo and Nai, I've known you since we were all little kids. You're truly such a wonderful couple, and I wish you a lifetime of happiness. To love!"

"To love!" everybody echoed.

Everybody, except Aileen. She hadn't touched much of the food on her plate, either.

Nai took a sip of her sweet drink. Hmmm, between her, Kristina, and Reese, they should manage to come up with something to help those two. Roman and Aileen had some bad history after dating in high school, but maybe with a sufficient nudge — okay, a push — they could find the same happiness she and Mateo had discovered. She'd have to pray about it.

Filled with joy and thanksgiving, Nai leaned against the chest of the man of her dreams. "I love you, Mateo."

"I love you, too. With all my heart and all I am. I always have, and I always will."

At last, she trusted Mateo and God enough to say it.

And to believe it.

THE END

THANK YOU FOR READING

I hope you enjoyed reading *Cherish Me*. If you did, please consider leaving a review on Amazon, Goodreads, or Bookbub. Positive reviews and word-of-mouth recommendations make such a difference as they give encouragement to authors, and more important, help other readers to find the Christian fiction they want to read. Every review, no matter how short or simple, is very much appreciated!

Thank you so much!

You can also read *Remember Me* (Book 1) by Marion Ueckermann and *Love Me* (Book 2) by Alexa Verde. *Choose Me* (Book 4) will release summer 2019. Make sure you don't miss any new releases by following our page Chapel Cove Romances on Amazon at amazon.com/author/chapelcoveromances.

SPANISH GLOSSARY

Abuela : Grandmother
Abuelo : Grandfather
Amiga : Friend (female)
Arroz con huevos : Rice and eggs
Nieto : Grandson
Primo : Cousin (male)

BIBLE VERSES
& OTHER QUOTATIONS

Chapter 12:

A ship in harbor is safe, but that is not what ships are built for.
~ J. A. Shedd (1928).

Chapter 16

"Come to me, all you who are weary and burdened, and I will give
you rest.
  Take my yoke upon you and learn from me, for I am gentle and
humble in heart, and you will find rest for your souls.
For my yoke is easy and my burden is light."
~ Matthew 11:28-30 (NIV)

About Autumn Macarthur

AUTUMN MACARTHUR is a bestselling author of clean Christian inspirational romances with a strong touch of faith. If you love happy-ever-afters, sweet romance, and Hallmark movies, chances are you'll enjoy her stories!

Originally from Sydney, Australia, she now lives in a small town not far from London, England, with her husband (aka The Cat Magnet), two guinea pigs, and way too many rescue cats for their tiny house!

Visit Autumn's website for more about her and her books:
www.autumnmacarthur.com

Real romance, real faith!
USA Today bestselling author of heartwarming Christian romance.

You can also find Autumn on social media:
Facebook : Autumn.Macarthur
Goodreads : 8522441.Autumn_Macarthur
Bookbub : authors/autumn-macarthur
Amazon : amazon.com/author/autumnmacarthur

Books by Autumn Macarthur

CHAPEL COVE ROMANCES
Cherish Me *(Book 3)*
Marry Me *(Book 6 – Releasing winter 2019)*
Plus more titles releasing 2020
Other books in this tri-author series are by
Alexa Verde and Marion Ueckermann

SWEETAPPLE FALLS
His Father's Son *(Book 1)*
His Healing Touch *(Book 2)*
Plus more titles on their way!

HUCKLEBERRY LAKE
Calm & Bright *(Book 1)*
Imperfectly Proverbs 31 *(Book 2)*
Midnight Clear *(Book 3)*
More stories to come!

Books 1, 2, & 3 are available in a in a reduced price boxed set,
Come to the Lake.
Book 1 and Book 2 are also available in beautifully narrated
audiobooks, with audio for Book 3 launching soon.

A TUSCAN LEGACY
Dolce Vita *(Book 8)*
La Risposta *(Book 9)*
Innamorata *(Book 10)*
Other books in this multi-author series are by: Marion Ueckermann, Elizabeth Maddrey,
Alexa Verde, Clare Revell, Heather Gray, and Narelle Atkins

LOVE IN STORE
The Wedding List *(Book 1)*
Believe in Me *(Book 2)*
Least Expected *(Book 2.5)*
A Model Bride*(Book 3)*
Forget Paris *(Book 4)*
Invitation to the Ball *(Book 4.5)*
Teapots & Tiaras *(Book 5)*
More Than This *(Book 5.5 – yet to be released)*
Heart in Hiding *(Book 6 – yet to be released)*

Books 2, 2.5, 3, & 4 are also available in a reduced price boxed set,
London Loves.

THE MACLEANS
A Model Bride – *Mac's story*
More than Friends – *Catriona's story*
A Lesson in Love – *Fraser's story*
The Real Thing – *Brodie's story (releasing late 2019)*

TOGETHER FOR CHRISTMAS
This ebook-only boxed set contains one book from each of my
main series:
Believe in Me, A Model Bride,
Calm & Bright, and *His Healing Touch*

ACKNOWLEDGMENTS

Special thanks go to:

- Alexa, for her help with the first draft that made this book possible,
- Marion for her wonderful covers and graphics,
- Marion (again) and Jan for their excellent critiquing,
- Paula Marie for her support,
- my amazing editor Dee for how she takes my ordinary words and finds the shine,
- beta readers Trudy, Grace, Paula, Sarah, Debbie, Susan, & Renate for being the first to notice typos and other errors,
- all the members of Autumn's Awesome Readers on Facebook, and my email reviewer list,
- my husband for his patience (most of the time!) while I wrestled with this deadline
- and most of all to God, the Creator and Cause of it all.

Plus an extra special thank you to you as well, for reading!

To stay up to date with my book news and new releases, I'd love for you to join my newsletter mailing list

Just click on the QR code
or visit http://bit.ly/autumnsubscribe
to find out more

Made in the USA
Columbia, SC
11 June 2024

36973016R00157